LOVE ON THE ROCKS

ALYSSA JARRETT

Geek Chic Press LLC

Editing by Kristen Tate at the Blue Garret

Cover design by Nick Jarrett

ISBN: 978-1-963875-02-7 (Ebook)

ISBN: 978-1-963875-03-4 (Paperback)

Published by Geek Chic Press LLC

PO Box 24915

Oakland, CA 94623

❀ Created with Vellum

To Daisy, who taught me I'm exactly where I'm supposed to be.

To my brother Nick, for inspiring me to take the leap.

And to the tiny anxiety hamster in my head I call Hammy.
Because if I'm not going by a pen name, neither are you.

content notes

This book includes references to generalized anxiety disorder and panic attacks, death of a sibling (historical, off-page), parental estrangement, swearing, alcohol use, and explicit sex. Reader discretion is advised.

on free soloing

This story discusses and depicts the act of free solo climbing, otherwise known as free soloing, which involves climbing without ropes or protective equipment. As the author, I must note that while I, like many others, am fascinated by those who choose to free solo, I do not endorse this dangerous practice and do not recommend it to readers.

Ultimately, *Love on the Rocks* is a romance that requires you to suspend your disbelief, as some of the climbing portrayed is not only life-threatening, but at this point in time, physically impossible. This is a work of fiction, so please do not attempt to follow in these characters' footsteps. Climb safely and live happily ever after.

chapter
one

Unhappy hour. Drink your feelings hour. C-suite suck-up hour. I'm a marketing executive—shouldn't I be able to come up with better names for this event? All of my colleagues seem to be happy enough. It's the last day of our corporate retreat in Yosemite, and the presentations and brainstorming sessions are finally over.

You should be grateful, Tania Beecher, I keep telling myself. Everything in the bar at the Granite Grove Lodge spells luxury: the historic stone interior with exposed wooden beams along the vaulted ceiling, the warm lighting from elaborate chandeliers, the plush furniture perfectly arranged for cozy conversations.

If I'd stayed in journalism, I'd be in some grimy dive bar, commiserating over the latest round of pink slips at yet another dying newspaper. It took a decade for me to break into the tech industry and claw my way up to vice president of marketing at Habituall, one of Silicon Valley's hottest tech companies. But as I sink deeper into my tufted chair, clutching an exquisitely expensive Napa cabernet, I feel not satisfied, but suffocated.

Everyone on my team is giddy and getting along, clustered

together in a boisterous group near the bar—I just can't bring myself to join in the festivities. Harris Shepherd, one of my top content marketers, meets my glance and I quickly look away. Not just because I can't handle chitchat right now—*shit*, he's walking over—but also because his soft, gray eyes are so gorgeous that it's hard to make eye contact.

"You think you got enough there, Tania?" Harris clinks his wine glass against mine, nearly sloshing Silver Oak's finest on the hardwood floor.

Harris has that thirty-something hipster vibe on lock: a dark, full beard and equally thick hair with a silver streak that matches those eyes I have to avoid getting lost in. I cough, as if trying to hack up my lustful thoughts. I'm his boss, for christ's sake. Get it together. "The bartender got generous with the pours. It's not like I asked for a double."

He takes in my nervous laugh. "Maybe you should have a double. It wouldn't kill you to enjoy yourself for once."

"I *am* having fun." I take a defensive gulp of my drink to make my point. "I'm a little stressed over Q1 planning—that's all."

Harris squints his perfect eyes with disapproval. "Come on. That's bullshit, and you know it. I've seen that fifty-slide deck you've been obsessed with. You've had every *i* dotted, *t* crossed, and penny counted since Thanksgiving. There's no way in hell you overlooked anything, and I would bet my Hydrow on it."

Okay, that gets me to laugh for real. Habituall gives every team member a two-hundred-dollar stipend each month to spend on fitness, and I've been approving Harris's expense reports for over a year, so I know exactly how much his rowing machine means to him. And from the way his toned arms bulge in his black Henley when he crosses them, I don't blame him. I remind myself for the hundredth time that he has a girlfriend—whom he met while he was DJ-ing on the weekends, of course.

"The content team's jumping in the hot tub after happy hour if you want to join us. No mentions of AP Style or SEO allowed. Bring your wine, and come unwind."

I should want to say yes. I should want to sit in a hot tub with a ridiculously expensive glass of wine and celebrate our breakneck period of record growth with my team. But the only feeling I can identify is this one:

I don't want to be here anymore.

"Thanks, but you go ahead," I say, passing him my wine glass. "Take that, and don't let it go to waste. I'm going to go for a walk and get some fresh air."

"We're around if you change your mind." He frowns but doesn't press the issue, which makes me think it was a pity invite anyway, then walks off to rejoin the rest of the marketing team.

Although I would describe myself as an "indoor cat," Yosemite in early January is absolutely awe-inspiring: calm and quiet, pristine and pure, ideal for a tightly wound workaholic who has to remember to take a deep breath every now and then. Maybe I haven't spent a single dollar of my fitness stipend, but I can take a stroll in this majestic national park outside. My longtime therapist, Dahlia, suggested I go on a walk to recharge when I texted her earlier today, and for once, I'll be able to tell her I took her advice.

I stride out the door into an Ansel Adams photograph come to life and regret my decision as soon as the icy chill slaps me right in the face.

If I was anywhere else, I would have no problem abandoning my plan and sneaking back up to my room to watch rom-coms instead. But as the sun dips over the mountains, illuminating the peaks in deep orange underneath cotton-candy-streaked skies, I have to admit that it's not just the thirty-degree weather taking my breath away.

It wouldn't kill me to take a walk around and enjoy the view, I think to myself.

Would it though? The little hamster of anxiety in my brain —I call him Hammy—butts in. *You haven't reapplied your sunscreen yet, and just because it's freezing doesn't mean your skin can't get burned in the elements. And you don't even have your trusty water bottle—what if you get lost and die of dehydration?*

Calm down, Hammy. I'm only stretching my legs. You've been doing so many mental laps that I forget I need to move my actual body on occasion.

You sure about that? he insists, his imaginary hamster feet sprinting endlessly on the squeaky wheel in my mind. *You do know you're wearing Ralph Lauren leather riding boots, right? You look like you'd be better off playing polo than going for a hike in the snow.*

I hate when he makes a good point. Lord knows I'm no equestrian—I haven't been around horses since I was a kid living on the outskirts of Fresno, feeding carrots to my neighbor's mares—but I'm even less suited for real winters. I live in the Bay Area, after all, so the only cold-weather attire I own is a stack of corporate-branded Patagonia jackets and the Ted Baker peacoat I'm currently wearing.

It's fine, I keep repeating as I scuffle away from the lodge and down a dirt hiking trail. There's not much snow on the ground, nothing I can't stomp through. Setting my smartwatch to outdoor walk mode, I set off toward the sunset, surprisingly upbeat considering there's no hot cocoa or fireplace in sight. But nothing makes me feel more accomplished than crossing items off my "I really should" list: Visit someplace new? Check. Do some cardio? On it. Connect with nature? Hell yeah.

Look at me, Hammy. All the kids these days talk about touching grass, and I'm out here like a natural adventurer.

I ignore his stubborn squeaks and power through the nerves, enjoying the smell of pine as I breathe deeper than I have in a long time. The muscles in my jaw slowly loosen and my shoulders fall away from my ears.

It occurs to me then that my urge to flee the not-so-happy hour earlier was just Hammy fretting. I'm not having an existential crisis, and I don't need to escape my job. I just need to take that six-week sabbatical I've earned after six years with Habituall. Maybe a few months from now, though—or even next year. It's not like I can peace out after we just got back from winter break—even if I spent most of it working anyway. You can get a lot done when the office shuts down, you know.

I channel Dahlia again and tell myself to stop thinking about work and pay attention to my body. My skin tingling in the cold, my feet moving down the path. The farther I go, the more limber I become, and it's downright thrilling to break out of the sedentary cast my desk job has molded around me. Are these the exercise endorphins everyone's always going on about?

The air stings my lungs and the increasing incline burns my thighs, but I move quickly to keep myself warm, not bothering to keep track of which paths I'm taking as the trail forks off. I resist the urge to pull out my phone and check the same five silly apps, remembering an article I read that explained how our phones had effectively replaced cigarettes as our go-to distraction. They give our hands something to do, without the cancer risk. I've felt enough compulsive twitchiness on this work retreat to know that a habit doesn't need nicotine to be addictive.

The sun's in the west, so I keep hiking further and further into the forest, knowing I've got that molten ball in the sky as my compass.

Do you though?

I stop in my tracks, branches snapping ominously under my boots. It's always worse when Hammy whispers instead of squeals. But when I look to my left and no longer see the sun, I realize he's right. Everything is indeed not okay. When I stepped outside, the mountaintops were illuminated like lit cigarettes, but now they're being put out as fast and unceremoniously as butts smashed into an ashtray.

When I pull my phone from my coat pocket and turn on its flashlight, those four trusty bars have disappeared. Meaning I'm by myself, out in the stark wilderness without any cell service, and it's getting colder and darker every second.

Fuck. Fuck fuckity fuck. I whip around, hoping to catch a glimpse of the lodge in the distance, but it must be miles behind me. With the sun officially set, I can't tell east from west, up from down, and it's not like I can get Google Maps to point me in the right direction. How could I be so foolish? Hammy doesn't have to scream to wake me up to the dire circumstances.

It's pitch dark. The flashlight on my phone is rapidly draining my battery. And, worst of all, it starts to snow. At first, there are just a few flakes sparkling in the light from my phone. But after just a minute they're not sparkling as much as settling. Settling in a flurry on my frigid nose, incessantly blinking eyelashes, and gloveless hands. They're conforming to my increasingly damp coat and piling up around my boots— and everywhere else.

The snowfall is heavy enough that the path beneath me has disappeared. I try to double back and return the way I came, but with my footprints getting covered as fast as I'm making them, I can no longer orient myself. Wherever I go, it's white snow on the ground and blackness all around me. I've never experienced the weather take a turn for the worse like this. I mean, climate change is real, but changing this quickly? Fucking unreal.

"Hey!"

Leave me alone, Hammy. I don't have time for this. I need to get back to the lodge before I succumb to exposure. It looks like there's an area up ahead where the trees thin—maybe I can tell where I am from there.

"Stop!"

Absolutely not. That's how hypothermia gets you. You stop moving, and all of a sudden, the warmth of oblivion envelops you before you have a clue what's happening. It's why folks are found frozen in their birthday suits, and I am *not* about to die literally naked and afraid. I keep moving forward up a slight rise. There are definitely fewer trees ahead.

"Can you hear me? I said stop!"

"And I said leave me alone, Hammy!" Wait a minute. I said that out loud, which means I responded to a real person, not my imaginary hamster. I've got a vivid imagination—that's undeniable—but even I stop short of actual hallucinations.

Milliseconds later, an abnormally strong arm pulls me back with so much force that I collide into a sheer wall of muscle.

"I don't know who Hammy is, but if he followed you any further, you'd both be falling down that cliff."

I aim my flashlight in the direction my rescuer is pointing. Just a few paces away, the ground drops off precipitously into a pit of rock and darkness.

I whip back around, and he holds up a hand to shield his eyes from the flashlight. "Do you mind turning that off? I've got it covered."

Quickly tapping the screen, I adjust to my surroundings, settling my gaze on the person in front of me. A man, who looks like he's about my age, with one hand on his headlamp and the other braced against my waist to keep me balanced.

Normally, I'd be startled by being held by a stranger, but my body's too frozen in place to step back in surprise.

"Who are you? And why are you out here?" My voice comes out shaky but holds onto its edge, clearly not as comfortable as my extremities to discover a source of warmth in the wild.

"That's supposed to be my line." He chuckles softly, crinkling his eyes and immediately putting me more at ease. His voice is warm and deep, like his embrace shielding me from the snow.

"You didn't answer my question," I project loudly against the wind. My accusatory tone makes me cringe, but he's not at all bothered.

"How about we get you someplace safe before formal introductions, alright?"

He charges down a path leading away from the cliff, but it's difficult for me to keep up. He's properly suited up for snow in several hooded, waterproof jackets and well-worn hiking shoes; whereas I can't get any traction in these ridiculous riding boots, so I'm slip-sliding across the slush and at constant risk of twisting an ankle.

He doesn't say a word when he realizes I'm not right behind him, just comes back down the path and takes my hand to help me around the most unstable areas. In any other circumstance, this might seem like a chivalrous gesture, but I'm reminded of my mother, who would tug me along at the mall when I was little to keep me from dawdling. I don't care how warm his calloused hands are—there's nothing romantic about them gripping yours so you don't fall on your ass and bruise your tailbone.

After who knows how many minutes, the trees thin out and we come to a clearing. I expect to see his headlamp shining on a quaint log cabin or at least a bare-bones Airbnb, but the only thing I can make out is a large white van.

"Are you going to drive me back? My company's staying at Granite Grove."

His eyes bulge, and a scoff escapes his lips in a foggy exhale. "Not a chance. It's pitch-dark, the road conditions are already not ideal, and out here a small snowstorm can become a blizzard before you know it. We're better off hunkering down tonight, and I can take you back first thing in the morning."

"Hunker down . . . where exactly?" I ask, my head swiveling in search of shelter.

We walk up to the van, and he slaps the side of it. "In my humble abode, of course!"

~

"WHAT YOU CAN LEARN From a Guy's OnlyVans Profile," by The Send-It Sisters on Thursday, January 6

WE GET IT. You were minding your own business when suddenly you came across a hottie's OnlyVans page. And being the progressive digital citizen you are, you're tempted to support this intriguing #vanlife creator, if only to get a sneak peek of what's under his hood.

But before you impulsively commit to yet another subscription, pay close attention to these four key areas. If you're selective about your sign-ups, you can avoid the van boys and drive home with a new van man.

1. **A picture is worth a thousand groans.**
   Reviewing bios for red flags is essential, but a profile picture can fill in what's left unsaid between the lines. He may have the eloquence of Shakespeare, but he's no Romeo if his neck has

so much beard it looks like it's never seen the sun.

2. **Perks worth every penny.** They say you get what you pay for, so don't cheap out with a lemon. If you want to evolve beyond van-surviving and enjoy van-thriving, pony up for premiums like sustainable energy, meals that don't require a microwave, and a bed big enough to unfurl from the fetal position.

3. **You can't spell GURL without URL.** Vans don't typically come with room for ring lights and tripods, so we don't expect dudes to be camera-ready influencers. But they better have a digital paper trail. So click those links, because a little cyber-snooping can be the difference between someone being all-American and on *America's Most Wanted*.

4. **Play a little game of "just the tip."** There's no ethical consumption under capitalism, of course, so we believe in supporting creators for their hard work. But if your van vagabond isn't adding more value than the space he's taking up in your driveway, might we suggest the only tip you leave is, "Get a real job."

chapter
two

Most of the time my brain is abuzz with all kinds of noise—the incessant chatter of Hammy and my inner critics, the steady ping of to-do items and checklists, the underlying drone of existential dread. It's as if my mind is hosting a large dinner party during a concert on an airport runway, and I'm trying to keep track of a dozen different conversations.

But in this moment, the record scratches, and all I hear is silence. As much as I would like to say it's blissful, I've become so accustomed to the mental chaos that this abrupt jolt is even more disorienting.

"I'm sorry . . . what?"

A man just saved me from tumbling over a cliff during a snowstorm in the dark but only now am I in freefall. I don't even know his name, and he's expecting me to join him in the literal Google search result for "pedophile van"?

He doesn't wait for me to agree—just slides the side door open and jumps inside, gesturing for me to follow.

Well, if this is how it ends—getting murdered by a mountaineering serial killer—I guess I had a good life. I hope he's efficient, because at least it'll be quicker than freezing to death.

When I step inside and the door's shut, I brace myself for the inevitable *CSI* episode they'll base on my death, but the warmth unfurls my clenched fists.

It's . . . cozy?

Other than the two front seats, everything inside has been converted for van life. In the middle is a makeshift kitchen with a sink, mini-fridge, and three-burner propane stove over an oven. Wooden cabinets flank the appliances, held shut with strange semi-circle metal fixtures instead of drawer pulls or knobs.

On the left is a bed, much larger than I expected to fit inside of a vehicle. Covered in gray sheets and a plush cool-blue comforter, it's about the same size as my full bed back home. A perfect size for sleeping solo, but manageable for visitors.

And that's when it hits me. I'm the visitor. And if I'm not hacked into a million pieces, we'll be getting up close and personal under those sheets.

Before I'm torn asunder by the erotic thriller playing out in my mind, I return to the most pressing issue. At the very least I should know the name of my lover-murderer.

"You didn't answer my question."

LED strip lights under the overhead cabinets illuminate the interior and give me a good look at my captor. He peels off two hooded, insulated jackets in complementary bright orange and blue, shaking off snow and revealing shaggy brown hair, tousled in every direction. He's long and lean, all sinewy muscle underneath his tight navy thermal, and he's staring at me with big eyes the color of hot chocolate.

I break our gaze, and my eyes lock on a large bundle of rope draped over the back of the driver's seat.

I guess I was right about the whole murder thing.

"That's not what you think it's for," he exclaims as he sees what must be panic on my face. "I'm Nolan Wells. Those ropes are for climbing. Not that I'd be opposed to using them for other purposes—I just don't meet many women in my line of work."

My eyeballs bulge out of my head. "You're not opposed to tying up your victims, but they're just hard to come by? That's the laziest serial killer line I've ever heard!"

"Who said anything about serial killers?" He throws his hands up and takes a step back, either implying that he's not dangerous or he's assuming that I am.

"What other purposes would you be talking about?"

He opens his mouth but quickly shuts it, and when he takes the tiniest glance at the bed, I know why.

Oh.

Heat rises from my abdomen, up my neck, and along the sides of my face. It's one thing when your pervy brain starts reenacting "Fifty Shades of the Great Outdoors" within minutes of meeting a stranger in a white van. It's another thing entirely when that stranger is on the same wavelength.

"So, um, Nolan, what is your line of work?" I refuse to acknowledge that we are both thinking dirty thoughts, and if there's anything I've learned from dozens of failed first dates, it's that there's no conversation topic more boner-deflating than day jobs. I will my eyes not to roll, expecting to hear that he's camping to distract him from engineering or accounting or whatever stable-yet-drearily-dull occupation our parents' generation pushed on us.

Instead, he looks at me, confused. "Climbing," he repeats, pointing at the ropes. "I'm a rock climber."

There goes that record scratch again. Every time Nolan opens his mouth, he stuns me into silence. He mentions he's a climber so factually, like he can't imagine what else he would do, but he might as well declare he's an acrobat or an archaeologist. These are jobs that technically exist but are as foreign to me as the assassins and mob bosses I read about when I get a hankering for dark romances.

"Like for a living?" God, I sound so irritating, but I can't help it. When I consider how expensive it is to live in California, all I can wonder is how someone can stay afloat on anything other than a tech worker's salary.

He nods, pulling a half-liter Nalgene water bottle out of the mini-fridge and handing it to me. "It helps when you keep that living pretty simple. Not many bills to pay when you live in your car, right?"

I wipe my mouth with the back of my hand after gulping down half the bottle, completely unaware of how thirsty I was until the cold water hit my parched tongue.

"Here?" I gasp. "By yourself?" The nosy part of me whirs with dollars and cents—holy fuck, all that money saved from not paying rent—but the even nosier part wants to know if he has someone to come home to.

Nolan shrugs. "Yeah, I guess. I haven't had a roommate since . . . well, it's been a long time. But I'm used to being alone, whether it's on the rock or . . . anywhere else."

He's got this sad look in his eyes, which is starting to convince me that maybe we'd both appreciate some company.

"Are you sure you want me to stay the night here? I understand if you're not thrilled to share your space with a total stranger." I omit the reason why I understand, which is that I haven't had roommates since college, because that guilt-inducing fact puts my privilege on full display, and I don't want to sound more out of touch than I already do.

He smiles, and I can't get over how adorable he looks when his eyes crinkle. "You wouldn't be a stranger if I knew your name."

My eyes pop. "How rude of me! Here I am giving you the third degree, without any reciprocation. I'm Tania Beecher—I live in the Bay Area, but I'm here in Yosemite on a work retreat. Please interrogate me as much as you'd like. It's only fair."

In my embarrassment over my etiquette faux pas, I stick out my hand to shake his before realizing how much of a square it makes me. Where the fuck am I—at a tech conference?

To my relief, Nolan doesn't make fun of me or leave me hanging, although I almost pull my hand back when his envelops mine. It's massive and warm, which I discovered on the trail. Now that we're inside I also notice a kind of dusty smoothness, like a permanent layer of chalk has settled into his skin. Once I get past how intimidating his grip is—seriously, this man could squeeze an apple like a stress ball—it's nice. I'm so accustomed to handshakes with rich, pretentious executives that it's refreshing to meet a man unafraid of getting dirty. Even if *I'm* afraid and want to wipe my hands with sanitizer as soon as he lets go.

"Work retreat?" He chuckles. "Isn't that an oxymoron?"

I snort in agreement. "You have no idea. I don't care how much fancy Napa wine they ply us with afterward, there's nothing relaxing about four-hour corporate workshops in the name of ten-*x*-ing our growth or whatever stodgy McKinsey consultants are obsessed with these days. But we get paid a quarter-mil in the tech industry to pretend to give a shit, so we keep on pretending, I guess."

Nolan raises an eyebrow, and I immediately regret the word vomit I've spewed. With all that business-speak and entitlement dripping off every word, I might as well have whipped out my tax returns and started ranting about the price of organic blueberries. Is that how I open on my first dates? No wonder I don't get many callbacks . . .

"Are you cold?"

"Excuse me?" I cough uncomfortably. Seconds ago, I was tearing myself apart, but with one question, I'm ready to be offended. Is he insinuating I'm an ice queen? It's not fair when some brogrammer refers to me as a frigid bitch the moment I admit I'm not exactly 420-friendly, but to hear it from someone I met today is uncalled for—

"Here, let me get that for you." My arm is outstretched, primed to point my finger in his face, and Nolan comes around to take off my soaked peacoat and hang it on the back of the passenger seat.

Oh. That kind of cold.

I rub the sleeve of my cream, cable-knit sweater. The dampness that's settled into my skin from head to toe causes me to tremble from something other than nerves. Expecting him to lecture me on my lack of real outdoor attire like I'm Paris Hilton on *The Simple Life*, I head him off by taking the self-deprecating route. "That's what I get for not checking the weather."

"That can only get you so far in the Valley. Yosemite is notorious for rapidly changing weather conditions. And if you're coming from the Bay for a few days, it's not like you need REI."

I tilt my head, puzzled. "I would think everyone in the Bay needs to care about real estate investing. Million-dollar homes don't land in your lap—you have to be proactive in such a hot market." I pause, fearful I won't be able to stop when I get on a roll about Bay Area housing. "Although I'm not sure what this has to do with snowstorms?"

Nolan laughs with such unbridled joy, like I'm a standup comic at the top of her game, that I question how much human interaction he gets in any given week. That's when I realize where I went wrong.

"You were talking about the outdoorsy store."

"The fact that you call it the outdoorsy store says every-thing I need to know about your lifestyle. What do the kids call it these days . . . bougie?"

He bends down to open a drawer under the bed, rooting around in the storage before pulling out—no joke—a Snuggie, without a hint of irony. Now it's my turn to raise an eyebrow.

"It was a gag gift from some climbing buddies," he says, with no sign of embarrassment, wrapping it around me and rolling the blue fleece sleeves until my fingers peek through.

"Joke's on them, because it's delightful. And for the record, I don't like fine wines and luxury hotels and wearable blankets because they're bougie. They're hygge—what the Scandinavians refer to as the cozy way of life."

Nolan considers the distinction. "Okay, but you have to admit that there's a big overlap. It's why the wealthy are always saying they're not rich, they're just comfortable."

The twinge of derision in his voice piques my interest, but I can't tell if it's because he grew up in a family who heard it a lot or said it a lot. My middle-class parents were fond of muttering "must be nice" around the well-to-do, but what if Nolan is a member of the "why yes, it is nice" club?

But since it's poor taste to ask whether you're living in a van because you're broke or a trust fund baby, I move on to more pressing matters: my growling belly. "You know what would be more comfortable? Getting some food. Whatcha got to eat around here?"

Nolan snaps his fingers. "Have I got the perfect comfort food for you. Mac and cheese!"

I clap my hands, more excited than I was hours ago when I remembered how good breathing was. "Omigod, *yes*. I love that Kraft blue box as much as I did when I was a kid. The spirals were my absolute favorite. I'll even throw in a cut-up hot dog if I'm feeling extra . . ."

I stop babbling when I notice the look of horror mixed with disappointment in Nolan's big, brown eyes. "Sorry, I'm vegan, actually."

"Ah." I try to mask how deflated I feel at the thought of

missing out on milk and butter and gloriously artificial cheese powder. But he sees it all over my face. I'm crushed.

"I promise, though, you're gonna love it. It was a big hit with the guys when we climbed across northern Norway on our last vacation, so if that's not hygge, then I don't know what is."

The idea of someone rappelling down a cliff for recreation is already bewildering, so I don't press Nolan's questionable opinions about comfort food.

I sit down on the bed, because there's nowhere else, and watch as he pulls out a small pot from the fridge, reheats the contents on the stove, and scoops out a serving into a nondescript white bowl. At first, I'm optimistic: there's elbow macaroni, although it's likely whole-wheat given its darker appearance, and even some kind of breadcrumb mixture coating the top.

But upon further inspection, I definitely get the feeling that I'm not in barbecue-loving Kansas anymore, because instead of Kraft's intense golden-orange color that could be used to shellac school buses, I can see pops of red pepper, yellow squash, and plenty of spinach. I know that we're supposed to taste the rainbow—and not the kind Skittles are always trying to sell us—but a part of me pouts on the inside, nonetheless. It reminds me of the times I've ordered pilaf at Americanized Mediterranean restaurants and been dismayed when they add peas and carrots. It may not be a cardinal sin, as much as I balk, but it's not how my Armenian mother makes it.

However, beggars can't be choosers. The last thing I put in my stomach other than the not-so-happy-hour wine was a dry, lackluster turkey sandwich during our working lunch, so I'm starving. And Nolan looks so earnest, awaiting my opinion like I'm a judge on *Top Chef*, van life edition. It wouldn't kill me to pretend to love it if it makes him happy.

I take a bite, and my "mmm" goes from affected to authentic in two-point-five seconds. Holy moly, it's good. Really good.

"Whoa, you're right. This doesn't suck!" I spurt out between shoveling spoonfuls of creamy non-dairy goodness into my mouth.

Nolan grins from ear to ear. "Why thank you for such a surprised vote of confidence. I knew that you'd come around to the idea. Don't get me wrong—I don't mean to hate on the blue box. It's got its charm, and when I was a little dude, it hit the spot like nothing else. But if I'm going to climb mountains, I need some real sustenance. Put into my body what I intend to get out of it, you know?"

Mmhmm. I can guess what Nolan could put in my body, alright. Moving up Maslow's hierarchy of needs as shelter and food are taken care of, I take a good look at him as he leans over the stove to scoop himself a bowl, savoring the moment while he's distracted to indulgently scan from the top of his bedhead to the bottom of his hiking shoes. It's obvious he works out—every waking moment is exercise for him—but he's not abnormally ripped like some bodybuilder. Every muscle is as hard as the rock he climbs, and I can imagine him effortlessly crawling up the sides of cliffs like Spider-Man— with as much superhuman strength but without the radioactivity and web shooters.

In comparison, I prefer to avoid thinking about my own body, but if pressed, I would classify it as charmingly average. It's not going to win *America's Next Top Model*, but to paraphrase the words of Tyra Banks, we're all rooting for it anyway. I've always looked precisely as good as I've cared to, which is to say good enough. Good enough to clock twelve-hour days at a desk job. Good enough to go out on regular dates with my online match of choice. And good enough to outrun the slowest person in the event of the zombie apocalypse. But not an ounce more than that. Throw my naturally curly hair into a ponytail, skip the makeup, and take advantage of having small tits by going out in public without a bra on, if I feel like it. If a man isn't expected to invest in his everyday appearance aside from basic hygiene, then I sure as hell won't either.

Speaking of hygiene . . .

Nolan takes a seat next to me on the edge of the bed. Curiosity gets the better of me, and I take a sly whiff as we're getting adjusted. Despite the obvious fact that there's no room in this van for a shower or even a toilet, he smells clean and earthy. No hints of cologne but enough notes of fresh alpine spring to know he at least cares about wearing deodorant. It's nice.

Everything about this moment is nice.

We enjoy our meal in comfortable silence, and for once, I can appreciate the bare necessities: hot food, a metallic roof over my head, and kind-natured company that doesn't care if I'm not dolled up. All in one of the most beautiful places Mother Nature has to offer, when she's not actively trying to kill us in a blizzard.

Who needs a bunch of chitchat on top of that?

That's what I keep telling Hammy at least, because all that persistent hamster in my brain wants to do is play a spitfire round of small talk: Where are you from? Do you have any siblings? What are your parents like? Are they still married? Where did you go to school? What did you major in? And on and on through the priority-ranked checklist of questions I ask on first dates, as if I can get the right answers, I'll unlock a special compatibility badge and get on the fast track to matrimony.

But this isn't a first date, and I don't even know if Nolan is single.

You could ask him . . .

Stop it, Hammy. It's okay to not know. We're just two people eating mac and cheese. Don't overcomplicate it.

If he's not going to ask us anything, then what are we supposed to do? Sit here and continue being strangers?

Again, my anxiety hamster has a point. You would think Nolan would be more interested in asking me a few questions. I mean, when you think about it, he's been cooped up in this van for god knows how long—weeks, months, maybe years. I can't imagine he would have many dialogues with anyone other than the occasional park ranger or grocery store checker. Can't even chat up the mail carrier without a mailbox—does he even have an address?

I wouldn't say I'm a sparkling conversationalist, but I can hold my own when given the chance. All Nolan knows is my name and some pretentious facts about my life in tech. Not that I need his approval, but it would be nice for him to know that I have more to offer than tips on the Bay Area real estate market or which Napa winery is the best bang for your buck.

At the end of the day, though, Nolan Wells is a guy, just like any other. His mind is probably preoccupied with mundane musings, like whether his gas tank needs refueling or if he's got enough almond milk for breakfast tomorrow.

"What would you do if you stopped pretending?"

"Huh?" I pick my head up from my ruined leather boots, unsure of how to respond.

"Earlier you said everyone at your company gets paid a bunch of money to pretend to give a shit. I'm curious why no one takes their money and goes off to do something they actually give a shit about."

Oof. That's hell of a lot deeper than I expected his mental talk track to be. Here I was thinking he was running through a to-do list in his head, but instead he's getting philosophical about my career.

I shrug. "Not sure, to be honest. I've been doing tech

marketing for a decade now, and it's never occurred to me—or any of my colleagues—that we could do anything else. Frankly, we're too busy to even contemplate it in the first place."

Nolan gives me the side eye while taking another bite of his vegan mac and cheese. I can tell he's not buying it, but he's too polite to say anything. Not that it matters, because if there's anything I learned competing in varsity speech and debate in high school, it's that I don't need to be invited to an argument to start one.

"It's not that bad—I don't know why I was complaining. Yeah, we run ourselves ragged, but the money's really, really good, and if you're going to work a stressful job, then you might as well get paid a lot to do it. They don't call them golden handcuffs for nothing."

I laugh, attempting to insert some levity into the conversation, but it comes out hollow. Everything coming out of my mouth makes me sound like Scrooge McDuck diving into what should be a pool of gold coins and hitting nothing but concrete on the way down.

Nolan considers what I've said, and I'm dying to get any kind of validation from him. I worked my ass off to finish grad school, break into such a competitive industry, and climb the corporate ladder. He has no idea how far I've come and what it took to get there. Why would I just up and quit the kind of job that everyone else would kill to have? Why can't he see that?

"So over ten years you never felt an urge to try something different?"

I roll my eyes, not bothering to hide my frustration anymore. "Sure, everybody does. But careers aren't as flexible as guidance counselors make them out to be. Not when you've got bills to pay and a retirement to fund and a house to buy some day. It's not feasible to make a pivot and start at the bottom of a completely foreign field. Regress all the way back to entry-level. Too much time has passed to enter something new, so now I'm just trying to exit as fast as possible."

Nolan finishes the last of his meal and sets his bowl on the kitchen countertop. "And then what?"

I sigh. We're running around in circles. Is this how all those guys felt on our first dates? Judged and interrogated for no reason?

"I don't know."

"I think you do," he says without a trace of snarkiness. It makes me want to scoop out his eyeballs with my spoon.

"I think you do," he repeats, "because you wouldn't be racing to an exit if you didn't know where you were headed to begin with. It's such a waste to spend your whole career waiting to do something else when you could be doing that thing now. It's easy to think you were put in those golden handcuffs by a cosmic force outside of your control, but you can take them off at any time, if you're willing to play by your own rules and not somebody else's."

"Oh yeah?" I sneer, standing up and tossing my now-empty bowl in the sink, secretly relishing the way it clanks against the stainless steel and jolts Nolan's attention. "You must have life all figured out, huh? Going off the grid and enjoying your moment of zen out here in the wilderness. We can't all be hippies sleeping in vans, so sorry if it's a major bummer to you that my job isn't manifesting spiritual enlightenment or whatever. Most of us are real people with real problems, and we can't simply run away from them because work sucks. So lay off, alright?"

Nolan starts to protest and reach for my arm, but I throw off the Snuggie and don't stop to hear him out. Powered by self-righteous indignation, I muster up all my strength to slide the van door open and slam it shut. It only takes a few freezing seconds stomping through inches of snow in utter darkness for me to recognize the irony of my tantrum.

Because if anyone is running away from their problems, it's me.

~

TEXT CONVERSATION between Tania Beecher and Dahlia Cruz, LCSW, on Thursday, January 6, at 8:00 p.m.

TANIA BEECHER: Have I been pretending this whole time? Has my career been meaningless and my entire life amounted to nothing?

NO CELL SERVICE DETECTED. MESSAGE NOT DELIVERED.

chapter
three

Out of all the messes I've gotten myself into recently—running over a nail driving home from the hair salon, missing a typo in our last email campaign, forgetting to pack my headphones on the bus ride to this retreat—this one takes the cake.

I don't know what I expected to accomplish when I stormed out of Nolan's van, but I've failed before I even started. Thankfully, the snow has stopped, but I'm not wearing any outerwear, the windchill is scraping my skin, and ice crystals are practically sealing my eyes shut. Not that I could see anyway, because there's no light other than the stars above, so I have no sense of direction.

And even if I did, where would I go? The lodge is miles away, and the only soul out here who could possibly help get me there is exactly the one I'm avoiding. I have two choices: either swallow my pride and head back to the van, risking the most embarrassing moment of my existence, or succumb to my fate, hoping the elements will kill me faster than any potential wolves or bears.

The fact that both options seem equally viable shows how

mortified I am. I know I can't dillydally all night, but I can't face him right now.

This decision is apparently not up to me, because I don't get farther than a few feet before I hear Nolan shouting behind me. "Tania, what in the world are you doing?"

I whip my head in his general direction. He's carrying a lantern and wearing both jackets, his face double-hooded for protection. It took him a minute, and he's more prepared than I was during this entire trip.

"I'm *fine*," I insist with all the confidence of an overambitious amateur, when we both know that everything is not fine. "I just have to go to the bathroom."

I don't know why I said that. It seems like a reasonable thing to blurt out if you want to get a guy to stop following you. It reassures him that I'm not leaving for good and gives me a few more minutes to collect my thoughts, sit with my feelings, or whatever else my therapist recommends when I'm struggling to regulate my emotions.

He holds the lantern up to my face, suspicious. "Have you ever gone in the woods before?"

I nod my head, but my scrunched-up look of disgust gives me away immediately. You don't have to know me very well to recognize that I'm not a fan of camping. My definition involves four-star hotels and high-end cabins, or at the very least, a decked-out RV with a full bathroom and shower. What's the point of having the amenities and luxuries of modern life, if you're going to abandon them to sleep in a bag on the cold, hard ground?

It seems insulting to forgo everything that folks in under-developed places would be dying to have—running water, indoor plumbing, Wi-Fi—just like it's insulting for Nolan to suggest I quit my lucrative career to chase some passing fancy.

"I'll manage just fine, thank you very much."

Nolan hesitates, not convinced by my response but not

deranged enough to stop me from relieving myself. "Wait here. If you're gonna go, you might as well do it right."

He bolts back into the van, and for a second I consider dashing off into the trees to escape his sight. At first going to the bathroom was merely an excuse to avoid confrontation, but now I'm confronting a different issue.

I actually have to go now.

Between heavy pours of wine, half a liter of water, and a bowlful of mac and cheese trying to make room in my gut, all systems are prepared for evacuation. I guess when nature calls, you need to respond at some point, so this is as good a time as any.

Before I know it, Nolan's back, handing me one of his jackets, a second lantern, and a black travel bag.

"I'm sorry for not minding my own business earlier. There'll be plenty of time for a full apology, but right now all I want is for you to be careful. If you head forty paces straight ahead, there's a small clearing where you can take care of things. You'll want to be quick and expose as little skin as possible—trust me, you don't want to risk frostbite in your nether regions."

He chuckles, and it cheers me up to have him act so casual, but I'm too horrified by the thought of literally freezing my ass off to find the humor in this.

"Inside this kit is everything you need. Take the trowel and carve a hole about six inches into the soil. The snow's fresh and not that deep, so you should be fine digging past it. Once you're done, you can use some of the toilet paper that I packed in here, but don't bury it. The cardinal rule of the outdoors is to leave no trace. Just seal it in one of the plastic bags, cover the hole, pack everything back in the kit, and come straight back."

I stare at him, humiliated that we're having this conversation. Regardless of his relationship status, whatever chance I had of Nolan viewing me romantically must be completely eliminated now. I'll never be anyone's number-one choice once they've pictured me doing a number-two.

"I know it's a lot to process. Do you want me to come with you? I can guide you, get everything set up, and, of course, give you plenty of privacy."

"No, no, no, absolutely not. I got it." I throw on the jacket and grab both the lantern and the bag from him before he can insist. I may be no camping expert, but I'm a grown-ass woman and I'll figure this shit out—pun intended.

I start counting my paces, speed-walking away from Nolan as fast as I can. It may be painfully cold, but the burning embarrassment in my chest powers me to the clearing. I manage to follow his instructions, going through the motions and trying not to think about how gross this is. And when I'm done, I practically marinate my hands with the sanitizer that's included. You don't have to tell me to leave no trace when I want to forget this whole incident ever happened.

As I'm walking back, I'm not just cooled down from the frigid climate. After enduring such a humbling experience, it's like the self-righteous wind has been taken right out of my sails. It's damn near impossible to stay mad when you're squatting over a hole in the snow. One minute I'm about to get in Nolan's face and demand who gives him the right to make judgments about my job, and the next I'm ready to bury the hatchet right along with my dirty business.

It may not feel great getting questioned by a guy I just met, and I've never had anyone see my career as anything other than winning the jackpot, but everyone is entitled to their opinion—even if they don't have a toilet and put red peppers in their pasta. We're living such drastically different lives that we're bound to disagree on almost everything.

Nolan Wells may be out of touch with the corporate crowd, but as far I can tell, he isn't some crypto bro or wellness guru trying to sell me something. I'm sure in his own way, he's just trying to help.

And he does help—at least with braving the wilderness. I expect him to have returned to the van, but he's right where I left him, holding out his lantern and waiting for me to come into view. As soon as I give him a small smile, letting him know that I don't hate his guts, he breaks out into a big, doofy grin. Without a word, he takes the travel kit from me and holds my hand to lead me back to his home on wheels, not caring where that hand has been.

I may have given him the nastiest olive branch I could have imagined, but I'm happy he enthusiastically accepts it, none-theless.

~

THE SEVEN PRINCIPLES of Leave No Trace (Rewritten for Silicon Valley Visitors)

1. **Plan ahead and prepare.** That means avoiding visiting during peak season even if you have to sacrifice social media likes. And don't bring your whole startup into the back-country—Tesla hasn't built electric emergency choppers, so saving your ass won't be sustainable.

2. **Travel and camp on durable surfaces.** Now is *not* the time to cross the chasm and walk the road less traveled. Stick to maintained trails and designated campsites that have way more permanence than your fundraising runway. We'll still exist in two years when your venture capital runs out.

3. **Dispose of waste properly.** You data nerds have heard the saying, "Dirty in, dirty out." To put it bluntly, if you have a pile of shit and you move that pile of shit, you still have a pile

of shit . . . in a new location. Make sure that location is in your RV and not all over the wilderness.

4. **Leave what you find.** We don't care about your astrology sign or the phase of the moon. Please don't steal native rocks and plants for your New Age altar of smelly sage and overpriced crystals. Unlike your woo-woo clutter, they actually have a purpose in our universe.

5. **Minimize campfire impacts.** Have you read the news lately? California's biggest wildfires have all occurred in the last five years, and Mother Nature gives zero fucks about your illegally cooked s'mores or pyrotechnic baby gender reveal. Light yourself on fire before you risk the lives of millions of people.

6. **Respect wildlife.** We're not about to bully your breed, but we will give you crap if you hike with Fido off-leash. Bears, wolves, and mountain lions have to eat too, and they'll munch on you and your fur babies if you make it easy for them.

7. **Be considerate of others.** Take the golden rule as seriously as you treat your golden handcuffs. This planet may not have stock options, but it's infinitely more valuable. Don't be a dick, and make the great outdoors great again.

chapter
four

I welcome the vibe shift when we get back to the van, as it's apparent that we're both determined to make sure the night ends on a happy note. Nolan quickly gets to work, storing the travel kit underneath the sink before washing our dirty dishes and placing them back in the overhead cabinets.

When I'm a guest in somebody's home, dishwashing is a task I gladly take off my host's plate, but before I can even offer, they're already cleaned and put away. All those soft-spoken lifestyle influencers would lose their minds over Nolan's bare-bones space—it's like minimalism on steroids.

So instead of commandeering his chores, I assuage Hammy's incessant curiosity by asking Nolan about the van— "a 2016 Dodge Ram ProMaster," he explains proudly—which has roof-mounted solar panels that generate just enough power to run the stove and lights, charge devices, and stay warm with an electric blanket for a few hours before going to bed. He points out the etched outlines of famous Yosemite landmarks on the inside of the doors and tells me that the makeshift drawer handles are repurposed climbing equipment called cam lobes.

"But this is where the magic happens," he declares

without a hint of irony, pointing to the item hanging above the door.

The pièce de résistance is his hangboard—which is exactly what it sounds like, a board you hang from. Obviously, climbers need strong fingers, but it never would have occurred to me that they train them.

"I stick my fingers in these holes and try to last as long as I can."

"You're fucking with me, right?" I snort, laughing so hard that snot almost shoots out my nose. Nolan's bewildered, until he catches onto the innuendo and turns beet-red, making me collapse into a fit of giggles all over again.

"Yeah, well, I take being good with my hands very seriously." He leans in, lifting the corner of his mouth in a coy smile like he's trying to tease me, and it catches me off-guard. There's not much room in here, so we're always in each other's personal space, and the air between us feels charged. Electric.

I gulp, preoccupied with fantasies of where else he could put those super-strong hands. I may not be able to confirm whether he's purposely flirting, but he's getting under my skin regardless.

Never one to make the first move, I switch gears to break the sexual tension and focus on making lighthearted conversation. Nothing as heavy as the heart pounding in my chest—just superficial topics like the books I'm reading and reality TV shows I can't get enough of.

"Wait, you're telling me people apply to get married at first sight?" Nolan's eyes widen with concern.

I nod energetically, delighted to be in my element and educating him on what I do best: gossiping about minor celebrities like I know them personally.

"Yep, that's how it got its name. They fill out a question-naire and put their fates in the hands of so-called experts in the hopes that they'll meet the love of their life walking down the aisle. The show follows them for eight weeks as they decide whether they want to stay married or get a divorce. It's completely deranged and *awesome*."

Ever since Nolan saved me from tumbling down a cliff, I have felt like a fish out of water, so it's fun having our roles reversed for once. He's been singularly focused on climbing, so it's wild how he has practically no knowledge of anything else. I feel powerful, walking through the finer points of pop culture like I'm Bruce Willis teaching Milla Jovovich in *The Fifth Element*.

Nolan looks like he can't decide whether he's intrigued by or terrified of *Lifetime*'s finest. "So, what's the success rate of the show?"

I chuckle devilishly. "The track record is as solid as a plume of noxious gas. But it's entertaining, and that's all that matters."

By now, we've gotten comfortable on his bed, our damp jackets draped over the car seats. Nolan hangs his shoeless feet over the edge and taps them against the side.

"I bet you don't see many guys like me on that show."

Is he curious or self-conscious? "It's definitely rare," I admit, flashing back to all the contestants. "Reality TV attracts quite a few schmucks. Lots of real estate agents and crypto nuts and day traders. But there was one couple that was off the beaten path." I pause, smiling at the memory. "She was a quirky doctor, and he was a dreamy playwright who lived in a tiny home, but they were so eccentric and cute, and it seemed like they legit loved each other. I don't think they're still together, though, which is a shame. They were my favorites."

The electricity in the air sparks again, and Nolan grins at my wistfulness. "I'm surprised you wouldn't have fallen for one of those real estate agents. I bet talking about down payments gets you going."

I playfully shove his shoulder, not sure if I'm more embarrassed by the idea of Nolan thinking about what gets me going or that he's not exactly wrong. Part of me wonders if it's weird, joking about sticking our hands in holes and being sexually suggestive with a complete stranger, but once we're on a roll, the conversation comes easy. I guess once you've broken the barrier of going to the bathroom in front of someone, nothing else is off the table.

We enjoy bantering, but even though there's no clock in the van, I can tell it's getting late when our laughs come out like yawns. Part of me doesn't want to be the first to call it a night, because then I would have to confront the stark reality of sleeping next to Nolan. Cramped and too close for comfort.

And the other, much smaller part of me is secretly looking forward to it.

My largest yawn yet escapes me, and I turn my head to cover my mouth so as not to make a big deal of it.

But Nolan doesn't let it slide. "Should we hit the hay?"

I pull on the sleeves of my sweater, nervously trying to stall. "I see how it is. I must be boring you with my encyclopedic knowledge of reality television."

"No, not at all. I love listening to people gush about what they're passionate about. You could be obsessed with something as boring to me as filing my taxes, but if it's what truly got you excited, I would want to know why. It's attractive when someone loves something so much that they can't help but talk your ear off about it."

A heat rises in my cheeks. I know that saying that something I'm doing is attractive is not the same as saying *I'm* attractive, but it's the first genuine compliment I've received from Nolan all night, so I count it as a win.

Nolan leans over the side to sort through the underbed storage. "I've got the perfect pajamas for you."

He pulls out a matching set of gray nightwear, with a long-sleeved fleece top that includes the tagline "The floor is lava," which makes me laugh until I stand up and realize that I can't go into a bathroom and change into it.

"Whoops, sorry." He turns around, getting the hint. "Take your time."

"No peeking!"

The tease comes out of me automatically, but as I peel off my clothes, that small, secret part of me hopes that he might. I face the front of the car so I can keep my eyes on him in the rearview mirror while I unclasp my bra, but Nolan's a total gentleman. Why is that so disappointing?

As I hold onto his pajamas, it occurs to me that I could *not* change. If I was a femme fatale in a sexy thriller movie, I'd strip down and tell him to turn around. Why couldn't I be one of those women who has one-night stands? It's not like I'll ever see him again. We'll get back to the lodge as soon as the sun comes up, and I'll join the Habituall team on the bus to San Francisco, with none of my colleagues the wiser. And what are the odds that I would run into a professional rock climber back home? The only rocks I've come into contact with are the whiskey stones at my favorite craft cocktail bar.

I think of my best friends, both within the company and outside of it, who would tell me to go for it. That it would be foolish not to hook up with a hot guy while spending the night caught in a snowstorm with him. Who cares if you have nothing in common, and he lives in a van nearly two hundred miles away from the Bay? It's not like you're going to marry the dude.

I take a breath. I'm gonna do it. I'm going to have meaningless, casual sex—if only for the juicy story I can tell at our next girls' night. For once, my BFFs are going to live vicariously through me and not the other way around. Thinking about their envy gets me psyched—it'll be like I'm starring in my own reality show instead of watching from the sidelines.

And that's when I see it, and my stomach drops. A small photo clipped to the air vent like the scented travel diffuser I use in my own car. Nolan has his arm wrapped around another young man with a bright orange and yellow faux-hawk. They're on a summit, with an absolutely gorgeous view of a green valley below. But it's not the scenery that takes my breath away—it's the fact that Nolan is kissing the side of this man's forehead in a display of pure love.

"Do you have a boyfriend?"

I immediately cringe, ashamed that my question slipped out, and with a way more accusatory tone than I intended. So what if he does? You're the one planning on seducing him without confirming his sexuality. He doesn't owe you anything.

"What? No—oh god, sorry!"

I turn around, bewildered by his apology, until I see what he sees. I never finished changing into his pajamas, so I'm in my baby-blue boy shorts, clutching the clothes against my chest.

"Jeez." I hold the nightwear closer to avoid a nip slip, while Nolan whips back in the opposite direction so I can quickly change into them. I would guess he's a few inches taller than me, just shy of six feet, and around my size. I tie the drawstring of the pajama pants, thankful I'm not drowning in them, so at least I don't have to worry about them falling off my curvy frame.

"I spaced out when I saw the photo on your dash. You're all good now. Sorry if I flashed you."

He slowly turns around again. "It's okay, you didn't." He says it to reassure me, but is my imagination catching a twinge of disappointment?

Nolan squeezes past me to unclip the photo off the vent and show it to me. It's in a clear acrylic frame, and it's slightly bleached from being exposed to the sun. But now that I can see the image up close, I can tell the two guys look too eerily alike to be romantically involved.

"Is that your brother?" The other's hair obviously sets him apart, and his smile is a bit more snaggle-toothed, but the facial similarities are uncanny.

Nolan nods. "My twin brother, Ryan. We're fraternal. I'm older by about ten minutes, and I never let him hear the end of it."

I chuckle with approval. "It's our right. I'm three years older than my brother John. If I was going to be my parents' guinea pig, then at the very least I should be allowed to gloat about being number one. So, does Ryan live around here?"

"He used to." Nolan pauses, rubbing the edge of the frame between his fingers. "This is the last photo I have of him before he died."

I double over like I got sucker punched in the stomach. How self-centered am I to get jealous of someone's late sibling?

"I'm so sorry to hear that." I peer closer at the background. "When and where was this taken? It looks familiar, but I've never seen a view so magnificent before."

He smiles, solemn but proud. "It was here, on the top of El Capitan, about a decade ago, a couple of months before our twenty-third birthday. We had broken our previous speed record on the Nose in less than four hours. Nowadays, the world record is twice that fast, but for a couple of kids right out of college, that was super rad."

Nolan catches me staring down, down, down the cliff where they're overlooking Yosemite Valley, and it's like he can sense me doing the scary mental math in my head of how high up they are.

"He didn't die on this trip, if that's what you're thinking. It was about a month later on the Matterhorn. Ryan and I had done plenty of alpine ascents—even climbed the same route the year before—but I was too busy studying for the CFP exam at the time, so I told him to take his new girlfriend, who was also a highly skilled climber. I was bummed to miss out, of course, but never in a million years did I think she would come back without him."

I'm left with so many questions: How did Ryan die? Did his girlfriend try to rescue him, or was she gravely injured too? And—embarrassingly, the one that intrigues me most—Nolan was studying to become a certified financial planner? It's so odd that a rock climber would have pursued that career, but it would be way too insensitive to grill him about it the second after sharing such a sad story. I may be a nosy bitch addicted to TV drama, but even I know better than to instigate it in real life.

"Thank you for trusting me to share that story." I parrot my therapist's preferred response to avoid saying the wrong thing. "I appreciate your vulnerability."

Nolan perks his head up from the photograph, an indecipherable expression on his face. "You know, I've been telling that story for so long, it's kind of refreshing for someone to not have heard it before."

Huh, I wasn't expecting that take. But after talking through my anxieties with various mental health professionals over the years, I can understand the weird allure of opening up to a stranger. You run the risk of the stranger making you feel even worse than you did before you divulged anything, and I would rather sew my mouth shut than accidentally put my foot in it.

"You look like you want to say something, Tania."

He gives me the same smile he gave when I was blabbing about *Married at First Sight*. "It's fine. Ryan's been gone for ten years now, and frankly he'd be annoyed if he wasn't brought up the first time I have a woman sleep over in my van.

Like he was missing out on the action—not that there'd be any, of course."

Nolan blushes, and I laugh, trying to ignore how my chest flips at the idea of any kind of action happening between us. And did he say the first? It's not like he admitted he was a virgin. I'm sure he's gotten laid outside the van, but given how much time he must spend on the road, climbing one summit after another, sex is probably not on the top of his to-do list.

But if Ryan was anything like my own brother, he must have been a real charmer, always up for a good time. Maybe in another universe, the four of us would even be fast friends, grabbing beers and Bavarian pretzels at the Granite Grove bar.

And if Ryan had time for a girlfriend, surely his brother must have dated?

Whether it's selfish desire, immature hope, or just simple curiosity, I can't help but want more in that moment. And, after all, the worst he can say is no.

"Would Ryan consider a hug as action?"

The sun has long since set, but I don't need any light to see Nolan's face illuminated from the inside out.

"Considering the only touch I experience is when one of the guys slaps me on the back after solving a sick boulder problem, he'll take what he can get."

He opens his arms, and I rush into them before I can chicken out again. Nolan's big reveal about his brother may have brought down the electricity in the room from high voltage to a low buzz, but the mood feels like it did when we were eating our mac and cheese. It's nice. Really nice.

Nolan envelops me in his arms, his abnormally large, strong hands drifting from my waist to the small of my back—and back to my waist after a moment of hesitation. I can only imagine Ryan's sigh of disappointment when we pull apart, instead of going any further.

Or maybe that's just mine.

TANIA BEECHER's morning routines

IDEAL

- 5:00 a.m. – Turn off old-school alarm clock because phone is out of reach to keep me from doom scrolling on social media
- 5:15 a.m. – Complete silent meditation and set intention for the day
- 5:30 a.m. – Upbeat online dance class to get the blood flowing
- 6:00 a.m. – Shower and shave, before blow-drying and straightening hair within an inch of its life
- 6:30 a.m. – Brush and floss teeth, get dressed, take vitamins, and finish ten-step skin care routine
- 7:00 a.m. – Full face of "natural" makeup while listening to NPR or a business podcast
- 7:30 a.m. – Healthy breakfast, either a homemade açai bowl or superfood smoothie
- 8:00 a.m. – Out the door to catch the bus to West Oakland BART into San Francisco
- 8:45 a.m. – Arrive at Habituall HQ with time to make a cup of Earl Grey while catching up on watercooler talk with the team
- 9:00 a.m. – Open laptop to achieve inbox zero yet again

TYPICAL

- 6:55 a.m. – Wake up in a panic before phone

alarm scares me first; immediately start checking email and doomscrolling

- 7:30 a.m. – Finally get out of bed, throw on nearest clothes, tie up curls into harsh ponytail to keep them out of my face, brush teeth, and wash face with same acne cleanser I've been using since high school
- 8:00 a.m. – Attempt an online yoga workout, spend most of the time in child's pose
- 8:15 a.m. – Abandon the news after one-too-many scary headlines and listen to the same five emo bands I've been listening to since high school
- 9:15 a.m. – Show up to work fashionably late after briefly entertaining running away from it all and joining a hippie commune

chapter
five

When I wake up the next morning, it takes me an alarming number of seconds to get my bearings. I'm definitely not at home, because I'm not sleeping on my special ergonomic pillow—as the dull, throbbing pain in my neck and jaw are quick to remind me. In fact, my muscles everywhere ache, and my head is pounding and spinning like it just finished a ballet hip-hop routine with Channing Tatum.

Did I drink too much wine last night? I remember at one point double-fisting two glasses—no, wait, that was Harris. Did I take him up on his offer and have a wild night in the hot tub?

The air around my face is cold, making my nose sniffle slightly, but the rest of my body is nicely insulated under the covers and a warm heat radiates against my back. Too warm to be normal, actually. Which means I'm not in bed alone.

I force my eyes open, afraid of seeing the inside of a hotel room that's not my own. For years I've been worried about letting loose around Harris and throwing myself at him after too many drinks. Not only does he already have a girlfriend, but also I promised myself I would never get involved with someone I work with, let alone someone on my own marketing team. I might as well brush off my resume because there would be no coming back from a mistake like that.

My eyesight adjusts to the sunlight pouring through the windows, which aren't attached to a building at all. Instead, I'm peering through the windshield of someone's van.

Nolan's van.

Nolan.

The aftermath of yesterday evening rushes through my brain, and I slowly run my hands across my clothes, taking note that I'm still in his fleece pajamas. If anything salacious had happened, I doubt I would be wearing any clothes, and I try to be more grateful than disappointed that I am. Even if this former Girl Scout is on birth control on the off chance she gets lucky, who knows if Nolan the van-life vagabond is just as prepared?

But then I remember the reason why we didn't do the dirty last night—and it wasn't because of a lack of condoms.

That's the last photo I have of him before he died.

I glance at the small picture frame on the air vent, replaying the end of our conversation as Nolan told me about his twin brother Ryan. If the many hours between my last glass of wine weren't enough to sober me up yesterday, that somber story certainly did the trick.

Officially brought back to reality, I'm torn between two forces, the first of which is the warmth down my back. There's not much room in this bed, so I'm not sure whether we ended up in a spooning position out of need or want, but it's surprising how quickly I can get used to this. Being in bed with Nolan is even more comforting than his unexpectedly delicious vegan mac and cheese.

It would be easy to sink in deeper against him and let our bodies decide how they'd like to spend the morning, but Hammy the cockblock is wide awake now, running on his wheel and ruining the mood with his strict schedule.

The Habituall team is heading back to the Bay at nine o'clock sharp. What the hell are you doing lazing around? Get up already—we don't want to be late!

Immediately, my anxiety hamster starts catastrophizing through potential disastrous scenarios.

What if we get left behind? Or worse, what if they think we're missing, and they call the police for a search and rescue? You'll never live it down if you're caught in bed with someone you just met.

Even if he's a climber with a body as hard as the rocks underneath him, I reconsider getting up, relishing how strong and solid Nolan feels draped behind me. But Hammy has a point, and it wouldn't kill me to check the time.

Thankfully, much of the van is within grabbing distance, and out of the corner of my eye, I see my smartwatch on the kitchen counter. I slowly stretch my arm out, so as not to disturb Nolan, and tap the screen, praying it didn't die in the middle of the night. The time flashes green: 7:15 a.m.

At first I sigh in relief, knowing that I've got over an hour before we jump on the charter bus, but Hammy's already calculating the mental math of my morning routine.

Okay, that's about one-hundred minutes until we head home, but even if we get back to the lodge in fifteen minutes, it'll take at least forty-five to shower, wash your face, brush your teeth, and attempt to make your hair presentable. And that doesn't even count putting on a face of makeup, which honestly you don't have the luxury of doing this morning, so that's on you if that boorish head of sales asks if you're tired because you didn't swipe on some undereye concealer.

I get it, Hammy, that's enough.

I'm not done yet. Let's tack on another fifteen minutes to pack up your shit, which you would have done the night before had you not gone on your little joy-walk and gotten yourself lost in a snowstorm. And then you need to check out and buy some grab-and-go breakfast, because if you don't put something in your stomach during that four-hour drive, best believe you will pass out. So adding all that up, we certainly don't have time to get in a quickie—in case you were thinking about it. You weren't thinking about it, were you?

Not anymore, I groan internally, leaning farther back into Nolan as if to escape the clutches of my own mind.

Until I feel something even more perilous digging against my backside.

Oh. Wow.

The cacophony of voices in my head start yelling over each other.

No-nonsense me is ready to be offended and declare sexual harassment.

No-judgment me knows it's just a bodily function and not worth taking personally.

No-shame me wants to reach around and wake him up in the horniest way possible.

And Hammy insists that everyone shut up and get a move on, already!

But before a winner can be determined, Nolan stirs and instinctively wraps himself around me.

He must still be asleep, I think, as his hard-on presses between my cheeks. We're separated by layers of clothing, of course, but there's no denying the sheer size of him. I don't have to recall the length of his muscular hands because they're splayed across my back—it may not be an exact match, but it feels pretty damn close.

Nolan doesn't seem like the kind of guy who would come on to someone without their explicit consent, and I don't want to freak him out for initiating a hot but harmless cuddle while he's unconscious. I need to wake him up—but how? Shrug him off unceremoniously and jump out of bed? Call out his name with increasing volume like one of those gradual alarm clocks? Turn around to face him and hope he pokes me closer to the belly button than the love button?

Nothing ideal comes to mind, so instead I try to slither out of his grasp as slowly and stealthily as possible so as not to disturb him. It'll be much easier to wake him up once there's a safe buffer between us.

But this proves harder than I thought—in more ways than one. As I attempt to inch away from Nolan, he reaches for me in his sleep. This would be adorable if we were dating, but I'm sure he wouldn't want me getting the wrong impression just because he's at full mast at the moment.

I jerk forward to escape, throwing the covers off of me and onto him, which wakes him from his slumber. "Rise and shine," I blurt out, hoping I sound more peppy than perturbed, as Hammy continues to spiral about making it aboard the bus on time.

Nolan blinks his eyes open, at first serene and then concerned. He glances down then back at me, and it's obvious he's coming to the same realization I did minutes ago.

"I, uh, I'm so sorry—"

I wave my hands to brush off his completely unnecessary apology. "Nothing to be sorry about. If anything, I mean, good for you, really!"

Shut up and stop babbling about how impressive his dick is. Nolan's flushed with mortification and arousal, averting his gaze, and in the deafening silence of the van, I can hear him taking deep breaths to steady himself.

There's no reason to draw things out and make the situation worse, so I grab my clothes from yesterday and change back into them as fast as possible.

Goosebumps prickle up my arms, and although pulling up the legs of my slightly damp jeans amplifies the chill, I know they're appearing because I'm imagining Nolan's eyes on my bare back as I slip on my bra. But erection or not, he's been too much of a gentleman to act on any desires—if he had them, that is.

Fully clothed, I'm afraid to turn back and find him distracted by his phone without so much as a glance, but when I meet his eyes, I suck in my breath, surprised by their intensity. The heat on his cheeks has morphed from an embarrassed blush to something much more. By the way he's smoldering, I know that he didn't look away from me for a single millisecond.

I was afraid he didn't have any attraction for me. And now I'm afraid he does. Anxiety can be a real bitch that way.

I gulp, grabbing the first thing I can think of—the travel kit. "I'm gonna go real quick before we head out."

When paralyzed by flight or fight, my brain will always pick flight—even when my body's thinking of another f-word entirely.

~

TEXT CONVERSATION *between Tania Beecher and Dahlia Cruz, LCSW, on Friday, January 7, at 7:30 a.m.*

TANIA BEECHER: Are boners a good indication that a guy like-likes you?

NO CELL SERVICE DETECTED. MESSAGE NOT DELIVERED.

chapter
six

After both of us have taken care of our business—me relieving myself and Nolan relieving himself of his boner—we pack up the van and drive to Granite Grove, arriving before eight o'clock. As we enter the lodge, I brainstorm excuses in case I run into a coworker who asks why I'm in yesterday's outfit, now in much need of laundering after surviving a snowstorm. Would it be convincing to say that I forgot to pack enough clean clothes?

But thankfully, it's early, so no one from Habituall has yet rolled out of bed. Everyone must have enjoyed themselves in the hot tub and need every precious minute this morning to nurse their hangovers.

"What up, Wells?" A college-aged guy in a beanie startles me, waving to Nolan with one hand and carrying a snowboard in the other. "Stay warm out there!"

Before Nolan can express his thanks, another passerby recognizes him, and then another. All kinds of folks—hikers, skiers, even hotel employees—come up to him and say hi, while even more drop whatever they're doing to watch him from afar.

"Wow, it's like you're a celebrity around here," I say.

Nolan gives me a strange smile. "You could say that . . . although it's hard not to be well-known among the locals when I rely on this hotel for civilization—a hot shower and indoor plumbing are hard to come by in the van."

I'm about to steer us toward the guest elevator, but Nolan instead leads me to the front desk. "I have my mail delivered to the lodge," he explains, "so might as well collect it while we're here."

We stop at the counter and are approached by a woman with a nametag that reads SUMMER. She's effortlessly gorgeous, with tanned skin, deep blue eyes, and strawberry blonde hair pulled up into a loose ponytail, wavy tendrils framing her face. I immediately tense up, feeling gross and inadequate in her presence, wearing second-day clothes and not even a re-application of deodorant.

"Hey, Nolan. What a surprise. I'm so used to you dropping by on Mondays." Clearly, he sticks to routines like clockwork, treating the Granite Grove Lodge like his pseudo-apartment. Does Summer beam at him like that every time he shows up? If she's his metaphorical door attendant, the territorial looks she's shooting in my direction make me think she'd like to shut me out.

I expect Nolan to be oblivious to this silent standoff, but he's tapping his fingers nervously on the front desk counter like he's aware of the shift in the air.

"Change of plans," he says, sounding overly casual. "I'm actually sending off Tania here. She's on a work retreat."

I give her a small wave, trying my best not to be intimidated when I'm desperate for a shower and a comb through my tangled curls. Nolan doesn't make a move to exchange introductions, so I take it upon myself. "Nice to meet you. I'm Tania Beecher, VP of Marketing." That last part comes out mostly from habit, but I'd be lying if I said I wasn't trying to puff myself up and sound more formidable than I am.

"Thanks for booking Granite Grove, Tania. I'm Summer McKenzie, Jill of all trades at the lodge—front desk manager, concierge, last-minute belayer if you're in a bind."

Nolan chuckles. "That was once, like years ago. I had no idea Tommy was gonna get food poisoning the night before, and you will never let me forget you saved the day."

She shrugs, a twinkle in her eye. "I'm just saying you're lucky you weren't doing a big wall, or you'd owe me for the time I bounced from work."

Mission accomplished. Now I not only know Nolan and Summer have climbed together, but they also go way back. Nicely done, girl.

"Anyway, how was your stay?" Summer looks pointedly at me, like she knows I wasn't in my hotel room last night. Not that it's any of her business.

"It was great. I'd love to come again as soon as I can." I give her a wide-toothed smile, hoping she catches the innuendo. There's absolutely no rational reason to spar over a man I met yesterday, especially one whom I might never see again. But Summer doesn't know that, and something—maybe her attitude or her enviably good looks—is making me feel a bit petty.

"That's wonderful to hear. I hope you get the chance." She flashes a smile to meet mine, but her eyes are unequivocally saying "not a chance." This undercurrent between us is strong, and as much as I want to tell her to take a hike, she's got me curious. She's clearly protective of Nolan, but as a future girlfriend or an ex-girlfriend?

Summer click-clacks on her keyboard, checking the screen in front of her. "Your company's checking out today, right? I've pulled up the group reservation so we can take care of that for you."

I shake my head. "That's alright. I've got things to wrap up, so it might be a while." Hammy's been spiraling the whole way here, reminding me of all the tasks I need to complete before I get on the bus back home. I haven't yet cleaned up the hair I've shed in the sink and shower, let alone packed my suitcase.

Summer looks at me, then Nolan, then back at me. "I think it's best if you check out now, before you regret it." Her smile's frozen, but there's no way to interpret her words as anything other than ominous.

Nolan's staring at Summer with a steely glint, like he knows what she's saying between the lines when I can't.

"You know," she wavers, "because of the long lines around check-out time." She reassures me that I'll have plenty of time to gather my belongings before the cleaners tidy the room up for the next guests. I relent, having run out of excuses to prolong my stay. I want to maximize every moment I have with Nolan, and Miss Yosemite Beauty Queen over here is getting on my last nerve with her twat-swatting.

I get the sense Nolan feels the same way. He continues tapping the counter restlessly with one hand, while the other is hanging at his side, his fist opening and closing. In my mind, I'm imagining him wanting to reach for me but holding back so Summer isn't provoked, but more likely he just has a nervous twitch and I'm overthinking things yet again.

"Hey, Summer, can you get Tania some snacks for the ride home? I'd hate for her to starve on the long way back to the Bay."

He gives me a warm smile, while Summer icily asks if I have any preferences.

"Whatever's available is fine. And hot tea, if you have it. I'm not a big coffee drinker."

"Me neither," Nolan adds, "so make that two."

Summer mutters, "Coming right up" and heads to an employees-only break room in the back of the lobby.

As soon as she's out of sight, I panic, wondering how to make the most of these last few minutes before Nolan walks back to his van. Should I ask for his number? Add him on social media? How should I say goodbye—is a kiss too forward or should I stick to a hug? What if a coworker interrupts us before I have a chance to make a move, or worse, catches us in the act and heckles me on the ride home?

I yank Hammy off his wheel to keep him from spiraling any further. Let's face it, I have never made a move in my life, and I'm not about to start at the front desk of the Granite Grove Lodge while checking out of a business retreat at eight in the morning. All I can hope is that Nolan will read my mind and take the lead.

"Thanks for driving me here. And for, you know, saving my life. And for the mac and cheese. And for, well, everything in between, too." Nice, Tania. Real smooth.

"Of course. And thanks for keeping me company. It was really nice. I, um, forgot how nice it was having someone around."

He looks down at me with his big, brown eyes, and I step closer, willing him to wrap me with his wingspan.

"Let me know if you're ever in the Bay and need a hot shower and indoor plumbing. I'd be happy to roll out the red carpet for rock climbing royalty." I say it with playful sarcasm, and he blushes so hard it's adorable. I can't help myself, so I rush in for a hug, summoning all my confidence to give him a farewell kiss on the cheek. Friendly, but flirty—a last-ditch attempt to make my intentions known and end the exchange on a high note.

But my utter lack of spatial awareness causes me to flub things in a split second. Because instead of planting a chaste kiss on the cheek, grazing his five o'clock shadow, I catch the corner of his lips mid-smile. Too awkward to be romantic, but too intimate to be platonic. Turn me into taxidermy and mount me on the wall of this mountain lodge, because I have officially died from embarrassment.

Before I can apologize or explain myself, Summer reappears with our tea and snacks, which I grab in a rush. I squeak out a quick "Okay, see you later" before dashing to the guest elevators, praying that I'm out of their sight so they can't watch me wait for the lift to take me up to my room.

Hammy's in overdrive, heart racing, and it takes me much less time to pack up my stuff than we anticipated. None of it is organized, of course, because my brain is too distracted replaying that cringey moment over and over again. But I'm not about to risk a sequel in case Nolan decided to stay a little longer to chat things up with Summer. Rather than getting to the lobby fifteen minutes before our departure time, as I usually would, I rush onto the bus five minutes before it pulls out, to ensure Nolan and his white van are long gone from the hotel.

When Nolan and I had first arrived at Granite Grove, I was afraid I was never going to see him again, but as I avoid making conversation with my colleagues on the long drive from Yosemite to San Francisco, I'm thankful after such a mortifying moment that I never will.

~

Search results for "Nolan Wells" on Friday, January 7

Nolan Wells – Wikipedia

Nolan Russell Wells (born August 17, 1989) is an American rock climber best known for his free solo ascents of big walls . . .

Nolan Wells: Updates Only (@FreeNolo)

New year, no fear. Need a keynote speaker to discuss motivation, ambition, and managing anxiety? Contact to book upcoming events . . .

WHY NOLAN WELLS Said No Thanks to Family Inheritance – *Forbes*

Elite adventure athlete Nolan Wells has conquered some extreme challenges, but none more daunting than turning away from his family's financial advisory business . . .

NOLAN WELLS – The North Face Rock-Climbing Rockstar

One of the most accomplished rock climbers of our time, Nolan Wells has his eyes set on higher sights. We roll out the red carpet with The North Face's latest line of durable climbing gear . . .

PEOPLE ALSO ASK

What is Nolan Wells's net worth?
Who was Nolan Wells's twin brother?
Is Nolan Wells still alive?
Who is Nolan Wells dating?
How big are Nolan Wells's hands?

chapter
seven

I t took a month to get over the embarrassment of meeting Nolan Wells, but eventually life settled into its usual rhythm. I'm not sure what I was more humiliated by—the perception that I went in for a kiss and botched it or that I must have been the only person on earth not to know who this man really is. I was a bookworm in school, not a jock, so the closest thing I get to exercise is the steps I get anxiously pacing at my standing desk. How was I supposed to know Nolan is one of the greatest athletes of our generation?

Eventually, after consuming about every interview and scrolling through all of his social media timelines, I escaped from the rabbit hole of research and tried to banish Nolan from my mind. Hammy already takes up too much space with his worrying, so there isn't room for another fixation.

Instead, I distract myself the best I can, catching up with friends, resuming therapy, and occasionally going on a medi-ocre date with an accountant, architect, or some other equiva-lent of a Toyota Camry—boring but reliable. Not as exhilarating as getting rescued in a snowstorm by a moun-taineer living the van life, but safety and security are underrated.

I imagine Nolan would strongly disagree with that sentiment. After learning that he's one of the top free soloists, aka climbers who forgo ropes and other protective equipment, I can't think of anyone else with whom I would have less in common. I consider driving up to wine country an adventure, and there he goes, hanging off cliffs where one misstep means certain death. It's wild and terrifying and foolish. And surprisingly hot.

"Get a grip, Tania."

I shake my head out of my inappropriate thoughts, taking in Harris standing next to me. He's chuckling, gesturing to my hands, which are white knuckling my desk. I was so consumed by imagining erotically thrilling scenarios with Nolan that it's like my body was holding on for dear life.

"Whoops, got distracted there. Guess I was racing against the clock again to get these last few emails sent."

I fully expect Harris to call me out on my blatant fib, but instead he nods in solidarity.

"I don't blame you. These annual company kickoffs are such a huge time-suck."

"You mean *House Party*?" I tease with dripping sarcasm.

Harris pretends to vomit. "I refuse to call it that. House parties are supposed to be about fun and free beer—not circle-jerking the C-suite's egos."

I don't reprimand him for the crude disrespect of authority, even if I'm technically a member of said C-suite, because he's not exactly wrong. Habituall's CEO Evan Chen has made giant strides as a leader, ever since he cleaned up his act as an eccentric tech founder and started dating Casey Holbright, a celebrity stylist and my dear friend. Two years ago, I couldn't convince him to ditch his cargo shorts for press interviews. Now he's impeccably dressed and, more importantly, our company's reputation has never been stronger.

But I understand where Harris is coming from. Ever

since the company went public, the bureaucracy and politicking have been at an all-time high. The corporate life is like being caught in a hurricane of board votes and earning calls and shareholder meetings. It's one of the many reasons my anxiety hamster is forever spiraling—trying to survive this much pressure and scrutiny on a daily basis is fucking exhausting.

I check my smartwatch, mentally congratulating myself for closing my exercise ring by simply expending my nervous energy in an upright position. "Circle-jerk or not, this kickoff starts in five minutes, so we better make our way upstairs."

Harris suddenly extends his arm out to block me from leaving my cubicle, and I have to roll back on my heels to avoid colliding into him. "Wait—there's something I wanted to show you."

He makes sure no one's eavesdropping before discreetly pulling a small, velvet box from his jeans pocket.

"Omigod!" I cut myself off mid-squeal to avoid causing a scene. "Is that—"

Harris nods excitedly, opening the box to show off a breathtakingly gorgeous engagement ring—a 1.5-carat oval diamond on a chevron-shaped, yellow gold, pavé-encrusted band. It's got that art nouveau look that's all the rage, not that I've been perusing those online create-your-ring builders when I'm alone on a Saturday night and have had a little too much merlot.

"I can't believe it's been that long," I whisper, trying to recall the first time I heard him talk about his girlfriend.

Harris nods again, eyes wide. "Almost two years. Can you believe it?"

I shake my head fervently, guilty with envy. I turned thirty-three nearly six months ago, and Harris is the same age. I know comparison is the thief of joy, but what have I got to show for the last two years? Sure, I may have reached the top of the corporate ladder, but achieving a huge career milestone feels empty when I don't have a life partner to celebrate with.

"Do you think Hannah will like it?" he asks.

As much as I want to gag—how sickeningly adorable does a couple like Harris and Hannah sound?—when he looks at me expectantly, hoping for my approval, I can't help but smile. "She's going to love it. Just as much as she loves you, I'm sure. Congratulations, Harris. I'm so happy for you."

He snaps the box shut and shoves it back in his pocket before anyone else sees. We exchange a deep but utterly platonic hug, then make our way to the all-hands area, Harris practically skipping like he's on cloud nine, and me begrudgingly following behind him.

It's all so final. Harris is getting married, and I'm never seeing Nolan again. In both cases, it's well past time for me to move on with my life.

The all-hands area is teeming with a restless energy as people get settled into the many chairs, sofas, and beanbags on the floor. The furniture is arranged in a semicircle, facing a large open patch of carpet where the leadership team hosts its town hall meetings every Thursday.

But it's the first Monday in February, the start of our fiscal year, so there's a much bigger sense of gravitas—especially considering that most of our rapidly growing company are new employees. With six years of tenure under my belt, I'm a Habituall veteran, so our internal kickoff doesn't hold as much shiny veneer for me. But even I'm bewildered by how much the team has grown in two years—more than doubling in size to five hundred San Francisco staff and just as many folks around the world tuning in via videoconferencing. I used to consider Habituall like a dysfunctional yet endearing family, but it's hard not to think even my own employer is outgrowing me.

As Harris and I take our seats on a couch in the middle of

the room, Habituall's founder and fearless leader Evan Chen takes the proverbial stage. Casey, confident and kickass as always, sits in the front row to cheer him on, proud of the outfit she's put him in: a crisp, white collared shirt with pinstripes that match his deep burgundy blazer, which perfectly complements his navy slacks and brown loafers. And yet with such an objectionably attractive man standing in front of his team, my mind wanders . . . has Nolan ever worn clothes that nice? Does he even own a suit?

"Welcome," Evan booms into the lavalier mic on his lapel, holding his arms out to address the group. "I can't believe it's already time to start another fiscal year. Ever since we began hosting our conference, First Party, we wanted to make our annual company kickoff a smaller, internal-only event. And thus, House Party was born."

The crowd claps, and I groan to myself. Thankfully, Marketing doesn't plan internal events, so I have no idea what's on the agenda of this kickoff, but any mention of First Party gives me emotional whiplash. It requires so much work for so many weeks, and all other marketing activities come to a screeching halt to make it happen without a hitch. The arrival of House Party means that First Party is only eight weeks away, and the period between the two events knocks years off my life every time.

Oblivious to my anxiety spiral, Evan powers through his introduction. "The theme of this year's House Party is *meta-morphosis*. We may be a global public company of more than a thousand teammates and a legitimate force to be reckoned with in our industry, but in many ways, we are a tiny cater-pillar on the journey to become a beautiful butterfly."

As Evan carries on with his metaphor, I dream about cocooning like a caterpillar. If two weeks in a chrysalis sounds super appealing, I must really need a vacation, but there's no way I'd be able to take one until First Party is finished. Getting my caterpillar on will just have to wait.

I snap back to attention when Evan asks, "Can you believe it's been a month since we gathered among the majestic mountains of Yosemite? As luck would have it, I met our keynote speaker in the Granite Grove lobby just minutes before we boarded the bus back home."

Don't tell me—

"If you've seen his *National Geographic* specials, you can imagine my surprise to be in the company of such a living legend."

You've got to be kidding—

"This man is the dictionary definition of metamorphosis, and I'm so excited to introduce him to you all today. Give a round of applause for rock-climbing royalty Nolan Wells!"

Hammy flies off his hamster wheel, shaking the bars of his mental cage as I consider making a run for it. I am no more prepared to see Nolan now than I was when we first met. I have always prided myself on deprioritizing my appearance at work, so I can maximize my time on the job I'm actually paid to do. But what I consider good enough most days—hair pulled back in a frizzy ponytail and little more than some concealer and mascara on my face—is absolutely not good enough for this day.

My gaze ping-pongs around for the nearest bathroom to hide in, but it's already too late. Nolan walks across the room, scanning the sea of puffy vests as he approaches the front, and spots me like the easiest *Where's Waldo* puzzle. He breaks out into a sunny smile and waves goofily at me, jolting my heart into a backflip. I should have let the gesture go unreturned, so everyone would simply assume Nolan was waving to the crowd generally, but my hand waves back before I can stop myself.

Harris raises an eyebrow, amused. "Something you forgot to tell us, Tania?"

I smack him in the arm and shush him, blood rushing to my cheeks. But the damage is done. Renowned rock climber Nolan Wells has graced Habituall with his presence, and he singled me out specifically.

Even Casey's looking at me gleefully like I was crowned the winner of *The Bachelor*. I certainly can't run away now.

Evan shakes Nolan's hand before pulling him into one of his bro hugs, slapping him on the back with exuberance. After one of the executive assistants gets Nolan mic-ed up, the two men sit atop stools facing the crowd.

"Wow, what an opportunity to learn from one of the greatest talents of our time," Evan says, settling into his role as interviewer. "Everyone here knows how much of a huge gym rat I am, so this is like meeting Santa Claus. Thanks so much for joining us."

Nolan chuckles. "Thanks for having me. I'm stoked to be here. My van's not as big as a sleigh, though, so I couldn't bring gifts for everybody." He stretches the last word ever so slightly, with another glance in my direction. Does that mean he has something for me?

"Don't worry about that. Your presence is gift enough, that's for sure. There's no one else who embodies our theme better, with your transformation from future financial planner to the Steph Curry of climbing."

"Well, no offense to the Golden State GOAT, but no one has risked death playing basketball."

The banter comes easy between them, and within seconds everyone is captivated by Nolan's charm. It's precisely because he's out of his element that he's so endearing. I've been in marketing for a decade now, so I know immediately when someone's been media trained. Clearly, Nolan falls into that category—with the level of success he's achieved, I wouldn't expect otherwise. But watching his abnormally large hands fidgeting with the zippers on the knees of his convertible trail pants, I can also tell he's nervous speaking in front of people.

Evan segues into the meat and potatoes of the interview. "Now, Nolan, Habituall is a marketing technology, or martech, company, so I wanted to kick off our conversation by asking you, as a climber, what's your relationship with technology?"

Nolan laughs. "Practically nonexistent. The great part of scaling big walls in the most remote locations is that no one expects me to reply to their emails."

The envy of hundreds of engineers and go-to-market gurus is palpable, but an anxious energy simmers underneath the surface. Everyone dreams of going off the grid for a long weekend, but any longer and my fingers would be itching to plug into the matrix again. Nolan's got a legit reason to leave folks on read, but what would I even do with myself if I couldn't infinitely scroll social media the second I'm bored?

Evan presses on. "So how do people get your attention if it's not through your inbox?"

"Mondays are when I visit Granite Grove to pick up my snail mail and run through any online to-dos in their business center. But honestly, the best way to get my attention is to stumble upon my van when I'm not climbing." He pauses, turning in my direction. "It rarely happens, so I'm not likely to forget you when it does."

Another laugh from the crowd, but only I can catch the hidden truth in that twinkle in his eye. *I'm not likely to forget you.* As if I could have erased Nolan from my memory if my life depended on it.

Evan runs through the rest of his martech-related questions, which Nolan answers with polite practicality—like when he's asked which consumer brands he admires most, and he responds he's contractually obligated to say The North

Face, as if his walking billboard of an outfit hadn't made it clear.

Only near the end of the interview do I realize Hammy's been surprisingly dormant, lulled to sleep by Nolan's comforting presence. It makes sense when I give it some thought—my preferred background of the meditation app I need to use more often is that of a peaceful mountain meadow. Nolan gets to live in that serene environment every single day, so even when he's suffering from a bit of stage fright, listening to his voice is soothing.

But then Hammy perks back up when his favorite topic arises.

"Not to end on a serious note," Evan continues, "but metamorphosis is an inherently scary process—to evolve from one thing to another without knowing how life is going to be on the other side. So when it comes to what you do, Nolan, what would you say is your greatest fear?"

For once, Nolan's lost in thought. It's not like he's never been asked this question before, but something tells me he won't be giving a rote response.

"Before I lost my brother Ryan, I would have joked that my greatest fear was public speaking for an event like this or maybe even asking a woman out on a date because, to this day, I've never been able to work up the courage to do that. Even years after Ryan's death, I side-stepped the question. Once you lose someone you love, what could possibly be more terrifying than that?"

He picks at his calluses before meeting my gaze, making my heart flutter like his long, dark eyelashes.

"But I met someone recently who was refreshingly honest with me, even if she couldn't be honest with herself. She reminded me of why I climb: it may be lonely at times, but where others see emptiness, I see freedom. So I'll say my greatest fear is being trapped in a life not of my own making."

My breath rushes out, like I've been kicked in the chest. He met someone recently who reminded him why he climbs? That doesn't sound like he's referring to that damn Summer chick, since they go way back. Did he have a meet cute while climbing a mountain? Raced her to the top, then made sweet love to her on the summit as the sun set? My heart would explode if it happened in a rom-com, but it's dangerously close to splitting in two if it happened in real life, and not with me.

Evan puts his hand on his chest, and not in a disingenuous attempt at flattery like most executives would, but out of sincere appreciation. "I think you stunned everyone into silence. Thank you, Nolan, for those words of wisdom. Such a great reminder to never give up—"

"Not exactly," Nolan interrupts forcefully. "Sorry, I'm sure you're all doing great work, but I would hate for my message to get manipulated to support some corporate mission. Because if you're like this clever, brilliant woman I met—who's in this industry, in fact—and you're getting paid to pretend to give a shit, give up immediately. My brother's life may have been cut cruelly short, but he spent every second of it doing what he loved most. That's not a tragedy. What's tragic is when amazing, witty, gorgeous women—excuse me, people—are too afraid to take risks. There's no virtue in living a smaller life just because it's safer. So I'm asking you all what I'd ask her again: what would you do if you stopped pretending?"

My fingernails dig into my forearms, nearly breaking skin, in an attempt to pinch myself awake. This has to be a dream. Clever. Brilliant. Amazing. Witty. Gorgeous. The adjectives spiral around in my brain, bewildering Hammy's negative self-talk. I was so convinced I had made zero impact on Nolan— even if I had over two million search results like he does, there's no way he'd waste his time clicking through them in the middle of the night.

But that existential question haunts me like an echo, recalling images of us stealing glances over vegan mac and cheese. That clever, brilliant, amazing, witty, gorgeous woman —he was talking about *me*.

I may not know what I'd do if I wasn't working in tech, but with his question ringing in my ears, there's no denying it now. I have to at least stop pretending I don't care about giving him an answer. Because if Nolan Wells managed to sneak into my life a second time, I can't let him walk out of it again.

~

"What Climbing Etiquette and Dating in Silicon Valley Have in Common," by The Send-It Sisters on Monday, February 7

You wouldn't think there's much overlap on the Venn diagram between climbing and computing, but they both share a common problem: a gender gap. While indoor climbing has a more even split, only one-third of outdoor climbers are women—mirroring the percentage of female tech workers.

The cishet ladies living in that overlap know we have a long way to go, both on the clock and on the crag. If you're struggling to top out of the dating pool, feel free to send these tips to climbing Chads and brogrammer Brads alike—written in a language both can understand.

1. **Pay attention.** Half the battle of climbing and dating is simply staying focused on the present moment. If you wouldn't whip out your phone on the route or disrupt your flow state on No Meeting Wednesdays, don't attempt to multitask over martinis if you want to get laid.

2. **Don't spray beta.** What do advice and celibacy have in common? No one appreciates them when they're involuntary. You don't want unsolicited tips from a newb when you're perfecting a pitch, so don't be a backseat driver with your dates either.

3. **Sharing is caring.** Every climber needs a spotter, like every coder needs someone managing quality assurance. What makes a boring relationship, however, is when no one takes turns. To be a successful power couple, switch it up and let your partner take the lead for once.

4. **Keep your noises under control.** Men are loud enough without assistance, and the last thing anyone needs is them blaring music in the office or grunting like a wild boar in the gym. Being vocal can help—especially on belay or in bed—but don't over-index into obnoxious territory.

chapter
eight

Go over there, Tania. You haven't seen Nolan in a month —the least you can do is say hello.

But what if he doesn't want to talk to you? Hammy's critical self-talk holds me back. *What if you were imagining him smiling at you? What if he was saying all those nice things about somebody else, and you look like a fool assuming you're special?*

That seems uncalled for. Who else could he possibly be referencing?

He rarely visits civilization—it could be any woman who crossed his path.

But what if I don't go over there, and I miss out on my one chance at true love? Did my anxiety ever take that into consideration?

Hammy stops spewing poison, trapped in a catch-22, unsure of what's worse—taking one step forward or dying alone. *Now that you put it that way—*

"What are you waiting for, Tania? Did you need me to give you a push?"

I'm jolted out of my paralysis. "Casey!"

My most stylish friend jabs me in the side, gesturing across the room where her CEO boyfriend is chatting up Nolan while he signs autographs and takes selfies with the team. I look Casey up and down, dressed in a luxe navy shift dress to match Evan, her hair effortlessly blown out and her makeup flawless. By comparison, I feel so frumpy in my tech uniform. I doubt I could even get a job as an extra in one of those action movies that destroys the Golden Gate Bridge.

"I don't know . . . I'm not exactly power couple material right now."

Casey rolls her eyes. "Have you seen what he's wearing? He rolled straight out of a Bass Pro Shop. You could be wearing a burlap sack, and he wouldn't take his eyes off you. I don't think he did once the whole time he was speaking."

Blood rushes to my fingertips, and I shake them, hoping to expel my nerves. "But what do I say?"

"How about this—" Casey abruptly shoves me through the throng of people. "Hi, Nolan!" she shouts, loudly and with as much projection as she can muster.

The sea of puffy vests parts, and I stop short of colliding into Nolan, who's looked up from signing yet another corpo-rate-branded notebook.

"Hi, Nolan," I whisper, immediately cringing. God, I hope he heard me, so I'm not forced to repeat that oh-so-suave opening line. There's no way he would have called me witty after a moment like that.

"Tania—it's so great to see you again." He pushes past his fans to give me a big hug. I melt into his royal blue fleece jacket and take a deep breath, noting a hint of cologne under his natural musk of alpine spring and chalk.

I hadn't told him where I worked, so Nolan must have figured it out after meeting Evan. The company had taken over the lodge that week, and there weren't any other groups reserving room blocks. So that must mean he woke up this morning knowing he'd see me again—had anticipated it all month, in fact.

Did he wear cologne for me?

I brush away the thought. He may not do events often, but that doesn't mean he wouldn't make a simple effort when he's around the people cutting him a check for his time.

Before I can answer, Evan steps in. "Hey Tania, Nolan here is wrapping up, so I was going to escort him out. I'm sure he's got a busy day ahead of him."

"I can take him," I blurt out before Hammy has a chance to resist. "You've got to get started with the last fiscal year's recap anyway."

Evan is about to brush off my offer, until Nolan reaches out to shake his hand. "Thanks again for having me. It was a lot of fun."

Habituall's founder takes us in with curiosity. "Of course. Hope there's much more fun in your future. Come back anytime." He slaps us both on the back, and after Nolan grabs his sizable backpack, I pull him toward the elevators before my face turns as red as a traffic light.

As I push the button to call the lift, my mind shifts to logistics. "So . . . where are you staying while you're in the city?" Please don't say Outer Sunset or some other neighborhood that's hella inconvenient from downtown.

"I'm actually parked at Pacific Pipeworks."

The elevator chimes as its doors open, but that name doesn't ring any bells. "Is that some new hotel in Pac Heights?"

He laughs. "I'm not a fan of the indoors, remember? It's too far a walk from the bed to my pee bottle. No, it's a new climbing gym in Oakland."

I don't have the mental space to be mortified—either on his behalf, for mentioning his bathroom activities, or for myself, recalling my own bathroom journey in the middle of a snowstorm. Because his last word rings in my ears.

Oakland. I live in Oakland.

The second we enter the lobby of our building, I'm pulling up the map on my phone before he has a chance to reveal where this gym is located. Lo and behold, it's right off the Bay Bridge. In fact, I drive past it every time I get a late-night hankering for Taco Bell. I remember someone telling me when I moved into the neighborhood five years ago that the massive warehouse was once used for Burning Man art. I had no idea it had been converted into—

"The largest climbing gym in the country," Nolan explains as I pull up the gym's website. "Nearly fifty thousand square feet of terrain, so I'm stoked to try it out for the first time. I grew up in Berkeley, so I've been going to Touchstone gyms since I was a kid, at least until I graduated from Cal and moved to the park. This location opened in the middle of last summer when I was finishing the climbing season, and I haven't had a reason to visit . . . until now."

I'm not sure what's cuter, that Nolan calls it "the park" as intimately as we in the Bay call San Francisco "the city" or that he's staring at me with a boyish hopefulness. I refuse to admit I'm the reason he's making a pit stop at Pacific Pipeworks, but it feels nice to entertain the idea.

"I could go with you." The words fall out of my mouth like hand grenades ready to explode. What the hell am I thinking? I don't even own leggings I'd wear outside the house. "You know, if you need a belayer."

His eyes lock with mine, skeptical but intrigued. "You've climbed before?"

I shake my head quickly. If this was a rom-com, I'd be lying my pants off and antics would ensue as I tried to keep up the ruse, but he'd see through my deception as soon as I get in a harness. "I overheard some other marketers chatting about it the other day." Only partially true. I may have eavesdropped on that conversation, but I've been obsessing over the sport since we parted ways. Not like that research would make me any good at it in real life.

"It's a popular first date activity," Nolan says, "right up there with ax throwing and paint nights. Or at least that's what it seems like whenever I train indoors."

Nolan sounds a bit somber, like he both knows and doesn't know what he's been missing out on. How many first dates has he sacrificed to become the best climber in the world? With so much time spent against hard, cold rock, how much does he yearn for softness and warmth against his skin?

"I could get off early." Again with speaking before thinking. Hammy must be in control of my motor skills. I cringe at the innuendo flying out of my mouth, but I couldn't stand there and let him feel alone. "I mean, I have to finish up things at work, but I could meet you at Pacific Pipeworks—say around four o'clock?"

The winter chill jolts us awake the moment we step outside the building. Karl the Fog, our beloved weather companion, is draped over the city today. But the sun's broken through the clouds in Nolan's eyes, and I'd do anything to preserve that brightness.

"Rad! I was hoping you'd be up for it because I, uh, got you these."

He sets his backpack down and pulls out a smaller black mesh bag with climbing gear inside. "It's all the basics: harness, belay device, carabiner, and chalk bag. I guessed on your shoe size, but I've been doing this so long, I'd be surprised if I didn't get it right."

I take the bag in my arms, holding the gear as awkwardly as if he handed me an eight-pound bag of jumbo russet potatoes. Yes, I technically know what they are, but what the hell am I going to *do* with them?

"You didn't have to go to all that trouble. Don't climbing gyms have rentals?"

He scoffs, throwing his backpack over his shoulders. "What else are corporate sponsorships for other than getting free stuff?"

I nod, feeling silly to assume he pays out of pocket for any expenses when he's in the elite echelon of athletes. And a gift is still a gift, right?

They say love don't cost a thing, Hammy whispers, *but this sounds like the price of the friend zone to me.*

Not that there's anything wrong with having friends! I want to scream at my anxiety hamster. Even if there's an expiration date, and he'll be gone in the morning, it wouldn't kill me to get some exercise.

"Thank you, Nolan, that was super thoughtful of you. I can't wait."

Before I send him off and head back to the office, we exchange phone numbers in case one of us is running late. I'm so used to being around brogrammers with the latest devices that I find his first-generation iPhone SE endearing. It sounds blasphemous when you're working in the tech industry, but there's something sexy about walking around with an eight-year-old phone in a plastic case that's chipped around the corners like you don't give a single shit.

I go in for another hug before I chicken out. "Safe travels across the bridge, and I'll see you later."

"Awesome, it's a date."

He pulls away with a smile and starts walking toward the nearest parking garage, waving behind him, while I'm left mouth agape, his cologne still at home in my nostrils.

To this day, I've never been able to work up the courage. That's what he had said about asking women out on dates. And here I am, bamboozled into one. A date. I'm going on a rock-climbing date with the most celebrated rock climber on the planet.

I march back through the lobby, up the elevator, and into headquarters on the top floor, practicing my fake cough as I gather my things because there's no way I'll be able to keep working today when there's so much on the line. Praying that Casey hasn't left already, I make circles around the cubicles until I find her in the kitchen grabbing another cold brew from the fridge. She's made her career dressing celebrities, and now it's time to enlist her in her strangest assignment yet.

"I'm sick." I mime hacking up a lung. "And I need your help."

TANIA BEECHER's dating profile

- **Name**: Tania
- **Gender**: Cisgender woman
- **Pronouns**: She/her
- **Sexuality**: Heterosexual
- **Age**: 33
- **Height**: 5′ 7″
- **Location**: Oakland, CA
- **Hometown**: Fresno, CA (because no one knows where Sanger is)
- **Ethnicity**: As white as the 1,000-thread count sheets I hide under when I get the Sunday Scaries
- **Children**: Not even interested in being the "fun aunt"
- **Family plans**: Living with my friends, *Golden Girls*–style

- **Covid vaccine**: If I could get a monthly subscription, I would
- **Work**: All #girlboss-ed out
- **Education level**: Overeducated and overwhelmed
- **Religious beliefs**: Jesus—or somebody, anybody —take the wheel, I'm tired of driving
- **Politics**: The only thing I'm conservative about is diversifying my investment portfolio
- **Drinking**: The best Napa Valley has to offer
- **Drugs**: Someone once asked me if I "liked to party"—it took me way too long to figure out they weren't talking about karaoke
- **A special talent of mine**: Waking up five minutes before my alarm no matter how early I set it
- **Biggest risk I've ever taken**: Sent a marketing email without a third proofread
- **Typical Sunday**: Dreading Monday
- **We'll get along if**: "Roughing it" is not part of your vocabulary
- **We're the same type of weird if**: We pride ourselves on not being able to keep a plant alive
- **What I order for the table**: Extra napkins
- **Worst idea I've ever had**: Drinking the house wine
- **My greatest strength**: Being prepared in an emergency
- **My mantra**: What doesn't kill you almost kills you, and honestly that's sometimes worse
- **Most controversial opinion**: The Oxford comma is overrated
- **Most irrational fear**: That my irrational fears are entirely rational
- **My simple pleasures**: A cup of tea, a good book, and an industrial-size weighted blanket

- **Never have I ever**: Lost this game because I have never done a lot of things
- **One thing I'll never do again**: Leave the house without a water bottle
- **A non-negotiable for me is**: Being a bad tipper
- **The award I should win is**: Fastest jumping to conclusions
- **I'm the type of texter who**: Has perfect spelling and grammar even when drunk
- **I won't shut up about**: What we can learn about feminism from reality television. In this TED talk, I'll . . .
- **I'm weirdly attracted to**: People who are too cool for social media
- **Social causes I care about**: Protecting civil liberties, supporting women in STEM, and teaching dog people how to be cat people at my local feline rescue

chapter
nine

My therapist Dahlia is always harping on the importance of naming our emotions, but it's hard to come up with anything other than guilt at the moment. Guilt over playing hooky from work for something as superfluous as a date—even if my marketing team had no problem taking the reins for one day. Guilt over roping Casey and the rest of her entourage into this assignment—even though they raced over to my Oakland apartment the moment they heard a man was involved. Guilt over not having time to stock my fridge before they arrived—even though no one complained about ordering delivery from Belly, my all-time favorite Asian fusion taco joint.

Eventually, when everyone's successfully curbed my guilt and reassured Hammy into submission, another emotion manages to ignite in my heart, fueled by the oxygen I keep inhaling with each deep breath.

Excitement. Because it's been a long time since I've gone on a date that I was actually looking forward to.

"Omigod, I'm so full." Casey licks the last of the kimchi aioli from her pristinely manicured fingertips and pushes away her empty plate. "So glad I'm the one supplying the clothes, not trying them on."

Casey's ride-or-die best friend Alex Waterston-Gardner nods in agreement, and even though it's not her first time sitting at my dining table, it will never not be surreal to have Princess Alex, the world's most famous social media celebrity, in my actual home. Casey's been Alex's stylist since they were teens, and since then they've rounded out the quintessential glam fam with makeup artist Som Srisati, esthetician Victoria "Tori" Townsend, and hairdresser Glen Cooper, who always lets us ladies occupy the four navy-colored dining chairs while taking a seat on the small pink ottoman I use for storage.

"I respect your strategy, Tania," Som says with a wink. "Get us absolutely stuffed so we can get you absolutely stuffed." She wiggles her eyebrows suggestively, making my face flush as rosy as the ottoman under Glen.

"It's just a date," I insist, trying to get my breathing back under control. "And it's at a climbing gym—there will be no stuffing involved." I turn to Casey. "You saw what Nolan was wearing today. He's the last man on earth to care about fashion, so I'm not sure if all this is necessary." I gesture widely to the racks of clothes and boxes of beauty products squeezed in the spare space of the open-concept living and dining room. "I was thinking of just a pair of cute leggings that don't have holes worn into the crotch like mine have."

Casey stands up and moves her chair into the middle of the room, pushing me into it. "It's just leggings for *this* date, but what about all the other dates? Think about it, Tania: camping trips across the Sierra Nevada mountains, swimming in crystal-clear lakes, making love under the stars? Today could be the first day of the rest of your life."

I don't bother mentioning that not all those activities on her list require clothes, because the idea of hooking up with Nolan in a sleeping bag—unprotected from the elements and wild animals and god knows what else I'd encounter in the wilderness—sounds as far-fetched as the idea that there would even be a second date.

"But I don't have an athletic bone in my body. The only reason I even have a gym membership is because Habituall pays for it, and I've yet to find a hike with a view so amazing it makes me forget it's still exercise."

Tori laughs, that sardonic edge cutting through my fretting. "And you think we're a group of fitness freaks? Alex only gets on her Peloton to justify ordering pizza delivery on movie nights. Casey only goes with Evan to Equinox to make sure he doesn't add more muscle tanks to his wardrobe, and those two wine snobs over there spend more time cruising for guys at the gym than doing cardio. Every one of them has ulterior motives for working out, so you're in great company if you're only rock climbing to get your rocks off."

The tough-as-nails nail technician has a point, even if it sounds skeezy to pretend I give a crap about climbing just because Nolan's got an obvious effect on me. And how many mediocre men have I met who have feigned an interest in reality television to try and get in my pants? It's not like I ever hid the fact that I have nothing in common with Nolan—for goodness' sake, I assumed he was talking about real estate investing when he mentioned REI.

Casey rambles on about faking it until you make it, while I follow Tori's line of sight to Glen and Som picking out a bottle of cab from my wine rack. They always love coming over, because they know I have "the good shit" thanks to my wine club discounts, so I can't begrudge them for helping themselves. But the good shit requires respect.

"Let me get that." I jump up to grab my aerator to help the wine breathe. "Nice eye. I love that vintage from Honig." Glen places a third glass in front of me as I fill the two of theirs. "Who else is drinking?"

"You are, betch. We can see those gears whirring in that tightly wound brain of yours, and we need you to calm down and enjoy the ride."

"But it's only noon."

"I'm sorry—did you have somewhere else to be, darling?"

Glen's adorably posh British accent placates me, but not nearly as much as the terms of endearment. I've been hearing the glam fam call each other betch for two years now, and I don't even remember when they first threw the word in my direction, but it makes me feel like an honorary member, nonetheless.

I take a long sip from the heavy pour in my glass, appreciating some of the best wine money can buy. "Okay, fine. Let the makeover montage begin."

I HAVE TO SAY, at first I was skeptical about how this was going to turn out, since none of us had a single minute of rock-climbing experience between us. But if there's one thing the glam fam knows best, it's taking it up a notch. And while I was concerned about being too done up for such a laid-back date, when I look in the mirror, I'm relieved to recognize the woman staring back at me. Som has perfected the no-makeup makeup—bright and fresh, with a hint of blush on my cheeks and a touch of candied apple tint on my lips.

Admiring her handiwork, I'm already bracing myself for when my dewy complexion turns greasy once I'm at the gym. "And you're sure nothing will budge once I'm sweating my ass off?"

Som heads to the sink to dump a bowl of ice-cold water down the drain. "Trust me, after you dunked your face into this, your base layer was locked and loaded. I may be a Thai beauty goddess, but the Koreans have us beat when it comes to the Jamsu technique. You could withstand a monsoon with that second skin, so a little shine is nothing."

My hands are like moths to a flame, but Som would kill me if my fingertips contaminated her canvas, so I twirl them around my hair instead. I'm still sporting a ponytail to keep locks from falling in my face, but my curls are voluminous and glossy instead of frizzy and unkempt.

"It's so bouncy." I tug gently on an *s*-curved spiral, gleefully enjoying the way it springs back with vigor. "Now I understand, Glen, why you're always going on about how hair should have body, rather than the other way around."

The hair extraordinaire guffaws, running his fingers through his robust beard. "Only because this body has enough hair to bring all the boys to the yard. I'm not one to discriminate, of course, but I do love me a slip 'n' slide."

The image tantalizes me. I don't know where Nolan falls on the body hair spectrum, because the last time I saw him, we were in the middle of a blizzard—not exactly great for going shirtless. After sleeping next to him that night in his van, I know for a fact that his abs are rock-solid, but now Glen's got me wondering if Nolan's naturally smooth or got the kind of happy trail I wouldn't mind hiking . . .

I shake my head, curls springing like pom-poms, as I try to banish the thought from going any further. Nothing wrong with appreciating Nolan's body, a bicep curl here or a glute squat there, but it's best to stick to the parts visible for public consumption. Can't be getting too hot and bothered in an environment that's already hot and bothersome.

As for the rest of my body, Tori's got me covered. After the esthetician gave me a much-needed wax—again, only on the parts visible for public consumption—she trimmed and buffed my nails, cleaned up my mangled cuticles, and added a pearly pink coat that's feminine but not too flashy to climb up walls.

"And as much as it pains me to know you're gonna grub them up in filthy chalk," she says, "that gel is practically indestructible for at least two weeks. Just clean under your nails, for the love of acetone, please."

I nod obediently, a bit intimidated by her tattoos, piercings, shaved undercut, and combat boots. It's like getting a manicure by the lead singer in a punk rock band, even though I know Tori actually plays jazz during the gigs she picks up when she's not painting talons.

Casey's finished off the makeover with the cutest athleisure I've ever seen. After I rejected revealing crop tops and those R-rated leggings that ride up your ass to show off each individual cheek, she landed on deep purple yoga pants that tighten up all the right places and a lavender racerback tank with cutouts to accentuate my shoulders.

"Now don't slouch! I'm not breaking my rule of no gym attire for you to ruin this outfit with that heinously bad posture you techies have."

I instantly snap to attention, smiling. Two years ago she was hired by Habituall to turn Evan Chen from an exercise-addicted hippie into a real CEO. How ironic that two exact opposites managed to fall madly in love.

Is that how it could go with Nolan? Today could be climbing at Pacific Pipeworks and before I know it, we could be spending the summer gallivanting around national parks in his van. Well, if that future is ever going to come to life, at least I look as good as Kate Hudson in a Fabletics commercial.

Once everyone's packed their beauty gear, we wrap things up with a quick photo shoot next to the large window in my living room to take advantage of the natural light and commemorate my resuscitated love life.

"Tania, you are gonna make that boy sweat all right," Casey gushes, snapping pics like a mom sending her teenage daughter off to her first prom. "I have a good feeling about this. Nolan's exactly the kind of guy you need to get out of your head and into your body."

Glen fluffs my hair between shots. "Just report back when he gets into your body, betch."

I shove him playfully. "Don't get your hopes up—one day at a time."

He tops off everyone's wine glass, except for mine. I switched over to water, so I don't climb for the first time under the influence. My heart's already pounding a mile a minute in anticipation, but I can't risk a concussion on top of an alcohol-induced headache in the event I take a tumble.

Casey gives me the kind of encouraging hug you give someone before a theater performance or a sports championship. "It's okay to get your hopes up, and keep them there." She raises her glass in a toast. "To the first day of the rest of your life."

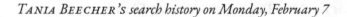

Tania Beecher's search history on Monday, February 7

How to rock climb
    How to rock climb indoors
    Why do climbing grades make no sense
    Climbing gym etiquette
    Why does chalk feel so gross
    Can your pants rip while rock climbing
    Is climbing cardio or strength training
    How many calories does climbing burn
    How sore will I be after climbing
    What if I have to go to the bathroom while climbing
    What the fuck is a poop tube
    Has anyone peed on someone while climbing

Do climbing harnesses have emergency eject buttons
Do climbing harnesses give you camel toe
Is chalk bad for a manicure
Is rock climbing an Olympic sport
What skills do you need to rock climb
What impresses rock climbers
How long do you have to rock climb before you're a pro
What if I'm a climbing prodigy without knowing it
How many people have died while rock climbing
How many people have died while rock climbing indoors

chapter
ten

I f this is the first day of the rest of my life, is it really going to begin in a rusted warehouse the color of spearmint gum that's been left out in the sun for too long? There's been no effort to update the exterior of the place, not even the ancient black sign that reads PACIFIC PIPE COMPANY in white block lettering. It has the same vibe as the broken-down mechanic shop in downtown Fresno where my grandfather spent almost every day of his life.

The exterior does not prepare me to handle what's inside. I walk through the supersized side door and enter an impossibly massive space—I feel like I'm on *Doctor Who* entering the TARDIS. As far as the eye can see are climbing walls, color-blocked in bright yellow and teal and fuchsia.

On my left are shorter, rounder structures with plenty of overhangs—those must be for bouldering since no one on that side has safety ropes and they're simply jumping down after reaching the top. Then on the right are fifty-foot faces where people are taking turns climbing and belaying—and falling when they hit a particularly tough spot on their route. These folks have ropes to catch them, of course, but they look so much higher in the air now that I'm up close. And Nolan regularly climbs El Capitan, which is three thousand feet, if I'm remembering correctly. I try to imagine the walls of Pacific Pipeworks sixty times taller, but there's no way I can properly compare this gym to a stone monolith that's double the size of the Empire State Building.

My heart is pounding in my ears at the sheer scale of this place and the impressive amount of skill someone like Nolan needs to make climbing their calling. And here I am, greener than a novice, calculating how many seconds I have to make a run for it before he sees me.

"Hey, Tania. You made it!"

Damn. There goes my chance to avoid embarrassing myself. I may look like a rock-climbing brunette Barbie thanks to Casey's impeccable styling, but no outfit can save me from the humiliation that awaits me.

I wave as Nolan approaches. I assumed he'd already be a sweaty, sexy mess after hours of climbing, but he's clean and freshly shaved. I spent the past three hours perfecting every inch of my appearance, but men are never expected to make that kind of effort. I'm genuinely surprised whenever a guy shows up on a first date to a fancy restaurant wearing a collared shirt, so I'm taken aback by how great Nolan looks—and at the gym, no less. I wonder what kind of product he's put in his hair to give it that effortlessly tousled effect.

"Everything okay? You look a bit shell-shocked."

I shake myself out my trance. "Yeah. You must have been climbing all day, but you look like you just got here."

Nolan blushes, smiling guiltily. "I was, but I jumped in their showers after my lunch break. It's been a couple of days since I had a proper shave, and I should look my best on a date, right?"

I break out in a big grin, nodding. Normally I'd hate to praise a man for doing the bare minimum to woo a woman. But it's written all over Nolan's face that he dates so infrequently—he needs confirmation he's not imagining this. "You look fantastic—almost like a professional."

He laughs at my teasing, because it's so obvious that everyone in the gym knows who he is. A few nosy nellies are whispering to their friends and pointing in our direction, but he must have already signed autographs for the most brazen because no one dares to approach him. Granted, it's not like Nolan Wells is as famous as Princess Alex—he has 5 million followers to her 500 million last I checked—but this isn't a fashion show or television premiere where you expect to run into celebrities. And yet a celebrity is exactly what he is here. Catching sight of Nolan at the largest climbing gym in the country is like seeing Gordon Ramsey at French Laundry. A thrilling chance encounter but not that shocking when they're in their element.

"Thank you," Nolan says gratefully, pulling me in for a hug. "But I must look like a loser standing next to you. You're so stunning I'm afraid I'll forget how to climb with you around."

I bite back the hollow scoff desperate to explode out of my mouth. The glam fam did their best, for sure, but I'd bet my entire 401(k) that these curious climbers would declare me the loser. My heart seizes at the thought of someone snapping photos of us and selling them to the paps. Nolan's a few inches taller than me, but we very likely weigh the same —a fact that can't be denied regardless of how much compression is built into my leggings. If they see what I see —a curvy, midsize woman so pale you'd think she sleeps in a coffin standing next to a bronzed Adonis—I can only imagine the hate comments I'll get once the images hit the web.

But I can take a compliment gracefully no matter how ridiculous it sounds, so I thank him for his kind words before following him to the check-in counter. The red-headed dude with the nametag JAKE staffing the desk is so giddy to see Nolan that I fear he'll have a little accident like a hyper puppy.

Nolan flashes his gym membership card. "Hey, Jake, I'm already checked in, but could you add Tania here to my reservation?"

Jake's initial joy that *the* Nolan Wells knows his name, even if it's attached to his uniform, quickly fades as he tackles this routine task with the gravity of someone who's been given the nuclear codes. "Absolutely. Let me take care of that for you, Mr. Wells." He tap-taps at his keyboard to pull up Nolan's account. "Wow, been a long time since you've used a buddy pass."

The photograph of Nolan and his brother flashes in my mind, and I'm this close to blurting out how wildly rude it is to remind someone of losing their closest climbing partner, but Nolan's chuckling like he's being heckled at a comedy show.

"Thanks, man, for pointing out I have no game. Hopefully, this isn't a one-time thing. We've got everything else covered, though—no need to ring up any rentals."

I lift up the bag of gifted gear. It's such a miniscule thing, bringing your own stuff instead of paying for it, but it does help a teensy bit to make me feel like I belong here.

But Jake frowns slightly, and I grow concerned that I'm going to get kicked out for being a climbing fraud. "If she's never climbed with us before, she'll need to pass our safety check. Let me see if someone can go through the procedures with her."

Nolan holds his hand up, declaring that unnecessary. "Come on, man. Don't make me pull the whole 'don't you know who I am' move and make me sound like an asshole. But you know who you're dealing with here. Tania is in the best of hands." The smile in his eyes hardens into a steely glint. *"The best."*

My breath releases in a slow exhale. Hot damn. I have encountered plenty of mediocre white men showboating like they're something special when they are very much not. But this is a man who has worked harder than everyone on earth to earn his place as an athlete and who will not be undermined. I have never seen that kind of ultra-competitive attitude on him —the edge in his voice, the way that vein pops out at his temple, the hard flex of his muscles—and it's so fucking sexy I want to yank him out of this gym and back to my place, stat.

Once he puts Jake in his place, Nolan grabs my hand, weaving his fingers through mine, and leads me toward an open wall while everyone at the gym stares at us. I'm pretty sure I catch a camera flash out of the corner of my eye, and I know for sure my face is going to be online now. As Habituall's publicist, I'm well acquainted with the world of PR and crisis communications, but I've always protected my employer's reputation—not my own. I can only hope the climbing community isn't as toxic as tech when it comes to how it treats women.

Nolan sets his bag down and chivalrously takes mine off my shoulder. "Sorry about that. I was not about to let some rando waste our time strapping you in and showing you the literal ropes when I'm right here. But now that's out of the way, let's do this. How are you feeling?"

"Anxious." It's my default setting, of course, but in this moment my emotions and everything else around me are heightened. Now that I'm standing next to the wall, it looks so much taller than it did from the entrance. I scan up to the top, trying to see where the rope is hanging from, but even after getting LASIK surgery a decade ago, I can't get a great look at how securely our ropes are fastened.

"That's alright. It's completely natural to be afraid of heights. But top roping is the easiest and safest kind of climbing, because you will always be supported from an anchor above you." He points to a group of climbers to our right. "See how their ropes are following behind them instead of coming from above? They're doing what's called lead climbing. You can watch them clipping their ropes into those carabiners on the wall. Those points are called quickdraws— they're a climber's protection as they make their way to the top, preventing them from falling too far."

I gulp, or at least try to but my mouth is getting drier by the minute. Falling any distance is falling too far to me. And people consider climbing to be a recreational activity, one you do for *fun*?

Nolan goes through the motions of getting ready: giving me a heads up to remove my socks before putting on my climbing shoes, checking to make sure they fit properly, and reassuring me there isn't such a thing as 'too snugly' when I'm bewildered by how tight they're clamped on my feet.

"You'll break them in. Trust me—when you're balancing on tiny footholds, standing on your tiptoes, you don't want your feet slipping around your shoes and sabotaging your ability to get traction on the wall."

I half pay attention as he explains the rock climbing grades, a system of five-point somethings that designate how difficult a route is. Nolan gestures to a series of blue holds on the wall nearest us, telling me he selected a route that will be a 'piece of cake.' With just a quick glance, I've already spotted the gap between two holds that I suspect is too wide for my strength or reach.

This must be how my marketing team feels when I explain the intricacies of the AP Stylebook, if we were living in an alternate timeline where the Oxford comma could kill you. Because every time I try to observe Nolan's tips, as I'm sure I'll need them to avoid falling to my death or getting the rope wrapped around my neck, it's like Hammy is clawing at the inside of my skull, and his high-pitched squeals are drowning out all other sound in his desperate attempts to get the fuck out of here.

And when I step into the leg loops of the harness Nolan has laid out for me on the mat floor, I can't even enjoy the sexual tension as he slowly pulls the contraption up my legs and secures it at my waist. His warm breath hits the back of my neck as his hands tighten the buckles, making sure each is double backed for my safety.

Come on, girl. He's intentionally taking his time, enjoying how snatched your waist feels under those leggings. Turn around and give him a sultry look through those long eyelashes that Som painstakingly applied four coats of mascara on. After all, you can't be forced to climb this wall if you get kicked out for swallowing each other's faces.

But there's nothing erotic about the way my body works itself into a major tizzy. Everything is happening too fast, like a train that's left the station and is barreling toward me while I'm tied down to the tracks. My heart's pounding so fast I'm afraid I'm going to go into cardiac arrest, and I can't get enough oxygen through my nostrils, and oh god, I have to get out of here *now*.

"Tania, are you okay? You're shaking like a leaf." One hand wraps around mine, while the other lifts my chin up, which I resist because I don't want Nolan to see my quivering bottom lip and the tears pinpricking my eye ducts.

"Hey, hey, hey. Everything's alright. Come here." He pulls me into as close a hug as he can with our harnesses clunking between us. "I would never put you in an unsafe situation. You know that, right?"

I nod into his shoulder, letting my tears fall onto his T-shirt. There's no way I'd be any safer than with the greatest climber in all of humanity. "It's so ridiculous. I've never even done anything like this before. It's not like I was traumatized taking a fall as a child. How can I be scared of something I have zero memories of?"

Nolan squeezes me tighter, deeply exhaling, which encourages me to let out my own ragged breath. We synchronize our breathing, in and out, in and out, until the urge to escape subsides. Even though I can't wiggle my toes in the vice grips on my feet, I've never got grounded so fast. One minute I'm on the verge of a panic attack, and the next Nolan's calmed me down enough to see straight again. I'm starting to learn he has an uncanny ability to pull me away from the edge, whether that's a figurative or literal cliff.

He steps back with an intensity that reminds me he's confronted real danger on a regular basis. "The body keeps the score even if you don't." The phrase has a familiar ring, and I don't know why I'm surprised. I don't need to search his eyes for meaning. Losing your twin brother in what must have been a horrific climbing accident would shatter anyone's mental health. Of course, he goes to therapy and has read the most pivotal texts on PTSD. It's not a revelation I should be aroused by, but damn is it rare to meet men in touch with their emotions.

Nolan catches my smile and lightens up the mood. "You wouldn't be ashamed of being hungry. You'd just eat some food. Fear is a bodily response like any other. It takes practice to regulate your fight-or-flight impulses. But I have no interest in coercing you into doing something you don't want to do, even if that something is my favorite thing on the planet. There's a taco truck outside the gym, so say the word, and we can grab some grub instead."

It would be so easy to abandon our climbing date and retreat back to my comfort zone with comfort food, even if it means eating tacos twice in the same day. Nolan's clearly got no stake in this. He got me to invite myself on a date with him, so he doesn't care about how we spend it. But even though he's not pitching this choice as a test, it still feels like one. His passion for climbing is not only palpable but also contagious, and I want to learn why it thrills him so—if only to show him that I can fit into his life. I mean, goodness knows I can't keep the charade up forever, but I should be able to pretend for a few hours at least.

Most importantly, I want to prove to myself that I can do hard things. And I'm not talking about the academic and professional challenges I've tackled over the years, like graduating summa cum laude or ascending to the C-suite. Somehow, those felt inevitable. Not a matter of if, but when.

This, though—getting on the other side of my generalized anxiety disorder—I know this will forever be the hardest thing of all. And I'm not so naive to think it will happen today if I manage to climb a fake rock wall. But like Nolan said, even if I can't conquer my fears, I can at least postpone them like I delay my lunch when I'm in the middle of launching a marketing campaign.

"Tania? You still here?" Nolan waves his hand in front of my face.

"Yup! Sorry, tacos were such a tempting offer I got distracted. But let's hold off on food until dinnertime. I'd like to give this a shot, if we can start with the tiniest of baby steps first."

He grins, throwing his arm over my shoulder and leading me toward a less intimidating wall, a 5.8 rather than the 5.10 he'd first selected. "You got it."

I look up, embarrassed to see a young boy, around seven or eight years old, scrambling to the top like it's not just a piece of cake, but the entire cake. When he comes down, Nolan gives him a high five, and even though I would rather be dead than pregnant, my heart warms to see he's good with kids. The boy doesn't recognize him, but his parents clearly do, and I'm not sure what's more adorable—the boy rushing to give Nolan a hug or his parents pumping their fists as they get the climbing Kodak moment on camera.

They let us take our turn, and Nolan walks me through tying a figure-eight knot, reassuring me how safe every single part of our literal connection is.

"The relationship between climber and belayer is symbiotic, like a pair of dancers. One may be leading and the other following, but they are equals on that wall. One can't succeed without the other, so they must intuitively trust each other. Do you trust me?"

"I do." The knot's been long tied, and he's triple-checked it, but his hands remain wrapped around mine. I don't believe in soulmates, but damn if this isn't a bizarre handfasting ceremony. Who am I to question the bond between climbing partners?

The 5.8 wall is half the height of the more advanced routes, but I still have to will my heart to beat slower as I take my position at the base.

"What do you say when you're ready?" Nolan quizzes behind me.

"Climbing," I parrot the command, feeling a bit foolish since it's obvious what's about to happen, but I can respect Nolan's adherence to the rules. It might be the only thing we have in common.

"Alright, climb on!"

There are an absurd number of bright orange holds, so I never have to stretch far to reach the next one above me. I'm going slowly, and I feel wobbly every step of the way, but it gets easier the farther I climb.

And Nolan's just as much of a pro guiding me up as he is climbing himself. Every move I make is horrifically amateur, but he peppers constructive feedback between encouragements so I'm able to quickly alter my technique without getting demotivated.

"Stand on your toes, not the sides of your feet. That's it, keep your range of motion as wide as possible."

"Don't work harder than you have to—lift with your legs, not your arms. There you go, you're doing great."

"Awesome, now reach around and grab some chalk. Yes, I know it's gross, but your fingers are slipping, and you'll want the extra grip."

"Aw yeah, you're halfway there. Now I want you to fall back."

I whip my head around, startled. "You want me to fall *on purpose*?"

He grins goofily like it's the chillest idea ever. "Yep. You said you trust me."

I roll my eyes. How dare he use my own words against me. "You know, when we're forced to do trust falls at work for team building, there are people right next to you to catch you."

Nolan nods. "I am right next to you, connected by a rope that can support more than two thousand pounds. Let go, Tania. You can do this."

I sigh, accepting that the sooner I fall, the faster I can get this exercise over with. It's ten feet up—even if I wasn't using a rope and safety harness, I'd most likely survive unscathed.

When I push myself off the wall, I expect to free fall for at least a few seconds, but I barely go anywhere. Swaying slightly, I look down to take in Nolan laughing at my confusion.

"I said you were in the best of hands. And I must say these hands have lightning-fast reflexes. Now go on and send the fuck out of this 5.8."

Within minutes, I've pulled myself back toward the holds and made it to the top without incident. But you'd think I broke an Olympic record the way Nolan's congratulating me.

"Hell yeah! Look at you. You are officially a climber."

It seems silly to feel proud of myself for accomplishing

what a child just did in a fraction of the time, but the rush of achievement fills my chest cavity all the same. It's even more rewarding than getting an A-plus on an exam or compliments from a customer on an article I've written—precisely because it doesn't come easily to me.

I didn't study or train for this task, and I hadn't climbed this route several times before, but the addictive thought flashes in my mind: What if I did? And all of a sudden, I understand why Nolan does this every single day, even if there's no one else competing with him. He's pushing himself past what he did yesterday to reach the furthest limit of his potential. And damn it, wouldn't it be thrilling to know what my potential is?

My forehead is as coated in sweat as my hands are in chalk, but I jump into Nolan's arms for a hug. "I did it. I can't believe I did it!"

He presses his forehead against mine and grabs my hands in his, despite my attempts to avoid getting my grossness on him. "Tania, that wasn't luck. That was *you*."

I raise my brows, hopeful. "Does that mean I'm a natural and I never even knew it?"

He laughs and laughs at the thought, but thankfully not at my expense. "Absolutely not. But neither was I. Now my hands may be freakishly large, and maybe that has something to do with my grip, but I didn't come out of the womb with climbing shoes on. I didn't even start climbing until I was ten years old, in a gym much like this one, so it's not like I'm a prodigy. I haven't broken records because I have a super-human body. It's because I eat, drink, and breathe climbing. I live for climbing, and I would die for climbing. And you can do anything, Tania, if you want it badly enough."

There he goes again. That fire in Nolan's eyes is spreading down his chiseled arms, through our laced fingers, until my entire body is set ablaze. In that moment, all I want is for him to want me that badly. There's no way on earth he wouldn't be the most passionate lover I've ever had when he talks like that. Once I ignite that spark and give him permission to explore my body as thoroughly as a first ascent, I know for a fact he would rise—literally—to the challenge.

Like a moth to a flame, I raise my hand to rest against his cheek, and he doesn't flinch even for a millisecond. Does he welcome my touch, or is he simply used to the feeling of chalk brushing against his skin?

We're pressed together at multiple points, from our glistening foreheads to our waists where his fingers have pulled me closer through my harness loops. I've even forgotten about the pain in my feet until Nolan shifts his shoe against mine. It would take no time at all to close the gap and kiss him—just a graze, a quick peck to know what his lips feel like. I'm positive the whole gym is watching us anyway, so might as well do what we already look like we're doing.

But Nolan Wells isn't an Olympic speed climber, racing to the finish line as fast as humanly possible. He climbs the most treacherous mountains for a living, trekking across vast terrains for as long as it takes to complete the mission. We may not have touched each other more intimately than a handhold, but I can feel it in my bones. He's the kind of man who takes his time.

I let out an exhale, sighing partly with disappointment that I can't capture his mouth here and now in the gym and partly in acceptance that it's only a matter of timing. A when, not an if. I run my thumb across the corner of his lips, promising to return to them when the moment's right, before pulling back and giving him a warm smile.

"Let's go again. I'm not done yet."

≈

Text conversation between Tania Beecher and Dahlia Cruz, LCSW, on Monday, February 7, at 7:00 p.m.

Tania Beecher: What do I do about this impending sense of doom I have?

Dahlia Cruz, LCSW: What's brought this on, Tania? You haven't been stuck in a social media spiral, have you?

Tania: Believe it or not, I'm at the gym. On a date. I am on a first date at a gym. It's much more fun than it sounds.

Dahlia: That's great. So what's the problem?

Tania: There is none, and it's freaking me out. My date is so sweet, and we're having such a good time, and it's been so long since I've had any chemistry with somebody, but it's definitely there. I'm not imagining it like I've done all those other times.

Dahlia: These are positive things, Tania. You're allowed to be happy.

Tania: I know that, but what if I fuck it all up somehow? What if this doesn't work out, and I'll never capture this feeling ever again, and I die alone?

Dahlia: I see. Sounds like we're overdue for an in-person session to touch base on the fundamentals again. Here's an article on catastrophizing to read in the meantime. Until then, take some deep breaths, and enjoy the present moment!

chapter
eleven

I t takes a couple of hours, but I finally get it. I mean, I don't think I'll ever understand why someone would abandon a house with four walls and all the creature comforts inside it to live in their van, but I get why Nolan loves this sport so dearly. Words are coming to mind that I have never, ever associated with physical activity: exhilarating, thrilling, cathartic, and—dare I say it—fun.

But it's way more than exercise. I couldn't have anticipated the mental challenge that comes with climbing. Determining where best to place your hands and feet to reach the top is like playing a particularly difficult game of Tetris or putting together a one-thousand-piece puzzle. And I love me a good puzzle.

And just like when I've got pieces scattered across my coffee table, when I can spend an entire day in pursuit of the finished image, Hammy is fast asleep. My anxiety hasn't vanished, per se, because I don't think that's biologically possible, but it's dormant. Doing something that requires full attention from both my brain and body is the tranquilizer I need to calm down my nervous system. And nothing yet has been as grounding and meditative as climbing has been today.

Nolan was overjoyed to watch me get the hang of it and ready to push me forward to harder routes, but I felt the urge to be as thorough as I could before moving on from one wall to the next. The people who know me best might have called it perfectionism, but it was more like confirmation that I knew exactly what I was doing. I didn't want to cut corners or squeeze through by the skin of my teeth. I didn't just want to send, but to fucking crush it every time. If I accidentally touched the wrong-colored hold or could only make it work with bad form, I told Nolan to lower me down so I could start again.

Once I mastered the fundamentals on the available 5.8 routes, I upped the ante and dominated the 5.9s. I know with Nolan's expert guidance, I could have hopped from one to another faster, especially since the gym members gave us plenty of berth. But I didn't want to commit to a route out of range of my ability and hog it from everybody else while trying to struggle my way through it.

Nolan hugs me after another successful run. I'm getting grosser with each send, but it doesn't stop him from having an excuse to put his hands on me. If anything, it's emboldened him to linger longer on the small of my back, to graze his lips against my neck. I'd be lying if I said his touch had nothing to do with me trying to do my very best.

"You sure you don't want to try that 5.10a I first picked out for you?" Nolan asks.

I check my smartwatch, psyched to be completing my rings several times over. It's almost seven o'clock, and the fatigue has officially set in. I can only imagine how sore my body is going to feel tomorrow, how every muscle will scream for relief. But whereas the pain would always deter me from making an effort before, it feels worth it now.

My stomach growls, reminding me it's got its own agenda, but there is one thing I'm hungrier for. Like my desire for food, it grew slowly because I was so focused on my own climbing, but then it ambushed me all at once. "How about you give it a go before we grab tacos?"

Nolan chuckles. "I had so much fun watching you send, I wasn't even thinking of swapping and taking you out of your element. Honestly, that might have been—" He bites off the rest of his sentence, but from the way his fingers are tracing the cut-outs of my tank top, I can guess what he meant to say. *The hottest thing I've ever seen.*

I untie the figure-eight knot to release me from the wall, my hands shaking to get a grip after being given the hardest workout of their lives. "Then you know exactly why I want to watch you. Why everyone in this gym has been waiting around for hours. We want to see the one and only Nolan Wells in action."

Nolan's smile peeks out like the sunrise, slowly spreading into an ear-to-ear grin. "Is that what you want? You sure you can handle it?"

I bite my lip hard, oh-so-tempted to march out of this gym and fuck him into oblivion, but if I have a chance to make Nolan mine, then damn it, I'm going to show him off first.

Taking a deep breath to project my voice, I wrap my chalked hands around my mouth and bellow at the crowd that's gathered on the perimeter around us. "Oakland, are you ready to see Nolan Motherfucking Wells conquer Pacific Pipeworks?"

A deafening roar echoes through the gym, bouncing off the warehouse walls and shocking my limbs awake. The biggest fans must have called all their friends because people have filled in every crack of empty space. The boulderers have left their makeshift rocks, and the few people using the tread-mills and ellipticals on the second floor have found something way more engaging than their cardio regimens. Even the staff have abandoned their posts because anyone who would need assistance is already on the floor. Everyone's got their phones out, cameras at the ready. I don't need to reiterate that I'm no sports enthusiast, but if there was a way to describe what it's like to witness a living legend in the wild—like if Michael Jordan showed up while you were shooting hoops at your local park or Serena Williams walked onto your country club's tennis courts—that's what it's like inside Pacific Pipeworks. The energy is electric, and everyone is waiting with bated breath to watch the performance of a lifetime.

"You did it now, Tania," Nolan whispers in my ear. "You put the spotlight on me, and I'm gonna look so *obnoxious*." He smirks, saying the word with relish, like he'd never willingly put himself in the center of attention, but if you're going to give it to him, he's going to enjoy every second of it. And so am I.

I lick my lips. "Do your worst."

Nolan doesn't break my gaze as he runs his hand through his mussed-up hair, nor when he peels his shirt over his head and tosses it at me. Every woman in this place, and a good handful of the men, whoop and holler, losing their shit at the sight of a Greek god. I run my fingers along his discarded shirt, and it takes all my willpower not to squeal like a horny fangirl at a boy band concert. And this time the striptease is all for me.

The spell is broken when Nolan swaps his sneakers for his well-worn climbing shoes. Wait a minute—he hasn't taught me how to belay yet. Should I ask for a quick lesson first, or should I find someone more experienced to take my place? But it's only when he removes his harness and clips the chalk bag to one of the belt loops on his shorts that I finally understand exactly what he intends to do.

Free soloing. The term from my internet stalking illuminates in my mind like a lightbulb. Nolan is going to climb the fifty-foot wall without ropes, without any safety measures whatsoever.

My breath catches in my throat, and Hammy immediately wakes up from his slumber. It's not often he's more afraid for somebody else than myself, but he rises to the occasion as if he was born to worry on another's behalf.

Hammy's not the only one tittering with concern either. The staff members standing off to the side are literally wringing their hands, conflicted between their eagerness to watch Nolan make Pacific Pipeworks history and their fear of an accidental death or disability lawsuit. I don't blame them for wanting to prevent the worst from happening—what awful luck would I have if the first guy I'm crushing on in a long time kicks the bucket before we can schedule a second date.

I lean in so no one can overhear us. "Are you sure about this? Wouldn't this be against the rules?" As soon as the words fly out of my mouth, I regret how cringy they sound. Nolan's shirtless, standing so close I could trace each individual ab, and I'm here ruining the mood like a Debbie Downer. If Nolan doesn't die from a horrific fall, I'm going to kill him by destroying the vibes.

But if he's disappointed in my straightlaced deference to authority, he doesn't let on. He gives me a wide-toothed smile, the twinkle in his eyes not dimming in the slightest. "This is nothing. I spent hours before you got here practicing this route on ropes. There is absolutely no reason for you to be worried." He turns to the Pacific Pipeworks staff. "I already signed the waiver." My eyes are boring holes into his skull when he adds under his breath, "And even if I didn't, I'd like to see them stop me."

Even after all the videos I've seen online of Nolan climbing, I wasn't prepared for this rebellious side of him. There's an inherent risk when scaling a big wall in Yosemite or any other major climbing destination, but in that footage, Nolan is in his element and nearly always alone save for a climbing partner. There's never a competitive spirit, at least not with anyone else but himself. To watch him throw up a metaphorical middle finger with a massive crowd of rubbernecking onlookers—I have to admit it's fucking sexy.

If signing away his rights to sue wasn't enough for the gym, no one who works here comes forward to call it off. Secure in his position of power over everyone in the room, Nolan turns his attention to the project in front of him, a 5.14a that makes me dizzy. There aren't many black-colored holds to begin with and those few are so spaced out that I don't think I'd even be able to reach them. They start clustering closer together near the middle until the wall juts out into a severe overhang. And that's only the first half. If he manages to grab onto the curved handhold above the lip and lift himself onto the other side without falling, he still has to reach the top using holds so rounded, I have no idea how you'd properly grip them in the first place. Honestly, I'm glad Nolan is so confident, because if someone said I had to climb this wall like my very life depended on it—because his does—I'd tell that person to take me out back and put me out of my misery before I waste anyone's time.

Nolan assumes his position at the base, and right when I expect him to jump into it, he turns back and smiles at me. "Climbing!"

I return his smile, touched that he'd go through the motions when I'm not attached to him and can't ensure his safety. In his own way, he's telling me we're still partners, together when we're apart. It's insignificant to anyone who's not paying close attention, but I'm deeply grateful that even in the moments when the spotlight's on him, he's thinking of me.

"Climb on!" I shout, and the crowd explodes in thunderous applause.

It's my first time climbing, so I don't know any of the

lingo or proper terminology. It may be inappropriate or cliché as hell to use animal analogies, but it's all I can think of as I watch Nolan make his ascent. He's racing through the first half like a mountain goat, completely at ease bouncing from one perilous hold to the next. When he reaches the overhang, he starts off horizontal like a lizard stuck to the wall. And then in a flash, his feet are dangling, and he's a monkey reaching for the vines that will get him to the top of the tree, before evolving into a sugar glider to leap onto the crescent-shaped handhold that will get him past the overhang.

The guy nearest to me, wearing a charcoal-colored graphic tee with the slogan LESS TALK, MORE CHALK, gasps louder than I do. "Holy shit, he got through the first dyno in less than five minutes."

Dyno? I don't think dinosaurs exactly fit into my animal comparisons. I make a mental note to research the definition when I get a chance, because I'm afraid if I do it now, by the time I look up from my phone, Nolan will already be done.

Setting aside the metaphors, I'm blown away by Nolan's athleticism. Every move he makes is so precise and methodical; he never exerts an ounce of effort more than he needs to. When he said he was going to be obnoxious, I expected lots of grunting and clapping so chalk debris fills the air. I didn't expect to be thinking of adjectives like elegant, graceful, and classy. Okay, one more metaphor: Nolan Wells is an orchestra. It wouldn't matter what year it is or what style of climbing is in vogue, he's timeless and I could watch him for hours.

"He's at the crux now," More Chalk guy says to no one in particular, which is ironic given the *less talk* part of his shirt motto. He catches my eye. "That's the hardest part of the route."

I nod, as if I knew what he was referring to all along. "He's gonna crush that crux."

More Chalk guy gestures toward the gym staff. "We

should call an ambulance just in case that crux crushes him though."

I inhale sharply, smacking him on the shoulder and leaving a white handprint on his shirt from the residue left on my hands.

"Ow!" More Chalk guy squeals, and I resist rolling my eyes. I have the strength of a mosquito, and I only gave him what his shirt said he wanted.

"Take that pessimism somewhere else, dude." I shoo him away before his bad vibes contaminate Nolan's climb. Sure, I was thinking along similar lines moments ago, but I'm not about to allow other people to will the darkest timeline into existence.

More Chalk guy walks off, complaining that Nolan Wells's new girlfriend is a real ball-buster, and I beam with pride. Girlfriend? To be determined. A ball-buster? Also up for debate. But damn straight do I like people thinking I am both.

With no more distractions, I can watch Nolan complete the route. He's about two-thirds up, taking a pause on a more substantial foothold, shaking out his arms, reapplying a thick layer of chalk, and evaluating how to tackle the rest of the project. Hammy's whispering conspiratorial thoughts, souring my mind against a positive outcome with images of Nolan slamming against the overhang and breaking bones and teeth on the way down. If there was ever a point where Nolan wasn't able to succeed, it would be now. And because he's at nearly the height of a three-story building, no one will be able to catch him if he falls.

The so-called crux is a series of moves involving several round or sloping holds, followed by two diametrically opposed holds. Together it's like they form the Bermuda Triangle, an area where climbers enter, never to return alive. Tackling it with a rope would already be horrendously challenging, but attempting it without one would be a death wish.

I'm not a spiritual person, but I cross every finger and throw all the hope I can muster skyward just in case.

With a burst of energy like he's exploding out of a cannon, Nolan jumps, shoving his right hand into the roundest hold, which I hear someone nearby call a donut, making it sound so much less intimidating than it looks. As he maneuvers around and reaches for the semicircle-shaped hold, his left hand misses its mark and he slips. All of us simultaneously gasp, unsure whether we're about to witness a tragedy that will make the ten o'clock news. Thankfully, his fist is locked tight into the donut, enabling him to swing to the side and secure his left hand on the second attempt. It doesn't leave any opportunities to match his feet, so they're simply hanging below him. I can't even enjoy his bulging biceps because I'm terrified his tree-trunk legs are weighing him down.

I'm not sure which voice in the crowd gets it started, but soon the whole room starts chanting his name—*Nol-an, Nol-an, Nol-an*—first as a quiet simmer then a rolling boil. But right when I'm about to join in, a man yells out, "Come on, Free Nolo, fucking send and kiss your girl, already!"

My mouth doesn't know if it wants to gasp, blurt out a retort, or tell him to mind his own business. As much as I'm over the moon at the thought of Nolan planting a big one on me after he stops shaving years off my life, they have no idea who I am. And despite the parasocial relationship they may have with Nolan online, his social media handle isn't his name, and they have no right to demand anything from him, even if it benefits me.

I fully expect Nolan to ignore the heckling and not waste a single breath on anything that's not climbing the remainder of this route, but he turns back, feet dangling, to lock eyes with me. "Is she on board with that plan?"

The gym goes quiet, save for the carabiners clinking from everyone's harnesses. They're waiting—he's waiting—for my response. My mouth's as dry as if I've got chalk coating my tongue, but I manage to croak out, "Yes, of course!" Get down here on solid ground, and let's go over safer second-date spots, like celebrating happy hour at a wine bar like normal people do.

I can see those adorable dimples from thirty-five feet off the ground, deepening the bigger he smiles. I've never had anyone ask for my consent under such life-and-death circumstances, and man would it suck if it were the last time. But if Nolan can't successfully reach the last two points of the Bermuda Triangle, there goes my desire to ever date a sports nut of any kind again.

Willing my anxiety-riddled PR and crisis communications brain to think of anything else than drafting Nolan's untimely obituary, I focus instead on everything else we have yet to do tonight: wash off the caked-on chalk from our hands, bond over delicious tacos from a food truck, maybe even take it back to my place for some drinks and a little over-the-shirt making out. But damn it, he's finishing this climb so we can finish this date and get on with the kissing.

And then what happens next is nothing short of miraculous. Instead of trying to grab the two upper holds with his hands like he's bowling and knocking down pins for a split, he lifts his full body weight into a handstand. For most climbers, it would indeed be obnoxious to take off your shirt because you're not pulling off moves like this, but instantly I understand how necessary it is for Nolan to avoid anything obstructing his vision.

He locks onto the right-hand hold with his foot, which gives him the leverage he needs to get his other foot to connect the triangle. For one brief moment he's starfished out between the three points, completely upside down, before he twists, moves both feet to the same left-hand hold, and backbends using all of his core strength to get into a standing position and grab the next handhold. Just like that, he's out of the Bermuda Triangle, and while everyone else screams their amazement, I let go of the breath I was holding hostage.

After the crux, the rest of the climb is underwhelming. Nolan doesn't even stop when he reaches the top to roar and pump his fist in the air. Instead he extends over to a much easier route and downclimbs until he's reached a safe distance, jumping down and slamming his feet to the mat.

People are throwing their hands up and slapping Nolan on the back, but he doesn't indulge in any of the bedlam. He clears a path, beelining straight to me, where my arms are outstretched, itching to confirm he's in fact alive and well. When he collapses his body against mine, I nearly bowl over, unsure who's more exhausted—him for accomplishing something I never entertained was possible or me for being so paralyzed at the thought that it wasn't.

Splaying my hands across his broad back and pressing him against me, I whisper in his ear, "I'm still on board if you are."

He laughs, looking so happy I have to squeeze the tops of his shoulders in case he died and went to heaven without me noticing. "I've never been more motivated in my life."

He cradles my face in his hands, swiping away tears I had no idea had come leaking out. I'm so relieved he made it down that I don't even care about the chalk transferring to my cheeks. As if we were in a fishbowl, I can hear the gym goers around us egging us on, but they're all white noise. The only sounds I direct my attention to are the blood pounding in my ears and Nolan's breath intermingling with mine.

One soft inhale, and his lips have closed the gap, and I'm taken aback how pillowy they are compared to the solidness of the rest of his body. Much like the springy mat beneath our feet, Nolan is a soft place to land. If the glam fam had asked me how I would describe the perfect kiss, not in a million years would I have answered at a gym after the most grueling workout of our lives. Well, my life at least. Nolan's broken a sweat, of course, but kissing him isn't nearly as messy as I anticipated. He's in such peak physical condition it's a crime to close my eyes during this kiss because then I can't admire every sinewy line and rolling muscle. But at least I don't need my sense of sight to answer what I know Glen's first question will be. Tracing my fingers down his glistening washboard stomach, I have firsthand confirmation of Nolan Wells's slip 'n' slide.

As much as I'm appreciating the male form, it's not just me getting a handful. As Nolan's hands roam across my hips and waist and down my backside, leaving white trails in his wake, his kiss is more wanton and urgent. His tongue slips past my lips, and he groans, dipping me into a backbend, at a much softer angle than the one he performed but with a much harder outcome as my crotch presses his. Immediately, I flash back to the morning after I slept in his van, reminded by the firmness greeting me the next morning. Before we can get carried away with the PDA, I pull back, uninterested in giving our onlookers that kind of show. While I'm sure porn exists for every sport imaginable, it's best if our first kiss is rated PG-13 instead of NC-17.

"I think we've overstayed our welcome." I smile, running my hands over his pecs and enjoying his racing heartbeat under my palms. His pulse slows, and he gulps, nodding. A tad guilty that I can't relieve his more immediate sense of thirst, I pull my water bottle from my bag and hand it to him. We've been at Pacific Pipeworks for nearly four hours, and ice still clinks inside the stainless-steel container as Nolan guzzles it down.

"It's pretty dark outside," he gasps between mouthfuls. "We can take our tacos back to my van if you'd like. That way, I can drop you back off in the city afterward."

I look at him quizzically, until I remember I never told him where I lived, so he's assuming I'm in San Francisco, close to the Habituall office. "My apartment's actually nearby. We can walk over."

Nolan's eyes bug out. "You live around here?" I brace myself for all the typical things I hear from my parents and well-meaning but ignorant colleagues: West Oakland isn't safe, there's a large, unhoused encampment down the street, and this is no place for a single woman (funny how people never say that to ladies who are several shades darker than I am).

But Nolan's laser-focused on something other than neighborhood crime rates. "I can't believe you're a stone's throw from the largest climbing gym in the country, and you've never been."

I laugh, grateful to avoid yet another lecture. "We'll have to come back. You forgot to teach me how to belay." After we make a pit stop at the restroom and wash up, Nolan grabs my bag, despite my insistence that he doesn't need to carry any extra weight after the ordeal he went through.

He shifts his shoulders, ignoring my pleas, lost in thought. "Why didn't you tell me? If I had known, I could have made a trip out here earlier, trained indoors for a while. We could have been—"

I search his expression for the words he stopped himself from saying. Going on more climbing dates? Binging Netflix over Chinese takeout? No, whether it's imagining ropes being used for not-safe-for-work purposes or being turned on while watching me master the beginner routes, I should know by now that Nolan never finishes his train of thought if it's approaching an inappropriate station.

It's written all over his flushed face. *Fucking each other senseless.*

～

"So You're Bringing Home a Spontaneous Gym Date,"
by The Send-It Sisters on Monday, February 7

HELL MUST HAVE FROZEN OVER, because the impossible has become possible: someone attractive and not-at-all creepy has asked you out at the gym, sweat and frizzy hair and all. And whether you grabbed a couple of burritos around the block or snuck into a fine-dining establishment wearing nothing over your sports bra, now the evening is transitioning from food to getting in the mood.

Here's a quick checklist when you're looking to get lucky back at your humble abode.

1. **Go as deep as you can handle.** And no, not that— we're talking about cleaning, you freak. The only thing that should be getting down and dirty are you two lovebirds. If you have a few hours to spare, it's time to get on your knees—and make sure those floors are spotless. Dust those bunnies, de-junk that drawer, and remove that gross ring in your toilet if you want to put a ring on it. If your date night was too impromptu to plan around, improvise with a few spritzes. There's nothing a little perfume behind the ears and Febreze in the air can't fix.

2. **Clear the decks.** If you want a love worth sacrificing yourself for on a raft definitely large enough for two people, you've got to give your undivided attention to your date. That means preoccupying your pets, kicking out your roommates, and putting a scrunchie on that door so no one unexpected ruins your good time. Even if you live alone, don't forget about your digital cockblock: silence that phone. No one gets laid if they're too busy checking their notifications.

3. **Prep for the morning after.** Yes, we're alluding to birth control here because nobody has regretted stocking Plan B in advance. But we're also referring to the literal morning

after—the best second date is breakfast after the first. Make sure your fridge is stocked with brunch essentials, the best of which always come in pairs: bacon and eggs, biscuits and gravy, and most importantly, champagne and OJ. After all, you just got laid, so cheers to a successful sleepover. You've earned it!

chapter
twelve

I'm psyching myself up the whole way home—practicing my breathing while we grab a half-dozen street tacos to go (carnitas for me and veggie for him) and focusing on the feeling of my hand in his as we follow the streetlamps to my apartment community. He releases my hand only to greet Stormy, the gray long-haired cat who is owned by the woman on the corner but who belongs to the neighborhood. As I unlock the door to my place, I realize my fingers are shaking— I hope he can't tell how nervous I am. If Hammy was fretting about not cleaning prior to the glam fam popping by, then he's close to a full-blown meltdown when I welcome Nolan in.

Take a chill pill, Hammy. This man lives in his car and walks through life with chalk fused to his skin. Any home he enters is already a major upgrade. And even if it's not, he's thinking too much with his dick to care that I didn't get around to dusting.

"Make yourself at home," I declare, quickly running through my mental list of tasks to make the mood more inviting. Dim the lights, light a few candles, and play Tori's soft jazz to break the silence and get a cozy vibe going. Nolan sets our gear down in a corner, and by the time he's placed our taco spread on the dining table, I've poured the best vintage—an Opus One 2019—from my wine rack.

"Thanks," he says, taking the glass I hand him but not drinking it. "You're so, uh, efficient. Do you, um, date a lot?" He bites his lip, adding quickly, "Not that I'd expect you to sit at home alone, of course."

I laugh, a bit proud I seem like I've been around the block more than I have and also relieved that Nolan's clearly more intimidated than judgmental because of it. "Oh no, but thanks for the confidence boost. This is what I do when I'm sitting at home alone. I'm all about that hygge life, remember? And home's not worth coming home to if I can't unwind with candles and good wine and the occasional bubble bath."

He takes a sip of his wine, expressing polite enjoyment. I can't tell if he's distracted by thinking about me in a bubble bath or if the wine's lost on his palate. Not the biggest deal. If I was going to waste a four-hundred-dollar bottle, it would be on Nolan Wells, the only man who could ever change my mind about the gym being fun instead of a chore.

We eat our tacos in comfortable silence, save for the beautiful piano track by my wonderfully fearsome friend Tori. She knows that pop-punk is my favorite musical genre, so she gifted me a cover album—instrumental jazz versions of my most played songs. When All Time Low's "Don't You Go" comes on, I don't know if I feel like laughing or crying. The original marches like a '90s anthem but this version dances like a romantic ballad. Tori's cover may not have lyrics, but I already know every word by heart.

"I don't want you to leave."

"Huh?" Nolan perks up mid-bite, eyes wide. Here I thought I was reciting the lyrics in my head, but I said the line out loud, and now he's looking at me like I'm getting way ahead of myself.

"Sorry, I meant tonight. I can't send you back out to your van when I have a perfectly good bed with your name on it here."

Nolan looks around. At six-hundred square feet, my apartment is way larger than any van you could live in, but it's no TARDIS. It's just as big as it appears. "This is a one-bedroom?" I nod. "So, technically, the bed has *your* name on it," he says.

I shrug off the semantics. "It's not the first time we've shared a bed, Nolan. And it's a full-size since I never got around to upgrading my childhood furniture set—don't laugh, anything that's not made from particle board is hella expensive when you're paying three grand in rent. My point is, it can fit us comfortably without being too overwhelming since you're used to such cozy quarters."

"It's not the size of the bed that's overwhelming," he says quietly.

At first, I'm terrified I misread the situation, and Nolan isn't interested in sleeping with me, literally or suggestively. But then he blushes and stammers in that adorable way that melts my heart. "I, uh, I really like you, Tania. More than I've liked anyone in a long, long time—which I know isn't saying much since I'm not around a lot of people to begin with. But as much as I'd like to, um, get to know you better in that way, I'm not a one-night-stand kind of guy."

The music playing in the background has me negotiating before I can think things through. "If that's what you're worried about, you can stay as long as you like. We can—" I almost quote All Time Low by saying we can mess around for two more days, but the words sound callous as they form in my mouth. Nolan and I may have washed off the chalk on our hands to the best of our ability, but we're not ones for emotional messes.

I look up at him, more resigned than I'd like to admit. "I

guess we're not one-week-stand kind of people either." It doesn't come out like a question, but Nolan nods with a small smile, confirming what I can already see all over his face.

I don't blame him. I'm not a fan of the term 'serial monogamist,' because it sounds way more pathological than it needs to be, but it's the only label that adequately describes my love life: a frantic period of first dates until I land on a suitable suitor, then clinging to them in a desperate attempt to justify my decision. I'm even capable of clinging on to a crush I've never even dated, like Harris.

Is that why I'm so intrigued by Nolan? Is he yet another guy I'm fundamentally incompatible with but pursuing anyway as a form of self-sabotage? I never thought of myself as emotionally unavailable, but now that I'm thinking about it, I do have a track record of—speaking in terms of tech marketing—nurturing cold leads that have zero chance of closing.

But what if Nolan is the combo-breaker? I may not believe in "The One," but leads are tricky things—one minute they're downloading your whitepaper with a junk Gmail and the next you learn they're an executive at a Fortune 500 worth millions of dollars in enterprise software. A deal of that size doesn't close in a week, so if I want to determine if Nolan is a whale, I need to extend the sales cycle.

"What if we were able to spend more time together?" I ask.

Nolan stares at me skeptically, probably calculating the fines he'd rack up parked illegally at Pacific Pipeworks for days on end.

"Not here, of course," I say. "We might have Salesforce Tower, the tallest building in the state, but it's only a third as high as what you climb in Yosemite—"

"Somebody's done their research." Nolan's clearly more impressed by my internet stalking than he should be.

I don't reveal how deep my rabbit holing has gone to avoid scaring him off. "I also learned this time of year, when it's often too cold and wet to climb, is your offseason. So I was thinking, it might—if you're up for it—be a good time for me to take my sabbatical."

Nolan blinks. "I thought sabbaticals were for academics."

"The concept originated in higher ed, but many tech companies offer them as perks to reward loyalty. Habituall awards four weeks of paid time off after you've been there four years, but they also let you postpone it to rack up more PTO —five weeks after five years, and maxing out at six weeks after six years. Which is how long I've been working there."

Nolan's eyes bug out as much as my colleagues when they learn how long I've stuck around at one startup without taking advantage of such a sweet benefit. "What's been the holdup? And why the hell would you want to hang around me when you could be sipping a mai tai in Hawaii?"

I laugh, tempted by the image. "Trust me, I know how ridiculous it sounds. Everyone I work with, all my friends and family, they've all been pushing me to take this break. I've blamed my busy schedule, but that's just an excuse. I've been putting off the sabbatical because I didn't know how to spend it."

The truth strikes a chord much deeper than the music coming from my speakers, and I take a long sip of wine. "I've had my career plotted out from my first entry-level marketing job to entering the C-suite, but I never thought I'd hit all my goals in just ten years, and I certainly never thought about what comes next."

Nolan smiles, taking my hand and rubbing his thumb along my palm. "Sounds like I'm not the only one who's been climbing this whole time."

I'm about to scoff and declare that comparison awfully

generous since I'm not risking my very life every time I go into the office, but I sit with the thought instead. Everyone talks about climbing the corporate ladder, but nobody ever discusses what to do when you reach the summit. And even if that journey isn't as treacherous, it can be just as terrifying to face the unknown.

"On one hand," I say, "six weeks sounds like a blissfully long time. It's the equivalent of three engineering sprints, so peacing out for that long would be pure indulgence. But I also know that it would be over in a flash, and I didn't want to take my sabbatical until I had a detailed plan for how to maximize every day, so I could return to work feeling accomplished, without any regrets. But obviously that hasn't happened yet. The market could take a nosedive and I could get laid off tomorrow without having a chance to seize this opportunity because I've been stuck in analysis paralysis for years. So this might be exactly the forcing function I need to take action."

Nolan abruptly releases my hand. "I don't want to force you to do anything. Especially if it's spending six weeks in the worst season with a guy who lives in his van and spends hours —even days at a time—attached to sheer cliffs like a barnacle. I'm not exactly the most riveting travel partner."

I chuckle, not deterred by his attempts to paint himself as a less-than-ideal date. As if I hadn't read all those articles glorifying his morning routine of waking up at four o'clock, eating a single meal of overnight oats, then spending hours on a training regimen more grueling than most of us mortals can comprehend.

"I'm not asking you to babysit me. We've just met, and I know nothing will ever come between you and climbing. The last thing I want to be is a distraction from you hitting your goals. But after being on the corporate fast track for so long, I need time to dream up new goals. To take things one day at a time, despite how torturous it feels to not have all the answers upfront. So don't worry about me. I have no problem keeping myself entertained. And if it doesn't work out, I promise I'll be out of your hair and back in the Bay way before climbing season begins."

That nagging thought in the back of my mind threatens to throw me off balance. *What if it does work out?* People think having anxiety is about worrying about negative outcomes, but there's horror in happiness too. Because if we fall madly in love, I will have to reckon with the fact that there's an expiration date—both on the sabbatical and our relationship. There's no way in hell Nolan is moving mountains for me when he's too consumed by climbing them. If anyone's disrupting their entire life, it would be me. But if I dwell on that, whatever's blossoming between us will be dead before it has a chance to live. I spent the last decade learning how to be agile when it comes to software development, so as my mother would say to get me to calm down as a child, we're going to have to cross that bridge when we come to it.

"But why me?" Nolan whispers so softly it's possible the question is rhetorical, and he never intended for me to hear it. It's bonkers for him to not consider himself a catch. He's an elite athlete with like three percent body fat—he'd easily have women lining up outside his van just to touch him. But it's obvious he doesn't see it that way. Perhaps his lack of dating experience makes him think he has little to offer. It's comforting in its own way, that no matter how rich, famous, or accomplished someone is, insecurity comes for us all.

This time I take his hand in mine. "You asked me what I would do if I stopped pretending to give a shit. This sabbatical is my opportunity to find that answer. I may not know what I want to be when I grow up, so to speak, but I know I don't want to pretend that I don't give a shit about you, Nolan. Because I do. So let me figure life out next to you."

Before I can ask Nolan how he feels, he's leaning forward

and kissing me. He's soft but certain, and I'm addicted to the way he cradles my face with both hands. It's like the roughness of his palms keeps me grounded, because otherwise the whirlwind in my head would whisk me away—especially when his tongue slips past my lips. Every nerve ending is on fire, and I find myself pulled into his lap, fingers making a mess of his already messy hair. Thankfully, we've finished our dinner because there's only one thing I'm hungry for now. Positioning myself on his chair with my legs wrapped around his waist, I can tell I'm not the only one ready for dessert.

I grind against him, just so I can hear him moan into my mouth. My leggings leave little to the imagination, and his climbing shorts are made of a thin, lightweight cotton with a touch of stretch, so I can feel every inch of his need. All the hesitation has left his grip, which has gravitated to my ass, where he's pulling me closer, rubbing me up and down his length until it gets harder to breathe.

"You sure you don't want to take this to the bedroom?" I gasp, leaving hot kisses up his neck and behind his ear.

Nolan reaches up to undo my ponytail, removing my hair tie so my blowout falls around my shoulders. Bless Glen for finishing off the look with a spritz of perfume—by the way Nolan's breathing me in, I can tell those notes of peony and nectarine have lasted all evening.

"Are you saying your sabbatical starts tomorrow?"

I pull back, confused. "No, not exactly. I run the whole marketing team, so I can't bail so last minute without getting my ducks in a row."

"And how long will that take?" He continues rubbing himself against my most sensitive spots, distracting me from his question. Because if he's referring to how long it will take to get me off, it won't take any time at all if he keeps grinding like that. "Tania, I need to know when I get you all to myself."

Turning my brain to logistics isn't the sexiest foreplay, and it's not like I have my calendar in front of me, but it's not the first moment I've considered a possible timeline. "We've got our annual conference, First Party, at the end of March. Once I make sure my team can hold down the fort while I'm gone, I could be in Yosemite by next Monday. That way, I'll finish out my sabbatical by the time First Party rolls around and I can pick up where everyone left off."

"Mmm . . . next Monday is the fourteenth. How fitting that you'd be mine starting Valentine's Day." His hands glide up my waist and hover under my breasts, thumbs running across the band of my built-in bra.

"I'm yours right now, I promise. Put an end to this torture and take me already."

I'm surprising myself with how fast I want to jump into bed—or the shower, or on any available surface, to be frank. You would think I'd been hanging out with Glen and Som too much the way I'm channeling my inner man-eater. So when Nolan scoops me up, I'm squealing with glee on the inside. No one has ever picked me up for the sole purpose of ravishing me, and the fact that Nolan and I are similarly sized doesn't deter him, as he has no trouble lifting his own body weight. I grip his biceps, appreciating the way they flex underneath his T-shirt. If my anxiety got the best of me, I'd be hella nervous about hooking up with someone in such great shape, but I'm excited to have his rock-hard body all to myself.

But instead of striding into the bedroom and tossing me onto the plush comforter, Nolan takes a few steps before setting me onto the navy L-shaped couch in the living room.

"Okay, this works too. Let me just keep away any Peeping Toms." I make a move to pull down the blind on the nearest window facing my neighbors, but Nolan stops me.

"There's nothing I want more than your naked body on top of mine, but I can't tonight, not when you've got loose ends to tie up before taking your sabbatical." He threads his fingers through mine. "Being with you is like climbing, Tania —I can't imagine ever stopping once I start. The moment I learn how you feel, how you taste . . . " He swallows, his throat bobbing, as if his mouth is watering at the thought. "I won't be able to help it. I'll need you every single night. So I'm going to drive back to the valley and count down the days until you join me, because you're worth the wait."

When it he puts it like that, he makes sex sound way more sacred than any religious fundamentalist. And as much as I'd like to jump his bones in ten seconds flat, I can respect his desire to enjoy the journey as much as the destination. Nolan's so precise and methodical when he's climbing—it's no wonder he's the type of guy to take things slow. I've often felt pressured to put out by the third date, so it's refreshing to be with someone who makes hand-holding hot. When's the last time I made out without an expectation of something more? Definitely not since I lost my virginity in high school. And nothing about my time with Nolan has felt like going through the motions.

For once in my life, I've found something real, something special. Why would I want to rush that?

$\approx$

DATE: Friday, February 11, at 2:00 p.m.
    FROM: tania.beecher@habituall.com
    TO: marketing@habituall.com
    SUBJECT: Follow-up: Sabbatical send-off

HI TEAM,

Wow, I'm still shaking from your gesture today—literally, because you all scared me popping from under the conference table with that surprise party. Hats off to Harris for using the excuse of going over last-minute transition planning—very sneaky!

And even though you absolutely did not have to go through the effort of ordering Doughbies, I couldn't imagine a better send-off to my sabbatical than their gooey chocolate chip cookies with flaky sea salt on top :)

I was sincerely touched to see you all come together and embody Habituall's value of Teamwork, but now it's time for me to embody Balance and trust that all our hard work is in the best of hands. That said, I want to reiterate that I'll only be a few hours away, and I will do everything I can to make myself available to you in case of emergency.

Here are the best ways to contact me, in order of priority —details and links are pinned to my Slack:

- Personal cell number
- Personal email address
- Social media: Instagram, Threads, TikTok, Tumblr (I'm chronically online)
- Front desk at the Granite Grove Lodge
- Hotel email address

I've also attached a spreadsheet of my sabbatical transition plan, complete with key stakeholders who will be leading projects and running meetings in my absence. Please review what your role will be during this time—especially in the run-up to First Party—and if you have any questions, route them to your manager or Harris directly.

By now you must be sick of me of fretting about the next six weeks, which I know isn't that long in the grand scheme of things, but it feels like an eon when you've dedicated yourself to this team for six years. Even though it will be a personal adjustment to be away, I highly encourage everyone who's eligible to prioritize their much-deserved time off.

(Just don't get so used to me being gone that you don't need me anymore. That would really suck, and I don't think my ego could handle it, to be honest.)

Alright, and with that, I'm off! Thank you all for everything, and I'll see you soon.

~ Tania

chapter
thirteen

For days on end, Hammy's in overdrive, freaked out by everything I need to take care of before jumping feet first into this sabbatical. But by the time the weekend rolls around, he's at least acclimated to the water. Not so chill as to put his tiny hamster feet up on a pool noodle and sip a margarita, but subdued enough that I'm starting to think this whole thing might be a good idea.

It helps that everyone at Habituall is super supportive. I was terrified of what leadership would think of the VP of Marketing going on an extended leave right before the company's biggest event of the year, but we've hosted First Party so many times now, the playbook is well-worn and all the systems in place are locked and loaded.

Even my team is ready to take the reins. Sure, they might joke about not having to deal with my eccentricities—like my bad habit of emailing design feedback instead of marking it up directly in the PDF—but they're excited to run things on their own.

Harris especially has stepped up as my interim team lead, taking charge in meetings and being a project management mastermind. If I'm an experienced shepherd when it comes to herding cats, Harris is a whip-smart border collie, getting everyone to fall in line on pure intuition. He's a total natural, and even though we've already discussed his promotion to marketing director at the end of the quarter, he's easily clinched it by owning his role. And if I'm not mistaken, he's secretly thrilled to call the shots.

"Now I know my internet might be spotty," I mention for the billionth time that week, "but I already called up my carrier to increase the data on my mobile hotspot and add Wi-Fi calling to my plan. I'll check my email and notifications as often as I'm able, so don't be afraid to get in touch."

Harris rolls his eyes and shoves my notes aside. "Absolutely not. Tania, do you know the definition of a sabbatical? I sure hope so because I am going off the grid the minute I'm eligible. Remember, Habituall takes its corporate value of Balance seriously, so if we catch you commenting on Slack, I'm gonna have to report you for not embodying our culture."

I blink at him, unsure if he's kidding. Are employees really getting written up for working too hard?

But then he breaks out into a smile and gives me a purely platonic bro shove. "God, loosen up, will you? You're never going to keep up with *the* Nolan Wells if you're as stiff as a board when you're climbing . . . or anything else for that matter."

"Harris!" I shove him back a bit too forcefully, my cheeks overheating with embarrassment at the innuendo. I had never intended to tell my team the specifics around my sabbatical, but Casey couldn't help herself. One too many glasses of sangria during our Taco Tuesday happy hour, and now half the office has heard the gossip through the grapevine. Is that why they call it the grapevine—because secrets start pouring out once someone has had too much wine? "I'm still your boss."

Again, he doubles down on the eye rolls. That's what I get

for joining an early stage tech startup where corporate hierarchies are flat and HR is nowhere to be found. I mean, I'm not fond of brown-nosing, but a little deference wouldn't hurt.

"Yeah, and I'm managing up here. Trust me when I say you're the best leader and mentor I've had in my career. And when shit hit the fan and Evan almost got booted for the fake drug allegations, I couldn't have imagined anyone else taking up the mantle when 'LSD CEO' was trending for weeks. But despite your notes and reminders and spreadsheets and backup plans upon backup plans, there is no way you can eliminate all hiccups. Nothing is guaranteed, not in life and certainly not with these chaos goblins we call coworkers. So give up any semblance of control you think you have and enjoy the ride for once."

Every word out of his mouth makes me tense, precisely because he's right. Giving up control feels as impossible as meeting his request to edit the team's blog posts in Google Docs instead of directly in the content management system. Which is why I reply with a joke. "I guess I have no choice to enjoy the ride with a man who lives in his van."

"That's the spirit." It's Friday afternoon, and Harris leads me to the elevator to send me off. "Just avoid any positions where your head will hit the roof of the car and relax. Now with all due respect, Tania, get the fuck out of here."

So I do. Even before they kicked me out of the building, they grabbed the baton on my work tasks before I could finish them, so I spend most of the week tackling the rest of my to-do list: rerouting my mail, deep cleaning my apartment, and nailing down my living situation. After researching all available options both within and outside the valley of Yosemite, I bite the bullet and negotiate a long-term rental agreement with Granite Grove. It's certainly not the cheapest route to take, but it's familiar and conveniently located in the heart of the park. And what's the point of having my supersized tech salary if I'm not going to spend it?

"Wait a minute," Casey says later that afternoon, stopping me in my tracks as we wander around REI during my first visit to the outdoorsy store. "I thought the point of this sabbatical is to get to know Nolan up close and personal. Why aren't you bunking in his van bed?"

I sigh, tired of explaining myself for the umpteenth time, mostly because Casey herself has loose lips about my fledging relationship with Nolan. "It's not that I'm against shacking up, even if a car is much smaller than an actual shack. But we've been on *one* date. Our chemistry may be off the charts, but nothing's going to ruin the mood faster than jumping from strangers to roommates without any warm-up. We've been living on our own for so long that I want to respect both his boundaries and mine."

Glen sticks his tongue out at me. "Boundaries and respect. Props to passing therapy with flying colors, but those are words I don't use to describe my extracurricular activities." The glam fam has joined our excursion, and before I know it, Glen is dressed in flannels and a vegan leather trapper hat like he's auditioning as a Nick Offerman lookalike for the Folsom Street Fair.

I brush off his disapproval. "I'll have you know Nolan makes consent sexy as hell. And I'm not saying we're not gonna hook up for six weeks. Who knows—he might appreciate getting down in a pile of down pillows on a real bed. I'm simply diversifying our rendezvous options."

All that talk about hooking up is getting them hot and bothered. Glen and Som segue into sage advice on the best strategies for having sex outside without getting caught or eaten by bears—"the bad kind, of course," Glen adds.

Meanwhile, Casey and Alex are so excited to be shopping for a love nest of any kind that I have to force them to only use one cart as we meander through the aisles. It's times like these that remind me Alex has never worried about the price of anything—before she was a supermodel and social media celebrity, she was the daughter of billionaires. But even if dollar signs aren't a deterrent thanks to her black AmEx, I only have so much room in my compact car. I spend more time putting items I don't need back on the shelves than I do taking advantage of Alex's hospitality. "Yes, I'm one hundred percent positive," I insist. "Even if Yosemite's lakes aren't frozen over in February, I don't need a wetsuit to fully enjoy them." And that's when Glen points out Nolan's slip 'n' slide and I regret ever mentioning what he looks like without his shirt.

Because I'd be lying if I said I'm not salivating over what awaits me in a few days. I've never had a Valentine's Day date worth writing home about, and now I'll be on the arm of a man who made *ESPN*'s Body Issue. I'd never admit it out loud, but it's partly why I booked Granite Grove in the first place. The petty, still-stuck-in-high-school part of me knows I'll run into Summer again. Even if she doesn't check me in at the front desk, there won't be many guests outside of peak season, which means she's bound to see me around and remember me from the retreat. I wouldn't be eager to come into contact with someone who clearly sees me as a rival, but if Nolan is to be my boyfriend, it's best if she learns that first-hand so she can't write me off as insignificant. I don't know if they were more than climbing partners, but if a little jealousy gets her to back off, all the better. Some might call that type of juvenile behavior "marking your territory," but I'm protecting a valuable asset. Since Nolan studied to be a certified financial planner, he'd understand. Staying at the lodge isn't an investment.

It's insurance.

~

Essentials to bring to Yosemite, from the National Park Service

- Map and compass
- Trash bags
- Sunglasses and sunscreen
- Food and water
- Storm gear
- Headlamp and flashlight (with extra batteries)
- First-aid kit
- Fire starter
- Waterproof matches
- Knife

The glam fam's packing list for Tania Beecher

- A sky chart so you can stare up at the stars and decipher what made you such a neurotic Virgo (Som)
- A bear canister—and no, not that kind, although if you find one of those while you're up there, send him my way! (Glen)
- A sun hat, hiking boots, and outerwear that won't make you look like an ugly lumberjack (Casey)
- And some sexy underwear in case he gets past your long underwear (Alex)
- A water treatment kit to filter out raw sewage and whatever bullshit that man is going to use to convince you to hook up in the dirt (Tori)
- Travel toiletries, no-makeup makeup, and the best skincare Korea can export to keep your face snatched (Som)

- A two-person sleeping bag to get extra cozy (Casey)
- Condoms and Plan B for a good time (Alex)
- Lube, a cock ring, and a bullet vibe for a *really* good time (Glen)
- Mosquito repellent that doubles as pepper spray just in case (Tori)

chapter
fourteen

D riving to my hometown takes about three hours from Oakland, and the journey passes by in several stages. Depending on when I depart, the first hour is insufferable bumper-to-bumper traffic leaving the Bay, which I manage to avoid this time by leaving early Saturday morning instead of Friday evening.

Once I turn onto the 99 and enter the Central Valley, most of the trip is a straight shot through rural farming communities along the San Joaquin basin. I know I'm getting close once I pass through what I refer to as the *M*-towns—Modesto, Merced, and Madera—which all blur together when you're gunning it at eighty miles an hour.

The last stage is when I turn onto the 180-East to exit Fresno and enter my hometown of Sanger. The freeway peters out into a rural road, and that's when I know I'm nearing my childhood home.

I take a deep breath, trying to soothe Hammy, who's dangerously close to getting caught in another downward spiral. What the hell do I think I'm doing? I spent my first date with Nolan ogling his washboard abs in the gym and grinding against him at my place afterward. Putting our animal chemistry aside, I have yet to find common ground with him. If we can't agree on how to make mac and cheese or whether homes should have four wheels, what makes me think we're on the same page about serious topics like religion and children, neither of which are my cup of tea. The adage that opposites attract is true when you're talking about magnets, but I'm deeply afraid that being too different will repel us faster than any other gravitational force. By the time I turn into my parents' cul-de-sac, my sabbatical feels less like a fun discovery of a new partner and more like a death sentence dooming me to repeat my failed romantic history.

You sure you don't want to turn around and abandon this haphazard plan of yours? Hammy says, squeaking through his distress. *You could avoid this unnecessary heartbreak and swipe through the men who share your dealbreakers—there's got to be a few left, right?*

It's too late for that, I telepathically tell him. My dad's already seen the car and is waving at us. No backing out now.

At the very least, you don't need to tell your family about Nolan. That way when it falls apart, they can't give you a hard time and tell you that's what you get for dating an elite athlete as a couch potato.

I nod, pulling my car into the driveway and putting it into park. If there's one thing that Hammy and I agree on, it's saving myself from everyone witnessing my inevitable embarrassment.

"Welcome home, pumpkin." My dad squeezes me into a hug the moment I exit my vehicle. "How was the fog?"

"I got lucky." I don't miss a beat, knowing he's not referring to San Francisco's cloudy friend Karl. The fog in the Central Valley is much more sinister, so thick during the winter that you can't see more than a foot of road at a time. Without streetlights, the best you can do is turn off the radio, roll down your window, and listen for oncoming traffic. These quiet country roads are full of memorials of people who didn't see the other car coming to hit them. "It dissipated by the time I got on the 99, so it wasn't a problem."

My dad's already grabbed the keys out of my hand to open up my trunk to help me with my luggage. "What in the world —why the hell do you have all this stuff? Are you moving cross country?"

I slam the trunk closed, taking the small duffel bag from the passenger seat instead. "You know how unprepared I am for real winters. The last time I experienced a lot of snow was when we celebrated Christmas at Shaver Lake twenty years ago, so Yosemite might as well as be Everest." I check my smartwatch to see it's a quarter past noon. I made good time. "But all that gear can stay, since I'll be out of your hair in the morning."

My dad rubs the back of his head. "Well, there's not as much hair as there used to be, but you can stay in it as long as you want."

He takes the bag and leads me inside the house, where I smell lunch on the table before I see it, the spicy earthiness of hot Italian sausage, crisp dough, and extra cheese. "You got Me N' Eds."

My mom gives me a kiss before setting the table—nothing fancy, just paper plates for my favorite pizza from my childhood. "Perfect timing. It was delivered a few minutes ago. Here, put these cups of ranch dressing out."

I take the plastic individual servings out of her hands, counting them. "Four? Are we expecting somebody else?"

That's when my younger brother John barges through the front door. "You didn't think I'd miss Me N' Eds, did you?"

I roll my eyes at his pretense he's here just for the pizza, when the hug he crushes me in gives away how much he misses me. Ever since I moved to the Bay a decade ago, I come home a few times each year. Of course, John and I talk way more frequently than that—he's a freelance graphic designer, and I've relied on his design eye to help me at every job I've had—but showing up on a random weekend in February is a welcome surprise for both of us.

I compliment him on his latest dye job, turning his natural brown hair as red as a cherry slushie. Between the haircut, tattooed sleeves, and inch-long ear gauges, he pulls off the pop-punk rockstar look effortlessly. My coworkers who have worked with John on design requests have wondered aloud how a Type-A goody-two-shoes girlboss and a Warped Tour reject could ever be related, but the stark differences are comforting in their own way. If I can have such a great relationship with my polar opposite of a sibling, why couldn't Nolan and I get along just as well?

Although it doesn't take long for the interrogation to start, making me question my resolve all over again. "So what the hell's going on, Tania?" John asks, mouth full. "You've been postponing this sabbatical for years and now all of a sudden you're packing up and bailing on us?"

I know he's not referring to our actual family, but our work one. He may be a contractor, but he's been as much a part of Habituall's marketing team as I have. His tone is more teasing than accusatory, but that doesn't stop a pang of guilt from shooting through my chest as I think of all the tasks that pile up on John this time of year as we prepare for First Party. If I let that guilt consume me, I'll crumble under everyone's expectations.

"There's never going to be a perfect time. And if I don't take my sabbatical now, I may never get a chance again. I'm not concerned about Habituall's finances, but who knows—the market could tank, and I could easily be a casualty, out of a job before I can use the benefits that are owed to me."

My dad grunts in disapproval. "Owed? That's the problem with you techies. You're already making more money than god, and you still think you're entitled to a six-week vacation. That's what's wrong with Millennials, especially the ones just graduating college. Nobody wants to work anymore these days."

I take a deep breath to steady myself. There's so much wrong with the word vomit he spewed—for starters, the unemployment rate's the lowest it's ever been, and new grads aren't even Millennials, the oldest of which are now in their forties—but he's simply regurgitating what's been spoon-fed to him on Fox News. I've been working sixty-hour weeks nonstop, save for a handful of getaways and the occasional drive to Napa Valley to enjoy the rolling hills when they're not up in smoke during wildfire season. And despite the hustle and grind, I've been laid off from multiple tech startups that went belly-up. I recognize my dad had a hard life, spending triple-digit summers drenched in sweat as a mechanic before he was forced into an early retirement when his gout got too much to handle. But what he doesn't understand is you can work your fucking ass off and still be treated as disposable, regardless of your industry or salary.

But I've gone down this road before, arguing back and defending myself, and it always ends in tears and visits cut short. So I bite my tongue and save my retorts for my next therapy session with Dahlia. John and I share a well-worn look of mutual resignation. He's the only one in my family who knows about my mental health struggles, and even though my anxiety is diagnosed and his is not, he understands the futility of trying to gain our parents' approval.

"Yosemite will be a nice change of pace. The fresh air will do me good." I'd never throw Oakland under the bus because it's not nearly as noisy, dirty, and crime-ridden as my father makes it sound—again, thanks to the racist commentary from conservative pundits—but I know if there's one thing we can agree on, it's the importance of getting outside.

Grateful to segue into a conversation about regional climate, my mom pipes up to fret about winter weather conditions. "You sure you don't want to spend your sabbatical at the beach instead—somewhere on the coast like Monterey or Pismo? Digging your toes in the sand sounds like a much better idea than digging them in the snow."

Under any other circumstances, she'd be right. If my white noise machine is any indication, nothing's more soothing than the sound of waves lulling me to sleep. But I'm already exhausted by my parents' prodding, so no way am I opening Pandora's box and revealing the real reason I'm going to Yosemite. You'd think between their criticisms of my high-powered job and the urban environment I live in they'd be tapped out of complaints, but I know they are ready to comment on my lack of romantic prospects with the smallest opening. If they found out I'm dating somebody, I'd never hear the end of it. They'd be counting down the days until they're grandparents, despite the number of times I've reiterated that they'll be waiting until they die, whether or not I have a partner.

"I actually had a great time in Yosemite during our company retreat last month. And a national park in the off-season is the perfect place to clear my head. There will be nobody around and it will be so peaceful and quiet that I'll finally be able to relax and hear myself think."

Glancing around the table, I'm not sure who's more skeptical, but I don't blame them. The words sound empty the moment they come out of my mouth. I've never had any issue hearing the cacophony of anxious voices in my head, and being on vacation has never meant being free of panic attacks. I can't recall a time in my life when relaxing came easy, even when I was a child.

But thankfully, nobody calls me out on it, until we finish up our lunch and I walk John out to his car, which is parked on the edge of the driveway, next to my dad's shop where he spends his retirement tinkering on '60s sports cars and woodworking art for the small Etsy store we set up for him. Now that I think about it, no wonder I have trouble enjoying myself for the sake of it when my father has spent his entire existence keeping his hands busy and monetizing his hobbies.

"Remember when Dad would make us pick up rocks as kids?" I reminisce, pointing at the ditch in the front yard where we would spend weekends and summers bent over, filling a plastic bucket.

John laughs bitterly, tapping his slip-on Vans against the back tire of his silver Monte Carlo. "He used to say it made it easier when he was tractoring, but he'd come up with any excuse to get us off the computer."

I nod, vindicated. "I told him we'd make good money with computer jobs one day, and look what happened."

John smiles. "That's what I've been saying. When are we gonna start that marketing agency together? Imagine how sweet it would be if we were our own bosses."

It's certainly a nice thought. We've always talked about going into business together, first as child comic book artists, with John drawing the panels and me writing the story. But ever since we settled into our careers of design and marketing, respectively, it's continued to be in the back of our minds, combining our strengths and taking charge of our destinies.

I shake my head. "One day at a time. Let me get settled in this sabbatical before we plan to take over the world, Pinky."

John chuckles at the nickname. "I don't know how many times I have to tell you, but I'm definitely the Brain, not you. That's why I'm not falling for your mountain woman act."

I kick a loose pebble down the driveway, avoiding his gaze. "What are you talking about? I'm getting away in the great outdoors. Why is that so hard for you and Mom and Dad to accept?"

"Because you've never found anything great about the outdoors. That one time a grasshopper flew up your shorts while Dad took us off-roading in Shaver Lake, and you wrote off camping forever. I love you, Tania, but you were born to indulge in the finer things in life. There's no way you're achieving self-actualization without sushi delivery and fiber internet."

I nearly shove him in the shoulder, but I can't get offended when he's right. I'll be safe and comfortable as long as I'm at the lodge, but all bets are off if I have to suffer through the backcountry. "So I prefer to have nice amenities rather than cosplay a caveman's lifestyle—that's not a crime."

John crosses his arms, matching my defensive stance, and smirks. "That's awfully rich coming from someone running away from life to shack up with a guy who sleeps in a van."

"How did you—" I whip my head toward the house, making sure our parents can't see us. "Who the hell told you?"

John rolls his eyes, opening the driver's side door. "We work for the same company. I may not get a W-2, but I've got the Habituall email address and I'm in your team's meetings. Who didn't express their excitement that you're dating Nolan Wells? I swear they're all stoked you're finally getting laid so they can goof off a little."

I'm not sure what's worse: that my younger brother is discussing my sex life or that my sabbatical has turned into a rom-com where I'm the harpy executive in need of a good railing and my employees are overjoyed to get me out of the office.

"Please don't tell Mom and Dad," I whisper, as if they can hear me through the walls and across the long driveway.

John comes around the open door and gives me a hug, slapping me hard on the back. "I may be your little bro, but I'm thirty years old. I'm not an idiot. Your secret is safe with me. And for what it's worth, Nolan seems like a cool guy. Not sure how you're ever going to keep up with him when you consider taking the trash out as exercise, but I hope it works out. You deserve to be happy."

I squeeze him back, living for these heartfelt moments, few and far between polar-opposite siblings who work together. We may give each other a hard time, but it's been us against the world, so we have each other's backs. "Keep the team in line while I'm gone, will ya?"

He gets in the driver's seat and starts the car, rolling down the window. "Hey, I'll keep cashing Habituall's paychecks until we start cutting our own. That's one positive to keep in mind when you and Free Nolo are enjoying that love nest on wheels."

I tilt my head, not following his point. "What positive?"

"We can run a marketing agency from anywhere. Including Yosemite."

≈

Transcript of the Climbing Clutch *podcast on Saturday, February 12*

Podcast host: Okay, now that we've covered your climbing journey up to this point, what's next for Nolan Wells? Any rad milestones you're looking to hit this year?

Nolan Wells: As I explain in any interview I do, I'm superstitious about revealing my upcoming projects. So all I can say is you'll know about my milestones after I've achieved them.

Host: Fair enough, bro. You're a private dude who likes to keep things close to his chest. Is that the same with your romantic life?

Nolan: Excuse me?

Host: Dan, pull up that image, will you? Looks like you're taking the climbing world by storm with these shots taken by gym members at Pacific Pipeworks in Oakland. Now we've seen you tackle some of the most death-defying routes, but nothing has blown us away like this—high-key macking on some chick like your life depended on it. So what can you tell us about her, Free Nolo?

Nolan: I, uh, can't speak to that at this time.

Host: Come on. Your hand is legit groping her ass in this pic. You can share a few tidbits. How long have you known her? Is she also a climber? Give us the deets!

Nolan: You know, my personal life is personal and, therefore, nobody's business but my own.

Host: Alright, bro, don't get your harness in a twist. We don't mean any harm by it. After all, our listeners are curious. But if you date like you climb, I guess we're not getting any confirmation until you've put a ring on it.

Nolan: Please, don't get ahead of yourselves. This is all super new. But for what it's worth, I'm happy. I'm very happy.

Host: Aw, you're gonna make us cry over here. You heard it here first, *Climbing Clutch* kids—Nolan "Free Nolo" Wells may or may not have a super new girlfriend and he's very happy. Congrats to you, man, and to your lucky lady!

chapter
fifteen

M y weekend in Fresno flies by, and before I know it, I'm treating my first day on sabbatical like I would any other Monday: waking up with the sun and racing from one task on my to-do list to another. I reply to any straggling emails in my work inbox to remind folks of my time off, make sure my autoresponder is set to catch anybody else who slipped through the cracks, and update my voicemail message and display names on Slack and social media. Once I've thoroughly fortified my digital forcefield, I pad into my parents' kitchen to make myself a cup of English Breakfast, settling for one of the tea bags I've packed instead of my typical bougie loose-leaf. Between acclimating to the guest bed and trying to will Hammy to get some shut-eye, I didn't get much sleep, so I can use the pick-me-up.

You love blaming me for everything, Hammy butts in, turning my inner monologue into a dialogue. *But it sounds like you're your own worst problem. You've already got the jitters, so you don't need caffeine's help.*

Or your help either, I argue. I wouldn't need an IV drip of Fortnum & Mason's best blends if you didn't keep me awake wringing your tiny hamster hands over every little thing. So, what is it this time, Hammy?

That's when my parents join me in the kitchen, banishing Hammy back to the recesses of my mind before he can tell me what's wrong. But not even my mom's breakfast casserole—a delicious nostalgia bomb of sausage, scrambled eggs, and cheddar cheese wrapped in crescent rolls—can dull my sense of dread. It only amplifies as I throw my small duffel bag back in my car, kiss my family goodbye, and peel out of the driveway. I tell myself that my heart will settle down now that I'm on the road, but it's racing faster the farther I wind into the foothills.

It's easier to confront acute anxiety because there's typically a tangible reason why it's appearing—being trapped on a crowded train, for instance—but this kind of nervous energy causes a subtler kind of suffering, keeping you worried and restless without a way to expel the feeling. It's as if your brain is a hair straightener you're not sure if you unplugged before you walked out the front door: is everything okay, or is your whole house about to burn down?

When I make a pit stop in Oakhurst an hour later to refill my tank, I have to park my car in front of the gas station and walk a couple of laps around the block to shake off whatever is plaguing me and identify what the ever-loving fuck is going on.

It can't be the fear of forgetting to pack something because I've triple-checked my list. And sure, I'm worried about work—simultaneously that everything will fall apart without me and that I won't be missed in the slightest—but there's nothing new about my desperate need to feel needed. That wouldn't have me folded over with my head between my knees to avoid vertigo.

Hammy's usually antsy before a date, but I'm not meeting a stranger. Nolan was gracious enough to let me pick the meeting spot tonight, and I chose dinner at Granite Grove. That way we can keep things simple, and I have plenty of time to primp beforehand.

When I arrive at the lodge and see it's not yet noon, even Hammy is reassured with how much buffer we've padded into this trip, with over seven hours to unpack, eat lunch, shower, and do my hair and makeup.

Heck, I don't even have to shave, thanks to Tori waxing everything below the waist—for free, might I add. Not sure if she took pity on me because I was legit freaking out to have hot torture strips near my lady bits or I needed reassuring that getting that up close and personal with a friend was no big deal when the glam fam has all taken the prone position in her presence. But I was grateful for her charity, nonetheless.

When I enter my hotel room, I'm hit with a blast of déjà vu. At least I've been upgraded to a bigger room with a better view as thanks for my long-term stay, but it still feels like I've been transported back to our retreat. It's difficult to turn off work mode and get in the mood for romance.

And yet, as I pace around the suite with restless energy, my anxiety feels more ominous than my typical corporate concerns. I'm contemplating the question the entire day, stressed about why I'm stressed. It's like a low mental hum, a radio static imperceptible to everyone else but myself. Any fully functioning person would have abandoned the quest, content to indulge in everyday distractions, but here I am, ruminating while applying a subtle cat eye and half-listening to an audiobook droning on in the background.

I'm halfway through taming my unruly frizz into bouncy waves with the Dyson Airwrap that Glen gave me for my birthday when it finally dawns on me. Much like the multiple hair curling attachments contained in this heavy, leather case that takes up the majority of my hotel room vanity, I have put all my hopes and dreams into one basket.

Even if this sabbatical—away from the hustle and bustle of the city—is the perfect chance to figure out what I want to do with my life, I can't deny the impetus for this journey of self-discovery is Nolan. My company knows it, my brother knows it, and now thanks to that blasted podcast, the rest of the world knows it too. Okay, at least the rest of the climbing world anyway, which is thankfully small enough that no one in my family's circle is sending that episode to my parents out of the blue.

But I'm not so oblivious to think there won't be ramifications with Nolan's loved ones. His mom, dad, friends, fellow athletes—they may not know me, but they definitely know of me now, and they'll know immediately that I don't belong. And that means the stakes are that much higher if our relationship doesn't work out.

Bingo, Hammy pipes up, smug and victorious. *When this door closes—and they always do—who knows if or when another will open?*

Weak answers tumble out—I don't know, I can't control that, am I supposed to avoid dating entirely?—but Hammy's unsatisfied with them all. I'm frustrated with the vice grip he's got on my psyche. I can't keep beating myself up for everything that goes topsy-turvy in my life. Why do I hold myself to such an unreachable standard that everything must go exactly to plan or I'm a de-facto loser?

The second I'm done with curling my hair, I stride over to the minibar, grab the first fun-size whiskey I see, and drain it in a single gulp. I could uncork one of the many bottles of red wine I packed and pour myself a glass like a proper lady, but something stronger is called for in this situation. The liquor burns my throat, and I'm going to regret the charge on my hotel bill, but it's what I deserve for letting my anxiety hamster push me around.

Get your shit together, Tania. Sure, our first date could be magical, with killer chemistry and the kind of all-night-long sex that '90s R&B musicians kept singing about. But every minute doesn't have to be perfect for it to be a night to remember.

Not to mention, Nolan may technically be a celebrity, but it's not like he's living a lavish lifestyle. Even if I didn't read all those articles about how he turned down his inheritance and donates most of his money to charity, I've heard firsthand how he has more conversations with granite than girls. If he shows up to a corporate keynote address for hundreds of techies in head-to-toe North Face, he'll likely be equally dressed down tonight. And if he's hella chill, then I should be hella chill, too.

Hammy scoffs. *Did that drink kill your last brain cell? Nothing about us can be classified as chill, and it's a fool's errand to think otherwise. It's only a matter of time until the jig is up, and Nolan calls off this whole charade.*

It makes sense then why I imagine Hammy as male. None of the women in my life would ever break me down like he does. I've got to channel my more confident friends in times like these, especially Tori, who gives the least amount of shits. I can hear her clicking her long talons together, telling Hammy to get fucked. If I don't hold myself in higher esteem, nobody else will. And if the glam fam thinks Nolan's lucky to date me, I should walk into the restaurant as if it's true.

I open the closet and can almost hear Casey's voice as I scan the pieces she selected. She's always going on about how women are judged more harshly for their appearance, so she has all the bases covered. She packed me an outfit for every occasion, from comfy, chunky knit cardigans to the kind of leather dresses that look more fitting for a dominatrix than a dinner date. It's such a fine thread to weave—the elusive balance between sweet and sexy, tailored but not try-hard, warm and a little revealing at the same time.

Nolan's so casual that the chances of him showing up in

climbing gear are pretty high, so he wouldn't care if I wore a trash bag. But now that the news of our relationship is out, the chances of getting photographed together are even higher. Nolan can be a walking billboard for his sponsors, but I'd rather be a tad overdressed than under-deliver on everyone's expectations of what Nolan Wells's new girlfriend should look like.

I throw on the winning number, spritz on some sultry perfume, and apply a fresh coat of wine-red lipstick, finishing my getting-ready routine at the exact moment Nolan texts me to tell me he's downstairs waiting for me in the dining room.

Hammy and I simultaneously gulp down our misgivings. No going back, no cancellations, no rain checks. Whatever happens will happen. I may be on display every time I'm with Nolan, but at least I'll look damn good while I'm there. If the world's going to watch us from the sidelines, let them stare.

Slack conversation in Habituall's #marketing-team channel on Monday, February 14

@HarrisShepherd: Hey everyone, our weekly team meeting is happening now. You can log in via the Zoom link I just shared.

@DemandJen: We're still doing those?

@HarrisShepherd: Um, yes, Tania's on sabbatical, not you. I'm hosting her meetings in the interim, remember?

@DemandJen: Shit, can we push to after lunch? I haven't finished my slides :(

@LondonLisa: That wouldn't be fair to the European team

@DemandJen: We could record the meeting for you!

@HARRISSHEPHERD: That's enough, Jennifer—we're skipping the demand generation team update if you're not prepared. Email your notes to @marketing by end of day

@SOCIALSARAH: Hey, side note—are we posting for Valentine's Day?

@DEMANDJEN: I thought we decided that was insensitive to unpartnered people by upholding the heteronormative industrial complex?

@HARRISSHEPHERD: For the love of god, just because your bf dumped you last week doesn't mean the world is out to get you. Now everybody, I'm not going to say it again, LOG INTO ZOOM.

chapter
sixteen

Nolan locks eyes on me the moment I exit the elevator and approach the Granite Grove dining room in my date-worthy look: a burgundy miniskirt that hugs every curve, paired with a black mock turtleneck sweater and matching suede thigh-high heeled boots. I'm as cozy and warm as a Taylor Swift music video during pumpkin spice season, save for the streak of silver-gray hair that gives me a mature edge and the tops of my bare thighs that are anything but basic.

I should be on cloud nine witnessing Nolan practically drooling over me, but I'm too busy drooling over him.

"Wow," he whispers, ping-ponging his eyes from the roots of my sleek waves to the tips of my stiletto heels. "You are stunning."

"Same." My reply comes out just as soft because my throat has gone dry at the sight of Nolan's black slacks, jacket, and tie. The man wore a suit? With a collared shirt and a fucking belt? "You have, um, literally stunned me silent."

Nolan tugs on his tie. It's not that he doesn't look great, because he pulls off formalwear as well as gym-rat rags, but he's so visibly uncomfortable that it's making me uncomfortable. And there's something about the fit of the suit that's off . . .

"Yeah, well, Granite Grove is notorious for its dress code."

Shit. I didn't even bother looking up the restaurant online. At our retreat, Habituall dined each day with no regard to what we were wearing. Several employees rolled up to the breakfast buffet in their flannel pajamas. After all, this is a mountain lodge, not the Four Seasons.

Nolan must see the panic on my face as I re-evaluate my choice in clothing. "You're fine. More than fine. You look amazing. It's mostly to curb tourists from waltzing in wearing grody T-shirts, cargo shorts, and flip-flops—which is pretty much all I live in during the summer when I'm not climbing. It's one of the reasons why I don't eat here."

I try to ignore the edge in Nolan's voice. Even if he's only perturbed at outdated hotel dress codes, it's hard not to take it personally. If he was so opposed to meeting here, why didn't he suggest an alternative?

All my friends would simply slap me on the back and encourage me to enjoy the evening. *He's not insulting your date idea, Tania. Just crack a lighthearted joke, and let's move on.*

"I get it. Too difficult to get your one suit dry-cleaned, amiright?"

His frown deepens, and he drops his head to fidget with one of the buttons on his jacket. "I never bothered buying another one after Ryan's funeral."

Oh god. That's why the suit fits too loose in some areas and too tight in others. I'm torn between apologizing all over myself and fleeing to my car, never to see Nolan again, but before I can make up my mind, the maître d' approaches and leads us to our table.

Despite the grand stone fireplace next to us, a chill causes me to shiver. I was hoping for a cozy booth so we could enjoy each other's personal space, but there are formal four-seaters as far as the eye can see in this vast, open dining hall. And because I've fucked up the entire mood, Nolan takes the seat across from me instead of one to my left or right. So now we're separated, both by the offensively large table and the emotional gulf between us. I shake out my napkin to place it in my lap, and the somber vibe hanging in the air makes it feel more like I'm waving my handkerchief goodbye to him as he retreats on the *Titanic* at sea.

"Whoa." Nolan's lips have all but disappeared into a thin line, and my breath catches in my throat as I wonder how the hell I've fucked things up further, but when I look up, his nose is deep into the menu.

"Is something wrong? Are there not vegan options?" Again, my brain is scrambling. Why, oh why, did I not do any research? I was more concerned with what lingerie I was going to wear under this miniskirt than making sure my date could eat something more substantial than a side salad.

"Um, no, that's not it. You know what, it's fine. What are you feeling?"

I scan the menu, and thanks to my parents who raised me modestly on a teacher and mechanic's joint income, I can hazard a guess why the menu is rubbing Nolan the wrong way. The sourdough bread to start is itself twelve dollars, and the prices go up the farther you read. I spot a vegan entree of seasonal vegetables for nearly forty bucks, a prime rib pushing sixty, and dishes at the bottom simply listed as "market rate." The wine list is impressive, but that just means I can't find a budget-friendly bottle. If I was dating yet another techie in SF, I'd feel no guilt springing for the Veuve Cliquot, but at that price, champagne becomes more of a burden than a celebration.

"I'm tired from the drive up here, so I don't need to drink tonight."

But before I can fold the wine list and set it aside, the sommelier appears at our table and opens a bottle of red. "Your bottle of cabernet sauvignon, Mr. Wells."

Even in the low light, I can make out the stag on the label as she pours me the customary taste, and I know what she's going to say before she says it. Stag's Leap. 2019 Cask 23 aged twenty-one months in new French oak barrels. Same vineyard that produced the bottle I have at home, but three times as expensive. It's been on my wish list for so long I don't bother swishing it around in my glass, instead gulping it down.

The sommelier walks away, pleased, and Nolan matches my sheepish smile. "While you were grabbing napkins from your cupboard, I snapped a pic of your wine rack. I hope you don't mind. This bottle's a winery exclusive so I made a pit stop before I returned to the valley. I don't know much about wine, but they made this one sound pretty special."

He drove two hours out of his way to pick up wine just to impress me? He may have allowed my apology from earlier to go unsaid, but there aren't enough words to express my gratitude. "It's perfect. Thank you."

Screw the cabernet—it's Nolan who's pretty damn special. Warmth spreads into my extremities, making my fingers and toes tingle. The heat inside me expands as wide as the boundaries of my growing comfort zone.

Before I moved to the Bay, "the valley" meant the Central Valley, the smog and dust bowl that is my hometown. And when I officially became a transplant, the valley included Silicon Valley and Napa Valley, the work-hard and play-hard destinations of my tech life. Now when Nolan refers to Yosemite Valley, the borders of my world are redrawn once again, etched into my heart. Perhaps with a little time, this valley can feel as much like home as all the others.

And if Nolan's moving mountains to make me happy, the

least I can do is learn to appreciate the mountains the way he does.

"Do you wanna get out of here?"

He grips the arms of his chair in surprise. "But we just sat down."

I nod, rummaging through my black clutch. "Yep, but do you really want to pay for overpriced carrot medallions while suffocating in a stuffy suit?"

"Not exactly." Nolan shifts in his seat. "But it's your first night on sabbatical and you deserve a nice dinner to celebrate."

"First off," I protest, "my company is paying tens of thousands of dollars for me not to work, so that's celebration enough. And I can't think of a nicer dinner than snuggling with you in the van and enjoying this bottle with your mac and cheese." My hand finds what it was looking for. "Ah, there you are!"

His eyes widen as I grab the Stag's Leap. "Do you always carry a wine stopper with you?"

"Mmhmm." I plug the stopper into the neck, sealing it tightly and wiping off any stray drops. "I mean, it's rare my friends and I don't finish off a bottle once we've opened it, but this is, as we say, the good shit. No way in hell am I wasting it when we've got the whole night ahead of us. What do you say?"

He smiles, his face awash with relief. "I bought a value pack of Kraft for when you stay over. The spiral kind, your favorite. And I got some hot dogs if you're feeling fancy."

He might as well have gotten down on one knee, because Tiffany's has nothing on the blue box of my heart. "I don't know how you're single, because you, Nolan Wells, know how to seduce a woman."

Our waiter comes by and before he can ask if we've made any decisions on appetizers, I'm tugging Nolan out of his seat.

"Change of plans. We've got to run. Please charge the corkage fee to my room, number 434. Now if you'll excuse us . . . "

For the first time, I'm willingly abandoning a four-dollar-sign establishment, a toasty fireplace, and my hygge way of life to rough it—with a rock climber, no less. Back home, I resented crossing the Bay Bridge for a date, even if he pulled out all the stops to wine and dine me, and now I've traveled hundreds of miles in the heart of winter to be with a man who last wore a tie when Obama was still president.

Is this settling down or just settling? That's a question for future-me to worry about, because right now, I couldn't care less. I've got a bowl of Kraft with my name on it and an adorably handsome cuddle buddy to undress.

~

"Your Ideal Sexual Position Based on Your Favorite Type of Climbing," by The Send-It Sisters on Monday, February 14

HAPPY VALENTINE'S DAY, limber ladies! If love is in the air, lust is on the rocks, because nothing gets us going like big, hard walls and the people who climb them. If you're looking for inspiration between the sheets, why not let the most popular climbing styles determine your next rendezvous? Strap in those harnesses and take your positions.

1. **Bouldering: Get up close and personal with some self-love.** They say you can't love somebody else until you love yourself. So enjoy your independence by laying out a mat and getting down with your bad self.

2. **Top roping: Go back to basics with missionary.** It takes two to tango, so if you've got a partner, this is the foundation you start with, whether at the gym or in the bedroom. It's not particularly adventurous, but it gets the job done.

3. **Trad climbing: Celebrate the spice of life with cowgirl.** Now we're talking. It may not be feasible to escape to the great outdoors every day, but it's the fun we live for. Take charge of both your safety and pleasure by bringing your own protection.

4. **Mountaineering: Prepare for the long haul with tantric sex.** Whether you're scrambling across red rock or ice-picking over alpine peaks, slow and steady wins the race. Practice your deep breathing and give your friends a heads up if they won't hear from you for a while.

5. **Speed climbing: Come in record time with a quickie.** Call it a burst of passion or a two-pump chump, but sometimes you've got to race to the finish line. Here function beats form, so your position doesn't matter so much as keeping your clothes on.

6. **Big wall climbing: Accept the ultimate challenge by standing up.** If you enjoy spending hours, days, or even weeks of your life in a vertical position, big walls and partners are for you. Hold on for dear life, and whatever you do, don't look down.

7. **Crack climbing: Embrace tight spaces with anal.** Let's face it—you're always sticking your hands into places they shouldn't be. It may not be for everybody, but the people who like it *really* like it. Bring lots of patience . . . and lube.

8. **Free soloing: Get dirty and dangerous by raw-dogging it.** We can't in good conscience recommend forgoing protection, but we get how sexy it can be to give into your basest instincts. But, as Coach Carr said in *Mean Girls*, if you do touch each other, you will get chlamydia and die. Fingers crossed a burn downstairs is the least of your problems.

chapter
seventeen

It's cozier in Nolan's van than I remember. I don't know if it's because the weather's warmer than it was the first time we met or if he's secretly installed a space heater since then, but it sure seems like he's been nesting. There's a weighted blanket on the comforter and a box of premium hot chocolate packets on the counter. Who knows what other little touches Nolan added to make sure I felt comfortable in his—

"Home."

Nolan perks up from the pot of Kraft spirals. "What's that?"

I gesture around the interior. "It sounds silly, but it took me this long to see this place as your home, not just your car."

He nods, handing me a bowl, complete with cut-up hot dogs. "I don't blame you. The mental shift was hard for me to adjust to as well. I see quite a few so-called digital nomads around the park during peak season, but it's not until you start picking their brain on how they handle healthcare or taxes without an address that they admit they've got a house back in LA that they list on Airbnb while they're climbing. Everybody wants the freedom and flexibility to go wherever and whenever they want, but very few truly cut the cord from creature comforts and untether themselves from society. And why should they? This kind of life is not for the faint of heart, but I can't imagine living any other way."

I let his words sink in along with the creamy goodness making its way to my stomach with each bite. "It must be lonely to not have anyone who fully understands what it's like. Not that I'm saying I do either, but I'm trying."

He looks up from his own vegan bowl and smiles. "Hey, you came back. That's more than I can say for most people. And now that I've reached a level of success, it's not so bad. Sure, there's always going to be some asshole who bangs on my door or climbs on my hood like he's entitled to bother me in my home just because it moves. But the IRS has stopped giving me a hard time, at least."

I chuckle. With his suit jacket and tie tossed over the driver's seat, Nolan's noticeably happier. Now that we're both more comfortable, I let my curiosity get the best of me and steer our conversation into uncharted terrain. "Hey . . . why were you studying to be a certified financial planner?"

Nolan gulps down his spoonful and a bell pepper catches in his throat, which would have validated my thoughts on veggies in mac and cheese if I wasn't concerned about him choking to death.

"Damn," he coughs, catching his breath. "Coming for the jugular. Whatever happened to warming up to the serious topics?"

I playfully shove his shoulder. "You interrogated me about my career on my first night here, so clearly we're not fond of small talk. And it's only fair."

He sets his empty bowl on the counter. "Okay fine, but where is that bottle? I'm gonna need a refill before this interview, Diane Sawyer."

He pours me another glass and takes a pause, mulling over his answer. "Strangers used to say Ryan and I were two peas in a pod, but once you got to know us, we couldn't have been more different. I was always the more organized and responsible one, even when we were teenagers going on our first expeditions. Ryan was the rebel, the life of the party. Because Ryan was always gallivanting around, his orange fauxhawk visible from outer space, our father assumed I was the more appropriate choice for taking over his advisory business. So when Ryan convinced me to take a gap year with him after college, Dad demanded that I stop dicking around. Just me, like he had already given up on his other son."

He grips his glass tighter, and for a moment, I'm afraid he's going to shatter it with his humongous hands. But he manages to calm himself down and avoid spilling red wine all over the bed. "Like I told you before, I was studying for the CFP exam that summer Ryan and his girlfriend climbed the Matterhorn. When he didn't come back, I don't know if I thought it was a sign or I just couldn't give a fuck about anything else, but I never took the test. I didn't care anymore. Climbing was the only thing that mattered to me apart from Ryan, and if he wasn't going to be around to do it with me, I'd do it alone."

I can't fathom losing someone that close to me, but I can understand his decision to lean into the chaos. Why make well-intentioned plans if the universe is going to tear them up and spit in your face? The cruelty and unfairness of it all would break anybody.

"Surely, your parents understood the importance of taking time to recover from such a horrific tragedy. You lost a brother, and they lost a son."

Nolan lets out a hollow laugh, draining his glass. "You would think, but no. They continued to emphasize focusing on my future, never seeing the irony that it was *their* future they were concerned about. They saw Ryan's death as proof that climbing was a foolish path to nowhere. Mom might have been fine with me taking a break—a grief sabbatical, if you will —but when Dad laid the hammer down and threatened to take away my inheritance if I didn't fall in line, she didn't stop him. After all, they run the largest independent advisory firm west of the Mississippi. Preserving the legacy of the family business is their priority, even if they sacrifice their family's happiness in the process. And when my father reminded me I'd be turning down twice the payout without Ryan around to claim his half, I snapped. Told him to keep his blood money and fuck off."

The callousness of his parents takes my breath away. I'm unclear on whether Nolan has broken all ties with his parents, but that's not important. If anyone was entitled to go no-contact, it would be him.

"Okay, Tania, it's your turn now."

I laugh nervously. "To what? Share the sins of Mr. and Mrs. Beecher? Whatever I spill will pale in comparison to your award-winning parents."

"Come on. I mean, I'm used to being number one at everything, including familial resentment, but you gotta give me something. Trauma bonding's what all the cool kids are doing apparently."

Alright, that was a good one. Nolan's got that dark sense of humor I like. Nothing gets me going like a guy in therapy.

"Well, I'm not expecting anything you'd call an inheritance —maybe just some rusted redneck rides on concrete blocks. But I know how it feels to be crushed under the weight of someone's expectations. I did the exact opposite as you— followed my parents' guidance to a tee—but it was never enough."

He goes to refill our glasses a third time, and even though I'm bracing myself for the hangover tomorrow, the cabernet tastes so smooth it's warming me from the inside out, much like connecting with Nolan on a deeper level. Knowing him this intimately is intoxicating.

"Did your parents push you into tech?"

I shake my head. "The only things they pushed were getting straight As in school and going to college, because my dad was a mechanic and never attended himself. You'll appreciate the fact that he worked for his own father and regretted every second of it. He's always been good with his hands, but he busted his ass so he could provide for us. It's not their fault he instilled an unhealthy work ethic in me and my brother. He just wanted to give us a better life than he had. Which meant college was a when, not an if."

"But what about after you graduated?"

I shrug, recalling the upheaval those early years of my career brought into my life. "I majored in English Lit because I liked reading, and I went to journalism school because I liked writing. I had these naïve visions of chasing scoops and reporting on juicy scandals, but when I landed my first job I was paid peanuts and my parents freaked out that I'd never be able to support myself. So I moved to the Bay and transitioned into tech marketing to make enough money to eat and pay rent at the same time. I ended up really enjoying the work, but it didn't matter to them that I was now earning the big bucks —not when I live hours away in the so-called inner city instead of in some stifling suburb next door to them."

I pause, trying to contain my bitterness. "I know it's hard being told to follow in your parents' footsteps, but it's just as hard when you desperately seek their approval, and it never comes."

Nolan reaches out, and that's when I realize he's left-handed. It's comforting, knowing we can hold hands without putting our wine glasses down. "I may be biased, but paying rent is overrated. A journalist's salary goes a lot farther when your house has a steering wheel."

That comedic timing, I swear. It never fails to cheer me up. "Thanks, but it was for the best. I'm way better at developing brands than breaking the news. And I genuinely like marketing because I still get to tell stories—ones that are so persuasive you can't help but buy whatever I'm selling. My brother is a designer, and we've even toyed with the idea of being partners. I'd run content and campaigns, and he'd take care of the creative. Starting a family business sounds appealing when it's a true collaboration. One we build on our own terms, and nobody else's."

Nolan smiles. "My parents could have benefited from that mindset, that's for sure. But yours must be proud that you climbed to the top of the corporate ladder, right?"

"They would say they're proud, but not even getting promoted to VP has been enough to cut me some slack. Now they're constantly harping on why I'm not married and giving them grandchildren." I hesitate, unsure if I should reveal why this has driven a wedge between us. But it's so core to my identity that it's only a matter of time before it comes up. Better sooner rather than later, I guess. "I've told them countless times that I never want to have children," I say slowly, "but they refuse to listen."

Pausing to gauge Nolan's response, I wait for the other shoe to drop. Too many times I've been burned by men in the past. The first few dates go great, but when I divulge I'm child-free by choice, I suddenly start racking up spaces on the proverbial bingo card. It's why the childfree community calls it getting bingo-ed in the first place—because their lines are so cliché we could make a game out of them.

"But you'd make such a great mom." The only things you know about me so far, Chad, are that I love pasta and have fantastic taste in pop-punk music, but neither makes me eligible for a World's Best Mommy mug.

"But who will take care of you when you're old?" Oh, I don't

know—ask the thousands of parents and grandparents neglected in nursing homes. I thought you wanted children, not an insurance policy.

"You're still young. You'll change your mind." Like I'm changing my number so you can never call me again.

I don't see any traces of judgment or pity in Nolan's eyes. He just smiles and squeezes my hand tighter. "Hey, I live in a tiny metal box and spend every waking moment clinging to a cliff—on occasion with nothing to prevent me from falling to an untimely death. I never felt like I had to spell it out, but me and kids go together like peanut butter and chalk. I can't think of a grosser combination."

Relief washes over me. This is the first time a man hasn't questioned my life choice or played devil's advocate. Not only has Nolan taken my decision at face value, but he's also planning on being childfree himself.

"Or mac and cheese and bell peppers?" I tease, to which he snatches the empty wine glass out of my hand and sets both on the counter.

"Now I know you're drunk because you're spouting off nonsense. Bell peppers are delicious. I bite into them like they're apples."

"God, I could take a bite out of *you*." Crap, did I say that out loud? Clearly, the alcohol has done its job of lowering my inhibitions.

Nolan searches my eyes. "If that's coming from you and not the wine, that . . . could be arranged."

I scoot closer and take his cheeks in my hands, inhaling deeply to steady my voice into sounding as sincere as possible. "I may not be able to pass a breathalyzer test, but I've wanted to jump your bones the moment I got a good look at your face. The booze has nothing to do with that. So I'm yours if you want me."

The relief on his face is palpable now that our waiting is

finally over. "By now, it's a need, not a want." Nolan pulls me into his lap and captures my lips in a deep kiss, cradling the back of my head. We vacillate between indulging in the taste of each other and ramping up the urgency, split between our desires to enjoy the current moment and race to the next one. After all, the only thing that could be better than Nolan's mouth on mine is the anticipation of it being everywhere else on my body.

When we come up for air, he gasps and I freak out, concerned I've knocked something over and spilled it all over the bed, even though our bowls and glasses are well out of reach.

"What's wrong?"

"Nothing at all," he insists, smiling, as if the apocalypse could be happening outside the van, and his answer would be the same. "I just forgot something."

I wonder if he's talking about protection, and I'm about to tell him I have a box of condoms in my bag when he flips a switch near the head of the bed. Suddenly, a string of twinkle lights turns on, bathing us in warmth.

"At first, I thought they were cheesy," he explains. "I always rolled my eyes when van life influencers used them to achieve some twee aesthetic, but I have to admit they make everything homey."

I grin from ear to ear at the sweet gesture. "Look at you— Nolan Wells setting the mood. I don't know why you make a big deal about not dating many women, because you're plenty experienced."

He blushes, fiddling with the zipper on my thigh-high boots. "I wasn't exaggerating my cluelessness. There have been a few women since Ryan died, but they were all casual flings, and only when I was traveling. When I'm here in the park, dating is just a distraction. I've avoided it for years . . . until now."

Part of me is rejoicing at the thought of being special to him, even if Hammy's whispering that I better enjoy it while it lasts. That it's only a matter of time before Nolan wises up and kicks me to the curb. "What's different with me?"

He continues wiggling the zipper back and forth. "It sounds pompous as shit, but when we met, you genuinely didn't know anything about me. From my parents to the press to everyone in the climbing community, the whole world has had specific ideas of who Nolan Wells is supposed to be. Because you didn't have any expectations, I could be myself around you."

Nolan wraps me in his Olympian-level wingspan. "And that's just how you make me feel—add in that you're wildly smart and successful in your own right, and so gorgeous my body aches harder than it does after I've climbed El Cap." He's not kidding, as I can feel every inch of that ache straining against his slacks.

But from the way he tenderly laces his fingers through mine, I can tell he cares as much about our emotional connection as our physical one. "Tania, you are legit the most beautiful, memorable woman I've saved from falling to her doom, so there was no way I wasn't going to fall for you."

If for any reason I had planned on keeping my clothes on tonight, his heartfelt speech would have made my intention fly out the window. I lean in for another kiss, but before I reach his lips, Nolan whispers, "Please tell me what you like."

This man, I can't. The swooning he incites with every word will end me. I lead his hand down my mid-thigh where my boot begins, having him pull the zipper down. "Climbing."

He flashes a smile, understanding the call and response immediately. "Climb on."

We kiss while he removes the other boot, along with my sweater and miniskirt. I must say I'm impressed—all that climbing by pure muscle memory makes Nolan a natural at undressing me with his eyes closed. It makes it all the sweeter when he opens them to find me in only my lacy black bralette and thong.

"Oh . . . no."

My hands fly up to my chest. "Are we moving too fast?"

"No!" Nolan shakes his head with a jerk. "No, for the love of—do *not* stop. It's just that . . . I can't imagine being able to last regardless of the pace. You're going to tip me over the edge before we even start."

I'm on top of the world, feeling like goddamn Wonder Woman. "We just need to build up your stamina."

I unbutton his collared shirt and slide it down his shoulders, before peeling off the undershirt in quick succession. It's not the first time I've seen his chiseled chest, but without the fear of him taking a fifty-foot fall, I can truly savor tracing my fingers over each individual ab—and not because I swear there's eight of them. Sports were never an interest of mine, but I get now why most people find athletes attractive. It's more than being built out of marble; it's appreciating the sheer effort and dedication it took to carve that body in the first place.

"You're . . . stunning," I whisper with the little air I have left in my lungs. I haven't even undressed his bottom half, and Nolan's already taken my breath away.

The twinkle in his eyes mirrors the lights hanging above us. "That's supposed to be my line." Nolan's hands follow mine to his waist, helping me unbuckle his belt and remove his slacks. My instinct during our first morning after was right on the money, because from the way he's practically bursting at the seams of his boxer briefs, he's working with quite a lot.

Usually, if I'm lucky to get this far with a date, I strip off my clothes and do the deed as fast as possible before I can chicken out. If I have too much time to think through what I'm doing, I'm at risk of my anxiety calling the whole thing off. But Nolan's watching intensely from underneath me, allowing me to take the lead. No matter what happens tonight, he's not going anywhere, and that reassurance gives me the confidence I need to tug off his boxer briefs and wrap my hand around him.

He groans at my touch. "Slack!"

It takes me a split second to recognize that he's not referencing the messaging app, but instead requesting a loose hold. Not a problem—if there's anything I'm good at, it's following instructions. And this time I get the added thrill of having a man like Nolan Wells at my mercy.

I take a comfortable position between his legs and run my tongue up and down his length, savoring the way he sighs. Most guys are so impatient they're shoving your head down as soon as their pants are off, so it's refreshing that Nolan wants to go slow. When I finally take him in my mouth, I let my fingertips roam—grazing his stomach, rubbing his thighs, stroking his shaft.

"*Fuck*, that feels good . . . just like that." If Nolan's pecs and abs are as hard as rock, then his dick ought to be made of diamonds. I'm reveling in how he feels between my lips, testing how deep I can take him just to hear him moan. His exhalations are so hot, I'm picking up the pace before I know it, and he grips my shoulder to stop me.

"I hate to pause mid-climb," he says, pulling me to him. "But if you keep going, I'll be ready to lower before we reach our peak."

I kiss him, and he doesn't flinch at his own taste lingering on my tongue. I have to admit bringing him so close to the brink has brought me right along with him, so I don't think I'm going to last much longer either.

"Hold on." Nolan playfully swats my hand away as I go to

peel off my bralette. "It feels like you're always undressing in my presence. Let me unwrap you like the gift you are."

My mind flashes back to our only-one-van situation the night we first met. Had I skipped the step where I changed into his clothes and instead threw myself at him, we could have hooked up without the excruciating wait. But even though I didn't know it at the time, Nolan was right. One night would have never been enough.

Nolan sits up so he can slide the straps of my bralette down, leaving a trail of soft kisses along my arms. I arch forward, urging him to unhook the clasp between my shoulders, but instead, he traces my nipples through the thinnest of linings with his tongue, leaving them as firm and wanting as his erect cock. With the way he's winding me up, Nolan's got me whimpering and grinding the underside of his shaft, desperate for more friction where I need it most.

Finally, he unleashes me from my lace prison. My nipples are hardened by the night's chill for a second before he warms them up with his mouth. As he lavishes attention on my chest, he grabs my ass, encouraging me to thrust against his stiffness. Nolan doesn't even have to slip his fingers past my underwear to find me already wet and ready to go. I'm dripping my desire all over his cock and down his leg.

After a few minutes that feel like an eon, I can't take it anymore. "Nolan, if you don't rip off these panties right now, I'll have to do it myself."

He blinks with lust-clouded eyes, his brain short-circuiting for a second. "Oh? Okay, yeah, I can do that." With barely any exertion, he yanks on each side of my G-string with two quick snaps and tosses the scraps to the side. I'm too impressed to be upset that he took my command literally, but my look of shock isn't what he expected.

"Oh, shit—you didn't mean—Tania, I'm sorry, I—"

"Shhhh." I shut him up by grinding my bare pussy against

his cock, eliciting a deep groan. "You never have to apologize for those ridiculously strong hands as long as you keep them on me. Now you better put them to good use and grab a condom before I lose it."

Thank goodness for his minimalist lifestyle because it takes him no time at all to reach into the underbed drawer and pull out a foil wrapper. Dying from impatience, I swipe it from his hand and do the honors. I'd typically be too self-conscious to start on top, especially when my softness folds and bends over a human slab of granite like Nolan Wells. But with all the blood rushing from my head to my inner core, if I don't get fucked asap, I will pass out.

I slowly set myself down with a long exhale, taking him inch by inch, until he fills me completely. Even with my pussy slick with anticipation, it takes me a minute to get acclimated. It wouldn't have mattered if I was in the best shape of my life. There's no workout routine I could have done to properly warm up to the size of him.

Nolan reaches out to rub my clit, turning the dull pain into a pleasurable ache. "Belay on." It's such an innocuous phrase without context, but it's Nolan's way of telling me I'm safe. He's got me and I can keep going whenever I'm ready. He sits up so he can kiss behind my ear and down my neck, while continuing the small circles with the hand that's not pulling me to him.

"That's it, Tania," he says as I start to ride him. "You can do this. *Yes*, you're doing so well." It's the same type of praise he gave me at the climbing gym, but the way he exhales his encouragement in my ear has goosebumps prickling my skin.

I pick up the pace, impaling myself on him until I'm close. "Tension!"

He obeys my command without skipping a beat, holding onto my ass with both hands so he can drive into me, tighter and deeper. He's got me moaning so loudly I'm grateful we're alone in the wilderness instead of annoying the adjoining guests in my hotel room.

"Almost there, I know, keep going," he says, one frantic thrust after another. "Don't you stop until you summit. I want to watch you send."

I chase that tightening in my core until I crest and feel like I'm being thrown over a cliff. "Oh god, *oh god*, Nolan—I'm falling." The waves of my climax hit hard, rolling through my limbs and making my fingers and toes go numb. As I clench around him, Nolan shudders with a feral groan and follows suit, spilling years of pent-up lust until he's spent.

He leans his forehead against mine, catching his breath. "I've got you. I've always got you, Tania."

I know it, deep in my bones. It didn't take an earth-shattering orgasm to trust Nolan with my whole heart. "We make the perfect team."

He pulls me in for a kiss, fishing for another condom in the drawer. Nolan must be in such peak physical condition that his cock doesn't even know what a refractory period is. It doesn't take long before he's standing at attention again. "Your body is by far my favorite expedition," he says, running his lips along my jawline. "And there's so much more to explore." His hands run up my waist and underneath my breasts as he bends down to take my nipple in his mouth.

"Climb on, then." Fuck me, this is gonna be a long night in the best way possible.

$\sim$

Tania Beecher's search history on Tuesday, February 15

How much sex is too much
   What defines nymphomania

Remedies for vaginal soreness
Can you sprain your vagina
How to build sexual stamina
What are Kegels again
Where to find condoms in Yosemite
How to get sterilized
Bringing up vasectomies with your new boyfriend
Sex and the City when Miranda's over honeymoon sex
Which SATC character are you quiz
Why does Miranda from SATC get so much hate
Career woman stereotypes
Well behaved women never make history quote
But what if you don't want to have it all
What if I'm a bad feminist
Bad Feminist Roxane Gay reviews
Does Nolan Wells call himself a feminist
Shirtless Nolan Wells
Can you fuck while rock climbing

chapter
eighteen

The first three days on sabbatical were pure bliss. Apart from the occasional trip to Granite Grove to shower and swap dirty clothes for clean ones, I was content to camp out in our love nest. The weather was cold but mild, so it wasn't a problem crunching through the snow on the half-mile walk to the Village Store, where we stocked up on condoms between marathon sex sessions. There aren't many tourists around February, so it didn't take long for the news to spread like summer wildfire that Nolan Wells and his new girl-friend were floating around the valley like honeymooners.

My closest friends are celebrities, but despite being an honorary member of the glam fam, I've never experienced fame myself. I had to admit it gave me a little thrill every time someone would greet me by name at the hotel. I almost wished to run into Summer, because there's no way she would have missed the gossip, and I wanted her to witness my well-fucked glow firsthand. Bummer that her shifts never lined up when I stopped by.

I wake up on Day Four feeling pretty smug, even if the 'bedroom' is brighter and the time of day earlier than I would have liked. I'm in the middle of the most beautiful valley on planet earth and basking in the glow of multiple orgasms from last night. Sure, I'd rather sleep in and enjoy a hearty breakfast in bed, but watching the sun rise through the windshield isn't the worst way to start your day.

Nolan catches me stretching out of the corner of his eye. "Come on, sleepyhead. Rise and shine." He pauses packing our backpacks to hand me a mug of tea and a bowl of overnight oats. I would prefer an everything bagel and a generous schmear of cream cheese, but I'm too overjoyed by the small gesture to say so. Thankfully, the chunks of apple and dusting of cinnamon make the mushy texture more palatable.

I shovel the food down and chug my tea as Nolan's restlessness becomes contagious. He's been a good sport these past few days, not pressuring me to make the most of my sabbatical. But from the way he rifles through his gear and triple-checks to make sure we have everything we need, I can tell he's antsy. The only cardio we've been doing has been between the sheets, and we're overdue on expelling the rest of our pent-up energy in the great outdoors.

Despite the early hour, I'm excited to move my body vertically instead of horizontally. I'm not so delusional to think I'll be any good at outdoor climbing after only one week of sweating in the gym, but they don't call it crunch time for nothing.

After my first date with Nolan, I spent my workdays blitzing through my to-do list as fast as humanly possible so I could spend my evenings at the climbing gym. Nolan had given me a head start by gifting me the gear I needed, but when I'm on a mission, I spare no expense and dive in, no holds barred. I switched my gym membership over to Pacific Pipeworks, hired a trainer for the first time in my life, and climbed until my arms and legs turned to jelly. As much as Hammy drives me nuts, at least he makes an excellent drill sergeant. And today we'll see how far that weeklong training montage gets me when I put fingers to actual rock.

"Remind me of where we're going again?" I ask Nolan while I get dressed, as if more information will magically make me more prepared.

"Literally in my backyard." He slides open the van door and points up. Not right or left. Up. "You can't do better than El Capitan."

My heart drops. "You've *got* to be joking." I don't know what the bunny slope of climbing is called, but that's what I was expecting to tackle today. Not a mountain so looming that if I leaned back to view the tippy-top, I would topple over.

"Only slightly," he says with a smile.

My breakfast threatens to evacuate, and I press my lips tightly together to prevent puking my guts out.

Nolan's face falls at mine going green. "Oh, Tania, I'm sorry—I was just messing with you." He grabs my hand to help me out of the van because my knees are shaking. "I mean, we will be climbing El Cap, but only at its base. The Pine Line's the perfect route for beginners."

"The Pine Line," I echo, strength returning to my limbs. I guess it can't be that bad if it sounds like a dance you'd do at a log cabin ho-down.

"Yup. It's a super-easy fingercrack, so it's a great introduction to trad, aka traditional, climbing and gives you the opportunity to practice core techniques. Not to mention, it leads to a ledge with a phenomenal view. You're gonna love it."

I stare blankly, massively skeptical on multiple points— that I'd agree with Nolan's definition of 'super-easy' or that I'd feel anything other than terror.

But when we throw on our hefty backpacks and Nolan flashes me a jubilant smile, eyes crinkling at the corners, I'm filled with motivation. If climbing is the way into Nolan

Wells's heart, then the Pine Line is the first step to getting him to carve out some space for me.

"ARE YOU SURE THIS IS A 5.7?" I ask once we reach the base of El Capitan, staring up, up, up at the wall that never seems to end. I know I'm not going to climb that much of it, but the forty-foot route in front of me still looks formidable.

"One hundred percent positive," Nolan says cheerily, helping me strap in. "Now, is the Pine Line more challenging than the 5.7s in the gym? Of course. You're outdoors, climbing on real granite, and laying your own protection. Not to mention, Yosemite's routes are notoriously sandbagged."

Images of emergency prepping for a hurricane cause my brain to short-circuit. "What does that even mean?"

He takes out a roll of white tape and starts delicately wrapping my fingers. "Back in the '60s, the Yosemite Decimal System only went up to 5.9, so routes are typically more difficult than their grade suggests. Plus, the rock faces are steep and slippery, so it's totally normal to ride the struggle bus for a while."

I raise an eyebrow. "Is this your idea of a pep talk?"

He laughs. "You're gonna be fine. And I'll be right here, tethered to you the entire way."

Nolan finishes wrapping my hands, and I observe his handiwork. "What is this tape even for? I didn't use this stuff at Pacific Pipeworks."

He points to the long crack leading straight up the wall. "That's the Pine Line. To climb it, you'll be jamming your fingers in that crack and placing nuts or small cams along the route to keep you safe and secure." He tugs on my harness, which has enough bits and bobs hanging off it to make me look like a busy janitor. "Granite's a climber's paradise, but it's not exactly, uh, the most comfortable for beginners. Most gyms don't even bother with makeshift crack climbing for that reason."

"Why not?" I step closer to the rock to inspect the crack, noticing how the pads of my fingers catch on the roughness of the speckled rock. Much coarser than what I'm used to. I sigh, the realization setting in. "I'm going to tear up my skin, aren't I?"

Nolan flashes a guilty grimace. "Some tearing is unavoidable, but at least the tape will prevent the worst of it."

I appreciate Nolan's attempts at a better bedside manner, but I can read between the lines. When he says most gyms don't bother with crack climbing, I can guess it's because blood is a pain in the ass to clean. My shins were bruised after one pole dancing class with the glam fam, so I can imagine how shredded my fingertips will be once the Pine Line has chewed me up and spit me out. And this is supposed to be fun?

Taking a deep breath, I brace myself. If I accept that most of this climb will suck, Hammy will hunker down and be resigned to his fate. My therapist often says anxiety is like a wave: if you try to fight it instead of riding it out, it will drown you. At least I have the best rock climber in the world as my lifeguard.

I assume the position. "Climbing," I say, hoping my shaky voice doesn't give away how scared I am.

After a final check of my helmet strap, Nolan grips my shoulder. "Climb on, Tania. You fucking got this."

That's what I repeat to myself with every step. I don't have any frame of reference, but the rock is somehow too coarse and too smooth at the same time. The holds are tiny compared to the ones in the gym, so I move on my tiptoes to avoid slipping. And for once, I'm glad I was never high maintenance because a manicure wouldn't last a minute in this crack.

After the first ten feet, Hammy starts squealing his objections: *Are you out of your mind? This is a ludicrous idea. You should turn your ass back around and return to the solid, safe ground.*

I make the mistake of peering down at said ground, which feels way too far away. Hammy's right. I should make Nolan lower me down and give up trying to be something I'm not.

But Nolan's looking up at me with pride, cheering me on, and I don't want to disappoint him or myself. My anxiety will have to wait until I complete this ascent.

It takes me way longer than it should, but I do, indeed, have this. Eventually, I become accustomed to the pain of moving my body weight up a sheer mountain and get in the zone. The climb is just as mental as it is physical, and once I get over the fear of relying on a few cables and pieces of metal to keep from falling to my death, I feel more confident. The trepidation never fully dissipates, but by the time I'm halfway up, I'm progressing less like a trembling fawn and more like a sturdy mountain goat.

After an hour that feels like a lifetime, I finally finish the route and pull myself over the belay ledge with an elated, exhausted groan. I'm gasping for air, my heart is thumping erratically in my chest, and I collapse in a heap, limbs turned to mush. But I did it. I fucking did it.

I may not have the strength to shout in celebration, but Nolan's hoots and hollers are loud enough for the whole valley to hear. "That's my girl! You showed the Pine Line who's boss! Nothing can stop you now!"

Sitting against the wall, I take in the view, laughing deliriously. The snow-capped peaks and vibrant evergreen trees are certainly a sight to behold, but they can't compete with the satisfaction that fills you when you push yourself harder and farther than you ever thought possible.

I'm usually not one to be present in the moment, not

when Hammy's too busy ruminating on my never-ending to-do list, so it's nice to soak up the winter sun and appreciate the stillness for once.

It's not until I feel the rope shift below me that I realize I've got a job to do. I crane my neck over the ledge and shout, "Hold on! I can belay you once I catch my breath."

But when I see the end of the rope attached to nothing, oxygen leaves my lungs. Nolan's carrying his gear on his back, but it's superfluous because he's not tied down to anything. He's climbing the Pine Line with just the chalk on his massive hands.

"What the hell are you doing?"

"Soloing," he replies without a care in the world. There's not a trace of annoyance at me for asking the obvious—just pure delight that this is his life. It makes me think of what all those cringey LinkedIn gurus declare about having a positive mindset. Whereas I *had to* climb El Cap, Nolan *gets to* climb El Cap. And at the risk of sounding like I'm jealous of an inanimate object, it's abundantly clear that Nolan Wells loves nothing more than this monolith.

I can see why, when he makes it look so easy. Might as well play "Miss United States," because he's beauty and he's grace. I marvel how comfortably his fingers grip the crack, how quickly and quietly he scales the wall. I'm retroactively mortified, sure that my grunts and groans must have made me sound like an elderly wildebeest.

He tells me he'll be up in a minute, and he means it. Right when the time changes on my smartwatch, Nolan pulls himself over the edge and slaps the extra chalk off his hands. "You've watched me solo before, Tania. Why do you look like you've seen a ghost?"

I hold onto his forearms, caring more about pulling him away from the edge than appreciating how toned they are. "The gym was completely different. If the worst were to happen, you would have had dozens of climbers to break your fall. Here, you'd—"

"Crack my head open like an egg? Yup." He pinches my cheeks as if to bring back their rosy color. "Good thing I can climb the Pine Line in my sleep."

He winks at me, and the butterflies in my stomach distract me from the chalk he's smeared on my face. The ecstasy of completing this route wears off quickly, and after witnessing Nolan risk his life climbing it, I've had enough action for one day.

"Well, that was fun," I deadpan, swiveling around in search of an exit plan. "Now how do we get down from here?"

Nolan returns a confused expression. "You can rappel down from this two-bolt anchor," he explains, pointing to a piece of metal sticking out of the wall. "Or you can scramble down the right side. But what do you mean? Don't you want to keep going? Or are you too pumped already?"

Out of all the climbing slang, pumped is the one that throws me for a loop. For most Californians, pumped means excited or stoked, like, "I'm so pumped to get a slice of Golden Boy Pizza." But Nolan is asking whether my forearms are too worn out and tired, and although that's the understatement of the century, I don't want to admit defeat so quickly and have him lose faith in me. "Oh, I was just wondering. I thought we were done with the Pine Line."

He nods. "You could say that. But technically, the Pine Line is what we call pitch zero of the Nose, so it's like it doesn't even count. The first real pitch is a 5.9, but it's nothing you can't handle."

My stomach twists into a knot. I appreciate that he thinks I can conquer multiple pitches on my very first day of trad climbing, but I just completed the hardest workout of my life, and *it doesn't even count*? I try to remind myself that Nolan and I have vastly different definitions of exertion, but I'm hurt, nonetheless.

I want Nolan to continue believing I can indeed handle anything, that I can conquer El Cap one day. But with the way my muscles are screaming for mercy, today is not that day.

"You know how it was for me in the gym," I say. "I prefer to pace myself and work my way up incrementally to the next grade. But I'm happy to belay for you if you'd like to keep going." I bat my eyelashes for good measure. "As long as you show me the proper technique."

I'm sure Nolan would have preferred to solo as far as his feet could take him, but he can't resist an opportunity to play teacher.

He ties an anchor around me to keep me secured to the ledge, then walks me through the finer points of feeding rope by giving and taking slack.

"The one thing to remember," he says, lightly knocking on my helmet, "is that none of these precautions ever replace your undivided attention. Listen and always be prepared, because our lives depend on it."

I'm not sure how useful I'd be in a real emergency, but I was a Girl Scout once, so you don't have to tell me twice. I ground my heels, countering my weight against the anchor. "Belay on."

Nolan continues his ascent, climbing the second pitch without incident, so easily in fact that I feel extraneous. He must have done this route a thousand times, and with his expertise, I can see now why free soloing is so appealing. If you're so good at what you do that taking precautions is simply a formality, of course you'll be tempted to forgo them. I don't begrudge all the equipment I'm wearing because it's the only thing keeping me tethered to safety, but the thought of tossing it all aside and relying solely on your own talent is powerful.

Nolan's instructions become less necessary as we get into a rhythm, and I find enjoyment in the calm and quiet. I haven't been away from modern comforts for that long, so my fingers are still itching to grab my phone for some indulgent doom-scrolling. But hey, Dahlia always said I need to get better at meditating, and there are worse ways to practice than staring at my boyfriend's impeccable ass.

Before I know it, Nolan completes the pitch with a quick acknowledgment that he's ready to be lowered. Because I'm not following him up, he has no choice but to come down. Once he's back on the belay ledge, he helps me rappel down to the base.

Under the midday sun, my belly growls, and I don't need to check my smartwatch to confirm that it's time to eat. If this were cardio with the glam fam, we'd be on our way to brunch with bottomless mimosas to celebrate a workout well done. But whatever Nolan's got in his fridge will be a worthy alternative.

"Ready to call it a day and grab some grub?" I say, my feet already marching back toward the van.

Nolan's swapped his climbing shoes for trail ones, but they don't move in my direction. "Oh, I packed some snacks." He unzips his backpack and pulls out an apple and a few protein bars—the ultra-healthy kind, with no chocolate drizzles in sight. "I figured if you're done with climbing, we could hike Old Big Oak. It's only five miles out and back."

Only. That word is going to be the bane of my existence. Nolan may be able to subsist on fruit and good vibes, but if I eat like a bird before attempting to walk ten thousand steps, I will pass out.

"We can . . ." I hedge, "but let me make you a proper lunch first. You're letting me cram into your space for six weeks, so it's the least I can do. And I found some scrumptious vegan recipes I've been dying to try."

It's not a lie. I did research what dishes I could cook with what's available at the Village Store, rising to the occasion as if I was tasked with getting the most bang for buck on a marketing campaign. The chance of putting Nolan into a food coma and dissuading him from the hike from hell is just a bonus.

To Nolan's credit, he's grateful to be doted on. He may not be used to a woman taking charge of the grocery shopping and making much-needed improvements to his spartan meals, but he takes the change in stride.

"You don't have to make all this effort," he says yet again as I stand at the van's kitchenette, putting the finishing touches on our lunch. I've upgraded Nolan's packets of instant ramen with sweet corn, green onions, and baby bok choy. I top his off with some silken tofu and mine with a jammy, soft-boiled egg that reminds me of the benedict I would be eating if we were at one of the Bay's three-dollar-sign brunch spots.

He gives me an apologetic smile. "I eat to live, not live to eat, so there's no need to roll out the culinary red carpet for me."

I hide a grimace behind my bowl as I hand him his. I know he doesn't want to be a burden, but all I can think is how sad a mindset like that is. If food is a love language, I'm fluent in prix fixe menus and Michelin stars. I can't imagine partaking in something three times a day and not enjoying myself.

But then again, none of the men who wined and dined me made me a fraction as happy as Nolan does. And I'd choose that spark over omakase any day.

Of course, another spark rears its ugly head the second Nolan exits the van to do his business—the codependent connection I have to my cell phone. Nolan may not feel the urge to beam up to cyberspace every hour of the day, but I installed a mobile hotspot as soon I unpacked. I'm—as they say—chronically online, and after an ordeal like the Pine Line this morning, I need to self-soothe.

Relishing a few minutes of alone time, I grab my phone off its charger. I could decompress by mindlessly consuming cat videos, but my unread notifications scream to be tackled instead.

Working for a tech company like Habituall feels very meta because that's how I'd describe the incessant tug to check my work email and Slack messages. It's habitual, and even though I rarely walk away in a better mood, I can't help it.

The executive assistants that the C-suite share have done a decent job of keeping my inbox clean from cold sales pitches and blatant spam, so most of my unread emails are unsatisfying cc's for 'visibility.' Just your typical office politicking and ass-covering in case a project goes off the rails.

It's my DMs on Slack, however, that suck me in. There aren't as many as I expected after nearly a full week out of office, so I scan through them quickly. A few of them from certain department leaders clearly don't care that I'm on sabbatical, but most are super apologetic. They're written in a timid yet frazzled tone, and I know they wouldn't have reached out if they didn't truly need my input or assistance.

I tackle the easy ones from my team first, answering their questions or redirecting them to other folks who can step in during my absence. But it doesn't take long to realize the error of my ways. I've signaled to people that I'm online, and they've taken my green status light as permission to open the floodgates. All the "you should log off!" chastisements quickly turn into messages of "well, now that I have you, could you take a look at this . . ."

They do have me—hook, line, and sinker. The requests keep coming, making it harder to disconnect. Even founder and CEO Evan Chen has tossed aside our company value of

Balance when word got out that I'm hosting unofficial office hours.

"Tania? You ready to get a move on?"

I look up from my phone, and it takes me a moment to recognize that it's Nolan speaking and not my boss rambling about event planning. My tunnel vision must have obliterated the rest of my senses if I didn't hear him return to the van.

A move on? That's right. He wants to go on a freaking five-mile hike. Even if my muscles weren't refusing to get off this bed, I can't leave everybody else hanging right now. I opened up the lines of communication, and I need to at least finish what I've started. It wouldn't be fair to them.

"Ugh, I can't," I reply, mustering up as much exasperation as I can. "Evan's getting carried away with this keynote for First Party, and I need to bring him down to earth before he breaks a blood vessel." I don't add that Evan never used to care about his speeches until he promoted me to VP of marketing, and I lit a proper fire under his ass.

"Isn't the conference at the end of next month? Can't he just hold off until you get back?" He stows the travel kit and washes his hands at the sink, giving me a knowing glance. "I always wait until the last minute to prep my speaking presentations, and the world manages to keep spinning."

Nolan's memorized every single step up El Capitan, so I don't know why I'm surprised that he remembers when First Party is taking place. But I'd much rather debate the finer details of a slide deck than hike until nighttime, so if laying it on a little thick is what's going to give me an afternoon away from the outdoors, then so be it.

"I wish, but I'm the only one who has the guts to turn down his harebrained ideas. If I don't put a stop to his nonsense now, then the keynote I'll be coming back to will be as cobbled together as Frankenstein's monster."

The disappointment on Nolan's face eats at me, and I

sense the irony. It's not fair to leave him hanging either. I rack my brain for a consolation prize. "What if we try to catch the Firefall tonight?" I propose, referring to when the sunset hits Horsetail Falls at the right spot and turns the small stream at the top of El Cap a molten orange. "I heard mid-to-late February is the best time of year to see it."

"I'd like that." Nolan smiles from ear to ear. I've never seen the Firefall in person, but I already know it won't compete with the way his face illuminates with joy. A smile like that is proof that even if he's witnessed the magic of the Firefall on countless occasions, he hasn't shared the experience with someone special. I can only hope that I'm worthy of being that someone because of how special he is to me.

Nolan starts cleaning up the kitchenette and washing the dishes. "And then, tomorrow we can go on that hike."

"Sure," I blurt out, before the word registers in my mind. Plastering on a smile, I try to mimic his enthusiasm. "Of course."

～

TANIA BEECHER'S Slack conversation with Habituall founder and CEO Evan Chen on Thursday, February 17

@EVANCHEN: Okay, I don't mean to be a dick on your sabbatical by sliding into your DMs, but I had a few ideas for the First Party keynote, and I need you to tell me how ridiculous they are. I can't get a straight answer with all these yes people around.

@EVANCHEN: Please disregard if you're doing a *National Geographic* documentary right now.

@EVANCHEN: Actually, if you are, could you ask them if they film tech conferences on the side? The guy we had last year kept shooting me from below, and whoever said there are no bad angles is a bad videographer.

@TaniaBeecher: That's a no. Both to *Nat Geo* and to whatever scheme you're about to propose.

@EvanChen: Damn, you've got some skill to be messaging me one-handed while climbing El Cap. Talk about dedication to your job.

@TaniaBeecher: I'll be as dedicated as you want if you save me from going on this ordeal of a hike.

@EvanChen: Are you telling me that your sabbatical is a waste of time, and instead you could've been in a bar, having a nice cocktail?

@TaniaBeecher: Shut up. I need Casey to take TikTok away from you. Now, what schemes have you been conjuring?

@EvanChen: Picture this: To sell the concept of our new AI marketing suite's "glass box" experience, I dive into a trap door while the floor panels show me traveling from one end of the stage to the other. It'll be a recording, though, and maybe we can CGI me into a rocket ship? Depends on the marketing budget, of course.

@TaniaBeecher: Yeah, makes sense to picture AI technology promising the moon and delivering nothing but a hole in the ground.

@EvanChen: So . . . that's a no?

@TaniaBeecher: Did you take acid on purpose this time? You're starting to make this hike sound less preposterous by the minute.

chapter
nineteen

O ne of the things that mental health professionals and wellness influencers are always touting to people with generalized anxiety disorder is keeping a gratitude journal. The reasoning seems to be that the more you focus on what you're thankful for, the less time you'll spend fretting about everything you don't have and can't control. Despite my therapist Dahlia's urgings, I've never been able to stick to the habit of counting my so-called blessings. But after three weeks of roughing it, I'm realizing I need to make another attempt.

As unconventional as my living arrangement is on this sabbatical, I honestly prefer to stay with Nolan instead of my hotel room at Granite Grove so we don't have to be apart. I've quickly grown accustomed to sharing a bed with him, to calling the van home. Sure, it's an adjustment being confined to such a small space, but it's not like my Oakland apartment is a sprawling estate. And if there's anything I take to naturally, it's coziness. Brushing your teeth in the same sink you wash the dishes, going to the bathroom in the woods, making hot chocolate with almond milk—it's amazing what you find yourself doing when you're falling in love.

Not that I'm about to get ahead of myself, of course.

But even paradise loses its luster at some point. As lame as it is for me to admit, if I were filling in a gratitude journal, I'd probably list my 9-to-5. It's not that I miss my day job necessarily, but it's rewarding to be included in something bigger than myself. I find it difficult to take myself seriously when I'm doing nothing more than propelling my body up a wall of rock, so when the siren call of work comes calling, I can't help getting pulled in.

At first, it was just a few harmless check-ins on my phone, logging into Slack to see what I've been missing. But over time, the occasional DM to my direct reports became more regular touch bases on how projects are going. It sounds silly to say that participating in the minutia of corporate monotony makes me feel productive and valuable, but it's the truth.

And at the very least, working remotely is way less physically demanding. Because after waking up at the crack of dawn every morning, climbing higher and harder than the day before until my muscles give out, then repairing my shredded fingertips with antibiotic ointment and bandages, my whole body is crying out for a break. I may not allow myself to say the L-word out loud so soon, but I should at least be able to request a rest day.

Sitting in bed with our go-to breakfast of fruit and muesli, I'm about to suggest we instead enjoy an indulgent brunch at the lodge in front of its roaring fireplace, when Nolan proposes his own plan. "We should tackle that route I was telling you about the other day, the one they call Grant's Crack."

It's not like Nolan's ever acted like a drill sergeant, coercing me into something I don't want to do. It shouldn't be difficult to tell him that I'm not feeling up to it, that what I'm craving most is comfort and softness. And yet time and again, I find myself afraid to speak up.

"Are you sure?" I pull out my phone to review the list of

routes nearby, sorted from least to most challenging. "What about Swan Slab Gully instead? That one looks fun." Not as fun as kicking up my feet with a mug of Earl Grey at the lodge, but perhaps if we top out fast enough, we can make it in time for afternoon tea.

Nolan proceeds to laugh in my face, but to his credit, it's more of a knee-jerk reflex than a malicious crack at my expense. "Yeah, if you're a child." He taps my phone screen to display the route's reviews. "One guy said his four-year-old climbed it clean."

"What's wrong with that?" I'm annoyed, but the question comes out embarrassed. "You said Yosemite's routes are sand-bagged anyway."

"Right," he says between bites of raspberry and rolled oats, "but you've made such amazing progress, there's no reason for you to regress to a 5.6. If you're dead set on that particular crag, though, let's at least start with Penelope's Problem for the first pitch. The routes are next to each other, and they top out in the same place, but it's a more technically challenging 5.7. It's a tougher face, so it'll kick your ass for sure, but after witnessing how far you've come in such a short amount of time, I'm confident you can master it like a champ."

I soak up the compliment like a sponge, grateful for how much he believes in me. I'd definitely add that to my hypothetical journal. As proud as I am to build my endurance and become stronger than I ever imagined during my sedentary techie lifestyle, the bigger fire fueling my determination is proving to Nolan that while I'm new to climbing, I'm no longer a newb. I'm a long, long way from climbing an entire big wall, but it's evident I exceeded his expectations of what a marketing executive was capable of.

But as much as I appreciate the new definition in my biceps and forearms, I'm bone tired. Day after day of jamming my hands in cracks, smearing my feet across slabs, pitch after pitch after pitch. I've broken about every nail, my fingertips burn from the constant scraping against granite, and with every pinch and crimp, my muscles scream in places I didn't know I had. My ass doesn't need kicking today—it needs to lie the fuck down.

The rational part of my brain knows I should tell Nolan to slow down. After all, I'm a grown-ass feminist who has no problem going head-to-head with the men in Habituall's C-suite to demand more budget and more sustainable work-loads for my marketing team. I'm more than capable of advo-cating for my employees—why can't I do the same for myself?

"Not to mention," he adds with a mischievous grin, "I'd hope you have more self-respect for me as an instructor than to make me suffer up the same path preschoolers can crush."

That's when Hammy rears his weary head. *See? If you admit you can't keep up, he'll think less of you. You're going to make him look bad if you pump the brakes now. You know who else would have no problem climbing that route? Summer. I bet the minute you reveal your limitations, he's going to run back to that tight, twiggy mountaineering supermodel because he can't stand being with an outdoorsy imposter like you. But you know what? Maybe I'm wrong. Go ahead and spill your feelings. We'll see what happens.*

In moments like these, it doesn't matter if Hammy is wrong, because I can't risk the chance that he could be right. With his never-ending negativity, he successfully torpedoes my self-esteem and scares me off from being honest with Nolan about how I really feel.

I take one last bite of my lackluster oatmeal, which has congealed into an off-putting mush. What I wouldn't do for a piping hot plate of thick-cut bacon and scrambled eggs.

"Alright then, let's do it." I gulp down what's left of my resolve with the rest of my sad breakfast. Maybe by the time

I'm done climbing Penelope's Problem, I'll forget about my own problems and be refocused on gratitude.

ON OUR FIRST date at Pacific Pipeworks, when Nolan explained to me that climbing put him in a meditative state, I was skeptical. As someone who had avoided most forms of exercise, I couldn't fathom reaching a zen-like state on a rock wall.

But by the end of that date, I became a convert. I learned firsthand how climbing was as much of a mental challenge as a physical one, and I appreciated the effort it took to concentrate on nothing but the next hold above me. And in the weeks since, I assumed that would always be the case—that my anxiety would subside, at least from the moment I strapped on my harness until I stepped out of it.

I should know by now that Hammy never lets me catch a fucking break for long.

By the time we reach the base of Penelope's Problem, the weather has warmed up and the morning dew has evaporated, so the only thing that keeps slipping isn't my grip on the rock but my attention span. I can't get into my typical groove no matter how hard I try, and it's frustrating as hell.

I'm annoyed at Hammy for spiraling out on all the reasons why I'm a lazy piece of crap and how inevitable it is that Nolan will leave me because of it. I'm annoyed at Nolan for not magically intuiting that I need to rest or recognizing that his carpe diem personality just makes me want to hibernate more. And, most importantly, I'm annoyed at myself because it's not Nolan's fault that my own insecurities are making me miserable. Especially if I'm too spineless to tell him how I'm feeling.

That's not to say the dam of anxiety doesn't almost burst. When I rappel down from my last climb of the day, curls frizzing and forehead glistening, I nearly pant out everything on my toxic mind along with my ragged breath. I can't keep pretending to be the athlete I'm not. I should rat myself out and let Nolan come to the conclusion that the jig is indeed up.

But then Nolan rushes to my side, concerned. "Tania, what's wrong? You're gasping for air. Do I need to call a medic?"

I shake my head vigorously, refusing to admit defeat before a team of clinical staff. I may not be able to keep up with Nolan "Free Nolo" Wells, but I don't need the entire valley to know about it. I can only imagine all the people like Summer rooting against me, and I'm not about to let them have the satisfaction.

"I'm fine," I exhale, trying to breathe through my nostrils instead of my mouth so I don't look so pathetic. "I've got some choice words for Penelope, but she's no problem for me."

Nolan laughs, scooping me up in his arms. "That's my badass girlfriend! I swear you're going to be as *obnoxious* as me one day. I love . . . that for you."

He blushes and sets me down, hearing what almost slipped out of his mouth. I should be elated. He may have stopped himself from blurting out that he loves me, but he can't hide what's in his heart. And yet Hammy won't allow me an instant of reassurance.

He called you a badass, which you're clearly not. So don't get your hopes up. He could never love the real you.

Any urge I have to open an honest dialogue and share our true feelings for each other is suppressed and set aside. We haven't been dating that long anyway, so that conversation can wait.

The days go by, and I'm determined not to rock the rowboat, choosing to divert my eyes to the sunny skies above and not the choppy seas below us. Channeling gratitude becomes more than a coping mechanism—it's my crutch. You can't have any conflict if you don't acknowledge it exists.

But between my body enduring beyond its limits and my mind suffering from Hammy's incessantly vile talk track, it's no wonder I find myself exerting my agency in more covert ways now. It's easier to avoid your problems when you're too busy working to address them.

For someone who was so excited to flee her responsibilities —all in the name of recovering from burnout created by late-stage capitalism—I'm surprised by how quickly I crawl back to corporate America like a victim of Stockholm syndrome. But after a week or so of getting increasingly sidetracked by Silicon Valley, what I'm not surprised by is Nolan's escalating concerns.

"Is everything alright?" after an extended bathroom break when I spend more time on Slack talking business than doing my business.

"Is that necessary?" as I refresh my inbox for the third time during dinner because I'm anxiously awaiting the results from the team's latest direct mail campaign.

"You said fifteen more minutes an hour ago," as I review the progress tracker in marketing's project management system from my tablet in bed.

I can hear the letdown in his voice, but I can't stop. How can I be in the present moment when there's so much going on at Habituall? If I don't stay on top of things for six weeks, I'm going to be that much farther behind when I return to the office. Nolan's never worked a 9-to-5, so he doesn't under-stand. He might not like that I work in tech, but sue me if I like feeling good at what I do. Climbing is his thing, and marketing is my thing, and my team needs me.

∽

SLACK CONVERSATION IN HABITUALL'S #incident-3825 channel on Friday, March 11, at 6:15 a.m.

@ADMIN-BOT: @marketing has been added to #incident-3825

@CISO_DREW: Alright, we never like when it comes to this, but it's all hands on deck now. @TaniaBeecher we need to deploy crisis comms.

@ADMIN-BOT: User @TaniaBeecher is unavailable. Away message set to "ON SABBATICAL: 2/14–3/25"

@HARRISSHEPHERD: Hey Drew, I'll be taking things from here. What's the severity of the incident?

@CISO_DREW: It's quickly escalated to Sev 1. Extremely high service impact of e-commerce customer Kooky Coupon Chick.

@HARRISSHEPHERD: What happened?

@VPOFENG_PAUL: What we know thus far is the customer distributed an over-privileged API key with their mobile app. This allowed any recipient of the mobile app to use the key, which is a violation of our complementary user entity controls.

@HARRISSHEPHERD: You looped in Marketing, remember? English please.

@CISO_DREW: It means a malicious party used the key to exfiltrate profile data. Put plainly, about 90% of Kooky Coupon Chick's ten million users got their personally identifiable information hacked.

@HARRISSHEPHERD: Shit, what kind of PII?

@CISO_DREW: Names, email addresses, locations, ages, and birth dates. We haven't confirmed whether financial info was stolen, but this already represents a significant security risk.

@HARRISSHEPHERD: It could be worse. Terrible

timing since we just confirmed the CMO of Kooky Coupon Chick to speak at First Party, but if the incident's limited to one customer with fewer than ten million users, it doesn't sound like a PR threat.

@VPofCS_Kevin: I'd like to remind everyone that we treat every customer incident with equal gravitas, regardless of size.

@HarrisShepherd: Yes, Kevin, I get that, but let's not kid ourselves. With only $100k in annual recurring revenue, they barely count as an enterprise client. I'm not going to call this a PR crisis when the press doesn't care about the ninth most popular coupon app. And if it's their fault they got hacked, why is this our problem in the first place?

@VPofCS_Kevin: Well, they got blocklisted by Spamhaus last week, so they can't send emails anymore. Notifying their customers via social media that a breach happened because of our technology might be the only method of communication left to them.

@HarrisShepherd: Fucking spammers, I swear. Okay, whatever, if it's only Kooky Coupon Chick we have to deal with, let's keep an eye on things and wait it out. Marketing will contact their CMO to do damage control and make sure they're not pulling out of the conference.

@CISO_Drew: So, this just in from the security team . . . turns out we had a lot more senders with over-privileged API keys than we thought. We're now at Sev 0—a catastrophic impact with 20% of our customer base affected. That's 400 million users hacked and counting . . .

@HarrisShepherd: FUCK

chapter
twenty

I wake up early but not at all bright on the Friday of our fourth week together. Nolan cheerfully explains it's going to be yet another day of warm weather, and I'm ashamed that my first reaction is despair. I'm not even religious, but I had been praying to any god, ancient or modern, indigenous or otherwise, for wind and rain, sleet and snow—any excuse to stay tucked into my down comforter at the lodge, with the heat cranked up and room service on its way.

I shouldn't be filled with sorrow. I should be rejoicing that I get to spend another day on the rock with the sweetest, sexiest man I've ever met, basking in the sun like lizards after ascending to the summit.

And I should be glad to be making progress, because after torturing myself to conquer the fundamentals and build up my strength, today we're tackling my first 5.8, a route called the Nutcracker. At five hundred feet and five pitches, it's not nearly the size and scale to be considered one of Yosemite's iconic big walls, but it's the biggest wall I'll have climbed so far. For all intents and purposes, the Nutcracker is the first step toward feeling like a real rock climber on my own and not just like Nolan Wells's girlfriend.

But all that becomes meaningless the second I check Slack and witness the epic dumpster fire Habituall's desperately trying to put out. The company is suffering through the largest security breach in its history, affecting nearly every customer with a mobile app, including the top music streaming service and that food delivery startup I can't quit despite its predatory fees. Even the mega-popular meditation app that's included in our benefits package has been hacked— boy, there's nothing calm about what that team must be going through.

I tell Nolan my stomach's been acting up from my abrupt shift into a mostly vegan diet—just a little lie to give me the excuse to take my time during my bathroom break before we head to the Nutcracker. After I make my way to the one reliable spot where I get cell service, I furiously scroll through the team's conversations to get up to speed.

And even though watching this chaos from afar is filling my gut with dread, I'm immensely proud of how Harris has stepped up to the plate. In the span of thirty minutes, he's executed flawlessly on the crisis communications plan I developed last year. He deserves every dollar of his promotion the way he's completed the first three stages of Habituall's response procedures: he's gathered all mission-critical information, assessed the severity of the crisis, and crafted a public-facing message in the event that reporters get wind of the breach.

I've almost finished reading the back-and-forth between marketing and legal on the message's language when I hear Nolan call my name and start the van. Crap, just my luck. I shove my phone in my pocket and step out from my hiding spot behind a tree, but so many questions continue to haunt me as we drive to the base of the route. What are the chances we're sued for being the common denominator behind our clients' mistakes? How many customers are so angry they want out of their contracts, and how much revenue is on the line if they succeed? What's the likelihood one of them breaks the news out of revenge?

But the one question I keep circling back to: if we're forced to issue our statement, who's going to serve as the company spokesperson? As VP of marketing, that role has always fallen on my shoulders, but I can't field hundreds of inquiries from journalists, partners, and investors if I'm hanging off the side of a mountain.

To Nolan's credit, he doesn't ask why I spent upwards of thirty minutes doing my business. He's cheerful as we make our way to our destination, but next to me and my somber energy, he comes off downright giddy. "Did you know the Nutcracker is one of the many routes on what's referred to as Manure Pile Buttress? Supposedly, back in the day, when traveling on horseback was the only way to get into the park, rangers used to dispose of all the horse manure here. Thankfully, it smells much better now!"

Under any other circumstances I would have been riveted by the origin stories behind these ridiculous rock names, but I don't have it in me to utter a polite, "Damn, that's wild." All I can think about is how much the fire's raging at Habituall and whether I'll even have a job when I get back. The financial hit the company might take due to this security breach could cost us our livelihoods. I wish Nolan would at least ask why I'm so quiet, because I desperately want to vent, but I can't bring myself to approach the topic without being prodded. I'm afraid he'll grow bored by the inner machinations of my employer, or worse, he'll dismiss my problems as unimportant and irrelevant.

I did this to myself. When we first met, I characterized my job as soulless and only worth the fat paycheck it provides twice per month. I didn't mention all the quirks of my team-mates—like how Sarah and I have near-daily debriefs on the latest Hollywood scandal or how Jennifer's desk is such a mess that FEMA should provide her disaster relief. If I talked about the positives, maybe he wouldn't express such skepticism when I act like there's anything good still worth fighting for.

But I can't expect Nolan to understand. It's my fight, not his, so I'll suffer in silence and deal with this data leak on my own. If only I can figure out how to do that . . .

He looks at me expectantly. "Ready?"

I nod, going through the motions. By now I can approach a route and put on my gear as if it's second nature. It's not until I grab my belay device that I realize I've made a wrong turn in our typical order of operations.

Nolan catches my hesitation. "Did you want me to go first? I know your first 5.8 in Yosemite can be tricky, so I'm happy to take the lead."

This is perfect. I haven't belayed much for Nolan during our time together, because he's been focused on improving my skills, but on the rare occasion I take the back seat, it's like I'm not even needed. As long as I move quickly, I can shoot a note to Harris and confirm who's taking on the role of spokesperson before it's my turn to clip in.

Once Nolan's got his helmet on and we double-check that he's safely strapped in, he gives me a quick rundown of the route. "Now, there are a few possible starts on the Nutcracker. I'll do the 5.9 variation, which has a more difficult finger crack, but you can stay to the left of that oak tree until you reach the ledge at the end of the first pitch."

From what Nolan's explained to me, a multi-pitch climb is like an intricate dance, with one person setting protection, then belaying their partner from above. The partner then removes that protection as they follow, rinsing and repeating the process each pitch until they've both summited.

But honestly, the first pitch is so easy for Nolan, he practically free solos it. Like his ropes, I'm unnecessary, off to the side for purely aesthetics. So when he gives me the signal that he's ready, I'm not at all concerned for his safety. It's kind of nuts when I think about it. A few weeks ago, I was freaking out about Nolan free soloing a mere fifty feet in the gym, and now I trust him to tackle ten times that height with or without my help.

"Climbing." He blows me a kiss, which would fill me with butterflies if I wasn't so antsy to get this show on the road.

"Climb on." Now how long do I wait before I furtively check my phone?

The answer is not long at all because as soon as Nolan's off to the races, I'm off to mine. I give him slack to cover him a while—admittedly maybe a little too much, but it's not uncommon for Nolan to take rope as fast as I feed it to him. I just need to buy myself time to make sure Harris has everything handled at Habituall until I get back to the hotel and its less-than-stellar Wi-Fi.

"Tension!" he calls out as I pull up my inbox. Yup, I hear ya, Nolan, just give me a second—

"Tania? Watch me on this." The way Nolan insists should make me want to redirect my gaze, but in the moment he sounds like a kid calling for his parents before he does something underwhelming.

I hear shoes scrape against granite, an unnerving sound when you're not expecting it. Wait—isn't 'watch me' a climbing command?

"Tania. Tension! Argh *fuck*!"

I don't have time to see what went wrong, because the force of Nolan falling lifts me off the ground, slamming me into the wall and flinging my phone from my hand. But as much as the wind's been knocked out of me, I have to brace myself against the rock as hard as I can to prevent him from falling any further. It's the only instance in which I'm thankful we're about the same size because if he weighed significantly more than me, I doubt I'd be much help at all . . . well, even less than I already was.

I lower Nolan down to the ground, expecting him to be pissed but walk it off, but he's in much worse shape than I assumed. Holes have been shredded into his pants, his helmet's got a crack down the center, and when he tries putting pressure on his right foot, he shouts in pain.

"Nolan, what happened?"

His face is pure fury. "What happened? I should be asking you that—what the *fuck* were you doing?" He balls his hands into fists, squeezing blood down his chalked fingers. I've seen every Nolan Wells interview by now, and never has he ever seemed capable of such rage.

"I, I didn't mean to. I thought you had it covered!" I stammer out a bunch of word vomit, but he follows my line of sight to my phone, which is lying in a pile of pine needles a short distance away from where Nolan is standing on one foot.

"You've got to be fucking kidding me." He leans down to grab the phone and shove it in my face. "At least it's not damaged—are you happy? I almost broke my fucking ankle, but as long as you were able to be a good little worker bee, then I guess it was worth it."

I fully deserve him chucking my phone at the rock wall and shattering it into a million pieces, but instead he drops it into my outstretched hands. Blood and chalk coat the case, but I don't dare wipe it off and risk his rightfully placed wrath over me caring more about an inanimate object than my boyfriend.

"Nolan, you have to understand. There was this huge data breach, with hundreds of millions of users implicated, and my team's been crafting this PR statement—"

"Just stop it, Tania. I don't want to listen to your excuses. I'm not expecting climbing to be your favorite thing, but I do expect you to give it your undivided attention because our very lives are on the line. You hear that? I may be an elite athlete, but I'm not superhuman. I'm a fragile sack of meat like everybody else, and I could have fucking died because of your negligence."

I nod, tears streaming down my face. "You're right. I fucked up, and I'm so, so sorry. It's a terrible habit, and I'll never do it again—"

"God, you don't fucking get it, do you? Biting your nails is a bad habit. Purposely being on your phone while you're belaying should be a goddamn crime. I've sprained my ankles enough times to know what I'm dealing with, and I'm looking at six weeks of recovery because of your recklessness. Rock climbing isn't a hobby of mine, Tania. It's my *job*. You know, like the one you're so obsessed with keeping tabs on? Except when you get sick or hurt, your employer keeps paying you. If I can't climb, there go my sponsorships and my entire way of life. And if I lose everything all because I took a whipper on the fucking Nutcracker like a clueless newb—"

He pauses to take a deep breath and sit on the ground, elevating his sprained ankle on a nearby log. He's not meeting my gaze, but I can tell he's holding back tears of his own.

Nolan lets the words tumble out. "I could have accepted mistakes if you were trying your best, but for you to throw away everything just to approve a paragraph of legalese or whatever the hell you were doing . . . I don't think I can come back from that."

Fear seeps into my nervous system, sadly giving me more cause for alarm than Nolan's fall initially did. "What . . . what are you saying?"

"I recognized you weren't a climber when we met, but you took to the sport like a champ, and you could be great if you keep at it. I really believe that. I've been so proud of the progress you've made in such a short time. Not to mention, you didn't know anything about me and my baggage, which was refreshing as hell. It sounds ridiculous, but I thought I found a unicorn."

All this talk using the past tense has got me hyperventilating. Nolan's already referring to me like a distant memory, as if he's having a conversation about me with somebody else, long after I'm out of the picture.

Nolan continues throwing wistful compliments like hand grenades. "And then I learned how smart and witty and driven and utterly sexy you were. A woman who had the potential to fit seamlessly into my life—"

"I still can, if you give me another chance!" I'm embarrassed by how hysterical I sound, but I never imagined I'd be tossed in the ex pile after only a month.

"Even if you can," Nolan says with a sigh, "the real question is, do you actually want to? Sure, our chemistry has been incredible, but the novelty always wears off. It already was for you, judging by the way I'd have to yank you away from your tablet at night. It was obvious you found your inbox more exciting than yet another day on the rocks. I don't blame you, because this lifestyle isn't for everybody, but it hurts when you're distant and disengaged. It's like you're rejecting who I am, not just what I do. And if you're only going to retreat further into yourself, I don't think I can trust you."

"You don't mean that." I regret the ridiculous line the second it comes out of my mouth. Nolan Wells is the most grounded, genuine person I've ever met. He never says anything he doesn't mean. This isn't a romance novel where the hero spits heinous lies to push his lover away for her own good. And even if it was, I don't deserve to be the heroine.

As the terror from taking potentially one of the worst falls of his life subsides, Nolan no longer looks angry. Just disappointed. And I've suffered through enough of my parents' guilt trips to know that's so much worse.

His brow furrows, but his lips remain steady in a firm line. "I've got the kind of ambition everybody calls crazy, goals that are unachievable by anybody but me. That's not arrogance. That's just a fact. It's not a mantle I take up lightly. But if you're going to jeopardize everything I live for—everything I'd *die* for—then I'm sorry, Tania. I can't let you be a distraction to me."

Every instinct I have makes me want to fall to my knees and cry a river of tears, but I can't prove Nolan right by collapsing into a desperate, distracting mess. Instead, I nod like I agree with everything he said, and let the tears stream silently. It takes all my concentration to bite back the sobs, so we wrap up the day without saying another word to each other. Not as I help him hobble to the passenger seat and drive him to the medical center to get his ankle checked out. Not as he returns to the van in a brace and crutches, and we make our way back to the spot at the base of El Cap he calls home. Not even as I pack my bag and wait for a hotel shuttle to take me to Granite Grove.

It's not until I lock my guest room door behind me that I finally fill the silence with my anguish. Like a dam bursting, my heart breaks open, and I'm left to drown in the wreckage, alone.

❧

TEXT CONVERSATION *between Tania Beecher and Dahlia Cruz, LCSW, on Friday, March 18, at 10:30 a.m.*

TANIA BEECHER: All this time, I've worried about everybody hating me, and it never prepared me for when it was actually true.

DAHLIA CRUZ, LCSW: Is that actually true?

Tania: I can't survey the entire world, but I'm positive at least a few people hate me because of how colossally I fucked up. I should just go home. I can't show my face around here ever again.

Dahlia: You're in control of your own life, Tania. But wherever you go, there you'll be.

Tania: So you're saying I'll never escape myself. That I'm stuck being this terrible monster who shouldn't have been allowed to breathe Nolan's oxygen, let alone date him. That I'm a self-centered, workaholic bitch who nobody will ever love because I deserve to die alone.

Dahlia: That sounds like shame talking, not compassion. Think of your best friends. If they were going through what you're experiencing now, how would you respond?

Tania: They never would have fucked up like this. I mean, they're all addicted to their phones too, but they've never put a person's life in danger because of it.

Dahlia: Let's assume they did. What would you say to them?

Tania: I would say I still love them, because I know they would never intentionally hurt someone, especially not someone they care about. I'd always be there for them, no matter what.

Dahlia: Agreed. If you wouldn't say those things about a friend, there's no reason to say them about yourself. Everybody makes mistakes, but it's how we learn and grow from them that matters. Because when we know better, we do better.

Tania: But how? How can I make amends after something so awful?

Dahlia: Sit with yourself, and trust that you already have the answers you're searching for. Before you seek forgiveness from others, dig deep and find it within.

chapter
twenty-one

As much as my heart wants to throw a pity party of epic proportions, complete with chugging down the minibar and peeling myself off the bathroom tile, I've never been capable of spiraling into a Bravo-level meltdown. Because as much as I love watching reality shows, I can't handle an ounce of drama when it's my fault I'm in this predicament in the first place.

Nolan was right: we both have jobs to do, and wallowing will have to wait. I arrive at Granite Grove by mid-morning and race to my room before anyone can notice I'm not hanging on the arm of my boyfriend. Ex-boyfriend now, I guess.

Pushing past the sting of rejection, I boot up my laptop and call an emergency meeting with the marketing team to debrief on the security breach. Harris has been a saint holding the team together these past few hours, and his notes detailing a real-time log of the latest updates are impeccable. I can't help but feel jealous of his fiancée. Seeing the way Harris handles himself in a disaster, I bet he'd be more understanding if shit hit the fan in his relationship.

And then I snap out of it. Harris has been dating Hannah

for years, and Nolan hasn't even known me for two months. He doesn't owe me anything. Especially after putting his life in danger.

After I confirm with our comms team and global PR agencies that all statements have been approved by legal and distributed through the appropriate channels, there's nothing else urgent to address. Sure, the social media managers will stay vigilant about negative sentiment, but now it's up to customer success to appease the clients and engineering to clean up the mess so nothing like this ever happens again. When I follow through on my duty to check in with every single marketer on my thirty-person team, they all give me the same spiel. We're fine, we promise. Please go back to enjoying your sabbatical.

Except there's nothing to enjoy anymore. Ordering room service used to feel like a treat, and now I'm scarfing down my lunch without tasting it just so I don't pass out. I consider filling up the tub with the peony-scented bubble bath I brought from home, but the idea of stewing with my thoughts sounds like torture. My therapist may recommend sitting with my feelings, but all that's going to do is make me feel like shit. Self-care isn't possible when I don't deserve compassion.

So instead I take the quickest required shower to clean off the chalk and reddish stains underneath my fingertips. And that's when I realize while Nolan may not have been gravely injured, I literally have his blood on my hands.

Even after I scrub my skin raw, the remnants of Nolan follow me wherever I turn. I can't drink the bottles of cabernet I packed because they remind me of the Stag's Leap we shared. I can't escape into the rabbit hole of YouTube videos because watching all of Nolan's interviews has screwed up my recommendation algorithm. My brain's got his last gut-wrenching words on repeat—*I don't think I can trust you, I can't let you be a distraction to me*—but when I give up on the waking world, Nolan haunts my dreams.

It goes on like that for over a week, with me subsisting on bland food between fitful attempts at sleep, despite my urges to pack up the car and drive back home. It wouldn't make me less wretched, but at least I'd be cocooned in my own bed. But I know Dahlia's right. If I want to do better, I should stay put for once and at least see out what's left of my sabbatical.

It's Tuesday morning on my last week in Yosemite when I finally pull open the curtains. Nolan typically picks up his mail on Mondays, and it's so snowy and stormy that I'm confident there won't be any unfortunate run-ins in the lobby. Ironic how the kind of weather that keeps people confined to their rooms is the same that's motivating me to leave mine.

I wish I could say that I quit my addiction to my work cold turkey, but without Nolan's ever-present disapproval, it's all too easy to fall asleep and wake up each day obsessively refreshing Slack and email. I'm damned if I do, and I'm damned if I don't, because I'll be ransacked with guilt either way. And it does feel like an addiction because I don't get the same rush of dopamine hearing the chime of a new notification that I used to, but I'm unlocking my phone to read it all the same.

Today, however, will be different. I can't break the cycle without a conscious effort, so I leave my electronic devices in my room and take a tote bag of books down to the lounge area. The sand-colored walls and rustic wood furniture give off the vibe that the hotel is much older than its nearly hundred-year history, especially as the long room is flanked by floor-to-ceiling windows ornamented with stained glass. Hygge may have been popularized by Scandinavians, but this hall is proof that you can find coziness in the Wild West.

I make my way to the back of the lounge and settle onto an ornate tufted sofa facing the large sandstone fireplace.

There may be dark clouds outside, but there's light coming from the fire and overhead chandeliers to illuminate my reading material. After a couple of false starts with a chart-topping guide on productivity (Why would I read about work when I could get actual work done instead?) and the latest romance novel to go viral (Hard to believe love conquers all when mine couldn't even conquer the Nutcracker), I eventually settle on the salacious tell-all from that child actor. Removed enough from my real life to be safe and engrossing enough to keep me occupied for hours.

"Can I get you a coffee, ma'am?"

When we lock eyes, her face looks as bewildered as mine must. "Summer."

We're sporting similar looks on this miserable winter day, loose ponytails and not a hint of makeup, but whereas I don't need a mirror to tell me I'm disheveled from prolonged insomnia and constant crying, she could have come off the cover of *Sports Illustrated's* snow bunny edition.

If I was feeling any better, I would have waved her off, content with my water bottle at my side, but the way my body's perked up at the mere mention of caffeine, I could use a cuppa.

"Tea, please, with sweetener if you've got it."

Summer gives me a curt nod, her expression neutral as she walks off. I should be annoyed by her uncanny ability to mask her displeasure, but I'm impressed. I've always had a terrible poker face, which has bitten me in the ass on more than one occasion, like that time I acted out when an investor requested I take notes in the board meeting when my male executive assistant was sitting right next to me.

But when ten minutes go by and Summer's nowhere to be found, I deduce she performs her passive aggression differently, by straight-up ignoring me. I give her mental kudos for a game well played and return to the chapter I was reading when she reappears in my periphery.

"I figured you were one of those Anglophiles who prefers the whole shebang." With a sarcastic flourish, she sets a tray down on the coffee table. On it is a teapot, cup and saucer, sugar bowl, and creamer in matching white porcelain with vintage blue florals. She even included the kind of shortbread cookies the Brits would call biscuits.

"Wow. Thank you." I reach out to pour myself a cup, appreciating the distinctive aroma of bergamot from a good Earl Grey.

"Don't take it as a token of kindness, Tania. I didn't recognize you at first, because I assumed after what you did, you would have checked out by now and slunk back to whatever gentrified wasteland you came from."

Damn. I got to hand it to her. That was good. But there isn't an insult she could fling in my face that I haven't already been beating myself with for the past week. "Blame your employer. I paid for every night here upfront and there's no way to recoup my losses if I check out a few days early, so I guess you're gonna have to deal."

The potential hit to my personal finances isn't nearly as motivating as learning to live with myself again, but that's none of her business. I stir in my cream and sugar, blowing the steam to cool the tea to the perfect temperature. I expect her to walk off but, to my horror, she sits down on the sofa next to me. "I've never seen Nolan so distraught, not since Ryan's death, which is honestly pretty damn offensive since you've barely spent any time together. And yet you've both got the same bloodshot eyes and puffy faces like you're in desperate need of a spa day."

Boy does that sound nice. But instead of destressing with a Swedish massage, I'm getting needled by a territorial nuisance. "What's it to you, Summer? Were you Nolan's last girlfriend, or do you just wish you were? Either way, you should be happy we've broken up, so you can pick up the pieces. From what it sounds like, you already know how he's coping, so at least you can swoop in and comfort him."

Summer shakes her head, looking up at the ceiling. "I can't believe that turd never told you about me."

I take a long sip from my cup, if only to keep me from tossing its contents onto the floor and retreating to my room. "I don't know why he would. It's bad taste for couples to ramble on about their exes."

She sighs, not trying to hide her frustration. "I'm *Ryan's* ex. If that's what you want to call the last person someone dated before they died."

I choke on my tea, hot liquid burning down my throat while the rest of my body goes cold. "Wait—what? In all the articles I read about Nolan and his brother, I never saw any mention of you."

She lets out a dark laugh. "Yeah, like how no one in the climbing media knows your name either. Because I was a new girlfriend of Ryan's, and Nolan is notorious about his privacy. As am I."

I can always tell when somebody looks down on my profession. It's that air of superiority when they declare they're not on social media, when they know I'm a marketer who has to play by the algorithm's rules. And I know that Summer's not on social media, because you best believe I looked her up on the bus ride home after the retreat.

"I'm sorry." The apology falls out with a thud, and she scoffs.

"For what, Tania? You weren't what killed Ryan, but do you know what did? He fell. One of the holds on the Matterhorn was more precarious than we thought, and when he went down, a large rock went down with him. Nearly took me out too since we were roped together but I managed to avoid getting hit. I wish I could say he died instantly, but he did not—"

She breaks off to take a big breath and fan back the oncoming tears. If she didn't hate my guts, I'd hold her hand or give a hug, but I don't want to impose where I'm not wanted. But it feels unnatural to not comfort someone, so without thinking, I hand her a shortbread cookie. Thankfully, she accepts it with the smallest of smiles, and we sit in silence as she munches it.

Once she's composed herself, she continues. "It's been a decade since, and sometimes the pain is as searing as it was back then. Especially when a happy couple waltzes in, and I'm reminded of what Ryan and I could have been, if only we had more time. Which is why when I heard that Nolan fell, naturally I was terrified of the life of another Wells brother getting cut short. But, believe it or not, I was also scared for you."

My eyebrows lift toward the chandeliers. "Me? Why?"

"Because if the worst were to happen and history were to repeat itself, I didn't want you to end up like me, a shell of what you used to be. I've been a mountain girl my whole life, so I thought I understood the risks, but nothing can prepare you for losing the person you love. Needless to say, though, when I learned you threw caution to the wind and were on your *fucking phone*, I lost any sympathy."

I nod, the shame so palpable I swear I can taste my tea getting more bitter with each passing sip. "I am sorry. Truly, I am. There are absolutely no excuses for being so careless, and I'll have to live with the consequences of my actions. As desperately as I hope that one day you and Nolan and the climbing community can forgive me, I don't expect anyone to, and I intend to make myself scarce for the rest of my sabbatical. But please know you're welcome to have tea and cookies with me anytime."

It just so happens Summer was reaching for another shortbread, and she chuckles at the timing. "I can see why you're in PR. That was an A-plus apology if I've ever heard one."

I thank her, glad my crisis communications experience could be useful for something other than crafting holding statements on security breaches. Ironic that what got me into trouble in the first place is the very thing that can help get me out of it, at least when it comes to keeping pissed-off climbers from grabbing their pitchforks. It just saddens me that I won't be able to stick around to win them over. I might not belong here, but it was nice to think I could earn a place and be part of a family other than the one I've made with my coworkers. But if Nolan won't take me back, then no one in Yosemite will either.

"For what's it worth," Summer muses, "I can't help but be grateful that Nolan will be out of commission for a while with that sprained ankle. He's been going so hard for so long to chase an absolutely batshit goal, that I'm honestly hoping if he's forced to take this climbing season off, he'll finally come to his senses."

All of a sudden, it's like alarm bells are going off in my brain, but I don't know why. Nolan's words return like an echo: *I've got the kind of ambition everybody calls crazy, goals that are unachievable by anybody but me. That's not arrogance. That's just a fact.*

"Summer, what is Nolan's absolutely batshit goal?"

Again, I expect her to roll her eyes, like I'm an amateur for even asking, but I've listened to enough of Nolan's podcast interviews to know he always sidesteps the question of what's next. He never tells the public what he's done until he's done it, but for once I'm glad Summer is close enough to him to know the real answer.

And she recognizes her honored position in his inner circle, because she leans in and whispers, "It's been his secret mission to free solo the Dawn Wall." I wish I understood the gravity of those words, but I'm coming up with blanks. She sees my vacant expression and puts me out of my misery. "The Dawn Wall is not just the hardest route of El Capitan—three-thousand feet, with more 5.14d pitches than the rest of El Cap *combined*—it's easily the hardest big wall in the world."

Delusional optimism sets in, trying to comfort me with mental bubble wrap. "But Nolan is the best climber in the world. I mean, free soloing El Cap's been done before—I saw the documentary. Surely, out of all the people who could do it again, it would be him."

Summer shakes her head. "That's the thing. I'm not discounting Alex Honnold, because that dude is a legit freak of nature, but he soloed the Freerider route, which is substantially easier at 5.13a. By comparison, in all of history, only three people have successfully climbed the Dawn Wall—and that's with ropes. Not to mention, it took the record holder Adam Ondra a total of eight days to top out. I can't stress this enough—there is not a human being alive who can do this, even one with as much unparalleled strength and skill as Nolan Wells. Free soloing the Dawn Wall isn't a dream. It's a death wish."

But if you're going to jeopardize everything I live for—everything I'd die for—then I'm sorry, Tania. I can't let you be a distraction to me.

The realization hits me, and I set down my teacup abruptly, causing it to clatter loudly against the saucer. "Summer, you have to drive me to Nolan. Now."

"What, are you nuts?" She looks out the window. "It's stopped snowing, which is great, but the weather's still miserable out there. Even if Nolan wasn't stuck in a boot, it's not like he'd tackle the Dawn Wall today. He's safe, Tania."

I wave my arms around. "For now! I know he and I don't go way back like you two do, but you don't need to be around him for that long to learn he's more machine than man. He's going to push his body beyond its limits, and the second he thinks he's in the clear, he'll be attempting the impossible. It's my fault he's in this mess—please give me the chance to talk him out of it."

Summer stares at me, long and hard. I'm contemplating who I need to bribe to let me borrow their car, until she finally relents. "Fine. Let me tell my staff I'm going on break." She scans my outfit—an oversized sweater over fleece leggings and sheepskin slippers—up and down. "Meet me in the lobby in ten, and go change into some outdoor-appropriate attire, will you? Nobody ever made a convincing argument in Uggs."

CONVERSATION IN THE R/CLIMBING subreddit on Tuesday, March 22, at 10:40 a.m.

POSTED BY @TheKillerClimber: Do you think someone will free solo the Dawn Wall in our lifetime? Just wondering what the experts here think the chances are. Answer my poll and comment with your thoughts.

VOTING CLOSED. Poll results:

- 5% say "Sure, why not?"
- 20% say "Maybe / I don't know"
- 75% say "Absolutely not"

@LightspeedLizard: Attempt? Yes. Survive? Fuck no.

@TopoutTroll: Classic newb question with major "just topped my first 5.8, I think I'm hooked" energy.

@SethStorm: Tell me you just binged ten climbing documentaries without telling me you just binged ten climbing documentaries.

@AtoZzzz: Accidentally voted yes because I thought you were talking about Freerider, and I was like, bro, where have you been.

@TrulyMental: There are way easier methods to off yourself.

@HardlyRoping: Not in our lifetime, but maybe in a thousand years when we can travel back in time and delete your dumbass question.

chapter
twenty-two

It should be strange to be riding in the pick-up truck of a woman who nearly bitch-slapped me thirty minutes earlier, but it's not. And when she starts streaming music from her phone to keep us company and my favorite rock band begins to play, the coincidence knocks the breath out of me. "You like AFI?"

She meets my bewildered gaze. "Uh, yeah, you know them?"

"Know them? Davey, Jade, Hunter, and Adam have played the soundtrack of my life for the last fifteen years. I've seen them live four times, on every tour since I graduated high school. I didn't peg you for a punk fan."

She laughs sardonically. "Yeah, the F150 tends to confuse people. But the only time I listen to country is when I go home for the holidays and my dad puts on Garth Brooks's Christmas album. You don't look like you rock out either, Tania."

I follow her glance to my outfit, one of the many designer ensembles Casey picked out for me: a plaid herringbone wrap coat over black denim and lace-up leather boots. I get where Summer's coming from. I might as well have walked out of a

Ralph Lauren catalog on my way to some country club brunch. "Yeah, the bougie bitch wardrobe tends to confuse people."

We exchange our first genuine smile, until the chorus hits on "The Leaving Song, Pt. II," and Summer blasts the volume so we can scream our lungs out. It feels sacrilegious to disturb the quiet of Mother Nature to belt lyrics about breaking down and burning now, but it's cathartic in ways I couldn't anticipate. By the time we park next to Nolan's van, it's like we've found equal footing on this narrow strip of common ground. My voice is hoarse, but my heart's full at this chance to redeem myself, even if I have no idea how to do so.

But this mission isn't about me. It's about getting Nolan to come to his senses, for his own sake and for everyone who cares about him.

Summer turns off the ignition. "I'll wait here for you."

I step out of the truck, turning back in surprise. "Are you sure? He's not going to be thrilled to see me after what happened. Since you two have been friends for so long, we could make this a group effort."

She shakes her head. "I've already drilled him about the Dawn Wall over the years, so he's effectively tuned out whatever I have to say. But no matter how grumpy he may act, he'll be glad you came. I wasn't exaggerating earlier—he's been a fucking mess without you."

The shame hangs in the air, and it's crushing me from both sides. Guilt for making him such a mess, and guilt for leaving him to sink into it. Either way, I feel like the villain, not the hero, but I don't argue with Summer.

Closing the truck door, I stride over and knock on the van —lightly as I'm reminded of Nolan's distaste for folks who disrespect his home. The side door slides open, and I have to force myself to breathe.

"Tania." Nolan's eyes go wide at the sight of me, then even

wider when he recognizes Summer's truck. "Were you abducted?"

I turn back as we both give her a friendly wave. "Believe it or not, this was my idea. Do you mind if I come in?"

He takes my hand to help me inside and puts the kettle on, which I take as a good sign that he's not going to immediately kick me out.

"How's your ankle?" I ask delicately, noticing he's still wearing the walking boot.

Nolan shrugs. "The ligament's only partially torn, which is a relief, but I've got four more weeks of recovery. It's driving me nuts that I'm stuck inside and can't drive anywhere, but I've never appreciated living in such a small space until I struggled to take a few steps . . . I, um, haven't had a chance to clean up."

That's when I take in the dirty dishes in the sink and the pile of plastic bottles on the floor containing a liquid that's too yellow to be water. Perhaps I should be thankful that Nolan broke it off so I'm free to date men who don't piss in old Poland Springs, but instead my eyes light up because I love having an excuse to make myself useful.

"No, please, Tania, you don't have to do that."

What's he going to do—chase me in that boot? Before he can block access to the garbage bags, I've snuck around him and grabbed one, tossing in the bottles along with empty snack wrappers and dirty paper towels scattered across the bed. I'm on a roll, dumping expired food from the fridge when the kettle whistles like a timer.

"Done!"

Nolan hands me a mug after I set the bag outside the van to go back with us later and wash my hands. "Alright, now that you've brushed your shoulders off on a job well done, you want to tell me why you're here? I get it if climbing's not your thing, but I doubt you've joined a cleaning service instead to pass the time."

I swish the tea bag around to help it steep. I'm not sure what it says about me that this is the second time I've been handed a hot beverage by people who are surprised I haven't bailed on Yosemite by now. "Summer and I had an . . . interesting conversation. Dropped a big bombshell, actually. Nolan, were you ever going to tell me?"

He sighs and gestures for us to take our discussion to the bed, where he puts his leg up and I help him adjust the stack of pillows to keep it elevated. "I honestly never thought it would be brought up, least of all by Summer. I mean, it was only one night, and we were both mortified it ever happened."

My jaw falls open. It's a miracle I don't drop my mug and spill scalding tea on my lap, putting us both out of commission with my second-degree burns. "I'm sorry—what?"

Nolan's whole face flushes red, and he doesn't move a muscle, like if he just sits still, I'll drop the subject. But with nothing to do on a dark and dreary day, I have no other items on my agenda. "That wasn't the big bombshell you were referring to, was it?"

I shake my head, aghast. "That you slept with your brother's girlfriend? No, Summer failed to mention that. I was talking about you free soloing the Dawn Wall, but with this one-two punch, I can't tell which is worse!"

Nolan rubs his temples. "Tania, neither are any of your business. You can't be angry with me over what I did in the past or what I'll do in the future."

That shuts me up. I haven't known him long enough to have any say on how he lives his life, and even I did, I definitely don't have that privilege anymore. "You're right. And I'm not angry. I'd just like to understand where you've been and where you're going so I can—" I force myself to finish my thought before I chicken out. "So I can love you better, in this moment. Even if it's the only moment I have."

I did it. I had never told someone I loved them first, because I wanted one hundred percent certainty they felt the same way, but Nolan is different. He hasn't given any indication he holds me in his heart, especially after what I've done, but I want him to know he's in mine all the same.

He doesn't launch into some heartfelt speech, professing his undying love for me, but he reaches out to hold my hand, the corner of his lip tugging upward despite his stoic resistance. The figurative door to winning back his affection hasn't been kicked down yet, but I can see it cracked open, which is more than I could ask for. Take the win, Tania, and don't push it.

We enjoy our tea in comfortable silence, and I relish the warmth radiating through my chest and down to where our fingers are intertwined. It might be wishful thinking, but the way his thumb is rubbing against my palm makes me wonder whether he's missed the heat as much as I have. His chest against my back under the covers. His body pressing into mine when cuddling turns into something more. I would give anything to have him one last time . . .

"Would you like to meet Ryan?"

There goes that record scratch again. Here I am fantasizing about seducing Nolan, and he's thinking about his late brother. Or at least I'm assuming there's not going to be an even wilder twist—

"I mean, visit his memorial," he clarifies, noticing my confusion. "I'm not that delusional to think his ghost is haunting the park."

Okay, phew. My constitution can't handle a run-in with the supernatural, but I can manage saying hi to someone's tombstone. We set our mugs in the sink, and I exit the vehicle to let Summer know about our plans.

"So . . . am I coming back to pick you up in a few hours?" Her voice carries as I throw the stuffed garbage bag in the bed of her truck to take back to the hotel dumpsters, which is why I don't see Nolan standing off to the side until I come around the corner.

He scuffs the snow with his good foot. "If it's okay with Tania, I was thinking she can stay with me tonight?" It comes out like a question but sounds as significant as a proposal.

Summer shoots me a side-eye and a smile. "Yeah, I guess, she's pretty good at getting people to root for her. You give her time, Free Nolo, and I might like her more than you."

He chuckles. "Wouldn't take long, especially since I accidentally spilled our—" He coughs with embarrassment. "Our history."

Summer blushes so hard that even her strawberry blonde hair takes on a reddish hue. "Oh god, you didn't." She turns to me, gripping my arm. "Tania, please know it meant absolutely nothing. It was weeks after Ryan's passing, and we were so drunk to get us through packing up his stuff, and it just happened. Grief is fucking weird, okay? But we regretted it immediately and were blubbering wrecks afterward. Trust me, Ryan and I may have never married, but this guy here is the closest thing I have to a brother. And I would black my eyes before I made that mistake again."

I grin, appreciating the Hawthorne Heights reference. Who would have thought that instead of raging with jealousy over Summer's one night stand with my hopefully-on-again boyfriend, I'd be thankful they had each other to get through the worst life could throw at them. "Don't worry, your secret is safe with me."

Summer restarts the ignition. "Good, because remember —I know where Ryan's memorial is too, and I'm not above digging two more graves if you lovebirds can't keep your mouths shut."

~

POSTED BY @TopoutTroll: Some morbid humor for the day [NSFW]

IF YOU'VE BEEN CLIMBING LONG ENOUGH, it's a fact of life that you've lost someone close to you. So let's have a laugh on their behalf: what are things that are equally appropriate to say during sex and at a funeral?

@**LIGHTSPEEDLIZARD**: I'm sorry, were you close?
  @**SETHSTORM**: I never thought it would be this hard
  @**ATOZZZZ**: It's okay if you need to cry
  @**TRULYMENTAL**: Can I get you a tissue?
  @**HARDLYROPING**: Thank you all for coming today
  @**LIGHTSPEEDLIZARD**: It just happened so fast
  @**TRULYMENTAL**: Lovely spread
  @**ATOZZZZ**: What a wonderful service
  @**SETHSTORM**: She put a smile on everyone's faces
  @**THEKILLERCLIMBER**: He's not here, but I know he's watching us

chapter
twenty-three

I was anxious driving on Yosemite's recently snowy roads, unsure of how far we'd be traveling, but after a couple of turns, Nolan tells me to throw the van in park.

"That's it?" I peer out the window, taking in more of El Capitan than we see when we're closer to base.

"Yeah, I'm never far from Ryan. If it wasn't for this busted ankle, we would have walked. Now come on and keep up."

I scramble out so I can help him get down, even if he resists my attempts at assistance. We hobble hand in hand, him leaning on my arm, until we reach a large log facing a stream, which is flowing fast enough to not be frozen over on this particularly frigid day. It's a picturesque stream, but the majestic and mammoth El Capitan dominates the view. I absorb its sheer massiveness and can immediately tell from the way it stands, proud and at attention, that empires will fall and humanity could go extinct, but El Capitan and the rest of its big wall companions will remain, long after we're gone.

"From this distance, climbers are nothing but ants up there," I say in awe.

Nolan brushes snow off the log and lays out a waterproof

camping blanket, pulling me close to him as we sit down. "And that's exactly what you feel like. It's funny how addicting it is to be reminded of how small and insignificant you are, but there's nothing better than topping out and appreciating that the world simply goes on regardless. You push the limits of human potential, and El Cap couldn't care less. Whether you succeed or fail, whether you live or die, it will still be there."

It's a nice sentiment, but my mind gets tripped up on the whole death part. "But doesn't that make life meaningless?"

He squeezes my hand, before leaning down to dig through the snow next to the large oak tree we're sitting under. Once I understand what he's doing, I take over the task, scooping snow with my bare hands until I reach the ground where a small memorial stone has been pressed into the soil.

Obviously, Nolan could recite the inscription word for word, but I say it out loud anyway. "In loving memory of Flyin' Ryan Wells. Life, if well lived, is long enough." I took Latin in college, so I recognize the quote from Seneca, but reading it in this context makes my eyes instantly well up. I let the tears fall, speckling the stone like melted snow.

"Ryan and I talked about death a lot," he explains. "When you do what we do, you're confronted by it every day. So when we weren't staring at it in the face, we'd be on this log, away from all the bystanders with their telescopes, skipping rocks in the stream and marveling at our mountain until we got cricks in our necks. To this day, he continues to bring people together. I'm amazed that the annual race up the Nose on our birthday gathers more participants every year. And when I drop off fresh wildflowers here to celebrate the start of the climbing season, his memorial is covered in bouquets—which I'm sure he loves because he was always the attention-seeker."

I nod, smiling through the tears and thinking of my own brother, and my parents and the glam fam and all my teammates and friends. And now Nolan, and even Summer. How lucky I would be if I touched half as many people at eighty-three-years-old as Ryan clearly did at twenty-three. "I wish I could have had the chance to meet him."

He holds both of my hands in his, the tears in his eyes sparkling so much brighter than the sun on the snow beneath our feet. "He would have loved you, Tania. How could he not when I'm so in love with you?"

I should be squealing and jumping for joy that Nolan returns my feelings, but there's something about him ending with a question that stops me, like something is missing.

"But—" Fuck, here we go. I knew it. Toss me in the river now so I can be pulled downstream and sink to the bottom of my breaking heart.

"But I can't give what you want."

His words land with a thud, and I'm getting riled up. "What the hell does that mean? How can you know what I want when I don't even know that for myself? I'm no closer to the answer now than when I arrived here. If anything, I'm farther away because your existence has thrown a wrench into mine."

"Exactly." He squeezes my hands, but I rip them out of his grip. "Tania, your life is daily planners and back-to-back Zoom calls from Monday to Friday and mimosa brunches and trips to Napa on the weekend. You work hard and play softly, surrounded by scented candles and weighted blankets. You may think you're some kind of failure for not having the next thirty years written in stone, but all I see is how fucking lucky you are to have the privilege to go on a journey of self-exploration in the first place. You can do whatever you want, live wherever you want, be with whomever you want, and it's a damn shame if you don't take advantage of it."

I have no idea how Nolan can make so much sense and yet

leave me so confused at the same time. "But what about you? You make it sound like I have ultimate flexibility, but nobody is freer than you. You gave your family the finger, and what few bills you have your sponsors pay, no problem. You don't have to answer to anybody—often literally because you live in an area with crappy cell service and people can't reach you. Why can't we forge our own path forward, together?"

He shakes his head, wide and slow and sad. "Because you deserve safety and security and a life without stress, and I can't give that to you. Summer is right about my goal. Free soloing the Dawn Wall has been a dream of Ryan's and mine from the second we first saw it. Here, on this log, watching the sun rise and light up the east face in all its glory. I don't have the freedom to walk away. I will push and train and tear my fingertips until they bleed. I will drive my body beyond its breaking point in the name of ambition because I don't care if I break anymore. I'm already broken. I have lost everything important in my life, and when I die—not if—I can't do that to you, Tania. I watched a part of Summer die the day she came back without Ryan, and I refuse to put you through that pain. I love you too much to do that."

I cross my arms, undeterred. "That's all nice, Nolan, but I refuse to budge. You're not some Marvel superhero, and frankly I think the whole pushing me away to protect me for my own sake is chicken shit. You say you lost everything important in your life, but I'm right here. I'm a grown woman who knows her own mind, and I know I love you. So if you're going to tell me you love me—I'm assuming that's the first time you've said that to a woman, period—only to leave me, then that's even more foolish than anything you could free solo. You're so used to climbing alone that you think you have to live your entire life that way, but you're wrong. So I'm going to keep loving you whether you like it or not because if there's anything I can wait forever for it's a well-deserved 'I told you so.'"

A bird calls above our heads, a thin, wiry song that ascends into a tee-hee-hee before collapsing into a chatter that sounds like laughter. And before it flies off, you can't miss the flash of yellow and orange atop its head. Not unlike a familiar fauxhawk . . .

We stare at the open space where the bird used to be, and I can tell we both sense the same presence. The silence between us isn't stifling. Instead, it's a comforting reassurance that not all is lost, even when it feels like it.

Nolan takes a deep, resigned breath before chuckling. "Sounds like Ryan agrees with you. Despite every urge I have to dig in my heels, I will relent for both your sakes. I'm not saying I'll be any better at being a boyfriend than you are at belaying, but if we make an equal effort at both, we might have a chance."

I pull him into a tight hug, amazed and relieved he didn't put up a bigger fight to break up with me. "Deal. But there's one key difference between the two."

"What's that?"

"When it comes to love, falling is encouraged."

With the dust settled between us like the snow on the ground, we spend the midday talking to Ryan and swapping childhood stories, reminiscing over our favorite memories until our bare fingers go numb and our butts nearly freeze to the log. And when we can't take the cold anymore, we warm up with nondairy hot chocolate and even hotter tomato soup with grilled eggplant sandwiches. The tug of war of our relationship —my tendency to avoid fear at all costs and his determination to seek it out—won't be something that will be resolved any time soon, but for now, I'm so happy to have Nolan back in my life that I'd give up grilled cheeses in a heartbeat.

~

TOP THINGS TO Know About Yosemite (Rewritten for Bougie Indoor Cats)

1. **Reservations are required.** Not all of them will be of interest to you—because lord knows you won't be camping or backpacking—but you'll need to make three specific reservations as early as you can: (1) to enter the park with your car that definitely doesn't have four-wheel drive, (2) to book the fanciest hotel your credit card points can buy, and (3) to sign up for the spa that might as well be your second guest room for how much time you'll be spending in it.

2. **Pack your patience.** The National Park Service says this because about four million people visit Yosemite each year, making this majestic valley as congested as a Disneyland parking garage. You can avoid this nightmare entirely by arriving at the crack of dawn and never leaving the hotel lounge.

3. **Keep wildlife wild.** You will be tempted to feed flakes of your morning croissant to any squirrels or deer that approach the patio where you're enjoying brunch. But you know how that goes—they'll tell all their friends, and then the news will get to the bears, and you'll have to explain why you didn't invite them or risk getting murdered. Not sharing is caring.

4. **Stay connected.** Cell service is extremely limited, so there's a good chance you won't be able to receive calls or texts in the park. But if you'd rather chop off your own arm, *127 Hours*–style, than be outdoors without a properly working phone, then don't leave the radius covered by hotel Wi-Fi.

5. **Drive responsibly.** Sorry, we meant to say drink, since

it's pretty clear that you'll be keeping your ignition turned off for the entirety of your stay. And if that's the case, you might as well drink irresponsibly. That hotel minibar isn't going to drain itself.

chapter
twenty-four

W hen I wake up the next morning in Nolan's van, it feels like the start to any other day I've spent in the park. The sound of birds chattering away has replaced my alarm clock. The early sunlight streams in through the windshield, diffused by the drops of condensation on the glass. The rays bounce off them, scattering around the van's interior like a disco ball.

And with the hope of a clean slate blooming in my chest, I could jump up and start an impromptu dance party right then and there—if it weren't for that blasted winter chill. The lack of central heating is even more apparent when I turn over to see Nolan already up and dressed instead of keeping me warm.

"Don't tell me I kicked you in the shin while asleep and pushed you out of bed." Hammy's prepared to list a host of possible reasons why Nolan's not spooning me—that he's reconsidered getting back together, that our makeup sex last night wasn't enough to convince him otherwise—but I force my anxiety hamster not to spiral into a tizzy when cramped quarters is the more likely culprit.

Nolan turns back from staring at the stove and smiles. "Morning, sunshine." He leans down to give me a tender kiss.

"And no, surprisingly no sleep-induced injuries. Just got up out of habit. It doesn't matter that I won't be climbing for a while—after years of waking before dawn, I've lost the ability to sleep in. Plus, I figured you'd want tea, so I got the kettle going."

As if on cue, steam pours out of the teapot with a piercing shriek. I chuckle. I'm not one to sleep in either, but even if I was, I can't imagine being able to with that sound reverberating in my ears.

Fully awake, I appreciate the generosity of Nolan's small gesture. Even though he can't move around easily with a bum ankle, he waits the requisite five minutes for our mugs of tea to properly steep before making mine exactly how I like it: with one packet of Sweet N' Low and a splash of whole milk. That can't be the same carton from two weeks ago. Did he make the trek to the village store on crutches? If he didn't know I was going to drop by yesterday, then he must have restocked on the off-chance I'd at least show my face again. Even with our relationship on the rocks—and not in the fun, outdoorsy way —he had faith in us. The glimmer of hope I felt when I woke up shines brighter, and it's like I'm falling in love all over again.

But before I can tell Nolan this, his mind is already planning out our itinerary. "What would you like to do today?" he asks, taking a hearty gulp of his tea. "I may be out of commission, but I could take you bouldering at Cocaine Corner."

I don't have time to comment on the hilarity of the route's name because he starts rambling about how the rock shouldn't be too slippery now that the recent storm has passed and that he'll just need my help setting up the crash mat. I nod along on autopilot, trying to psych myself up. My body could use some exertion after weeks holed up in my hotel room.

But then Nolan sets his tea aside to make us bowls of muesli, and that's when the déjà vu hits me. This is how the beginning of the end started—by me not speaking up and being honest with Nolan about what I want. And right now, I don't want to exert myself to climb a boulder and eat a bowl of mushy oats. Exertion is just another word for work, and the last thing I want to do—after the ordeal we've been through together—is get addicted to work again, whether it's his definition or mine.

"Actually," I interrupt him mid-sentence as he's about to pour muesli into our bowls. "I want to relax today." Good job, Tania. No bubble-wrapping with people-pleasing language, like, *That sounds like a great idea, but . . .* or *If you don't mind, I was thinking we could maybe . . .* I put on my boss hat and allowed the sentence to land with a commanding thud.

Nolan sets down his zero-waste-friendly glass jar of muesli. "Relax?"

Of course, he's going to stare at me like I've grown a second head. He thinks bouldering *is* relaxing. Our worldviews are so different that he'll never catch my drift, so I better get specific.

"Yes. I only have a few more days on sabbatical, and I could really use"—the words tumble out before I can register them—"a spa day."

"Like a whole day . . . at a spa?" he echoes, as if he's learning a foreign language and doesn't understand what I've said.

"Not a full twelve hours, obviously," I tease. "We'd have to start with an indulgent brunch—with bottomless mimosas, of course, or it doesn't count. Then once we've got a good buzz going and we can feel the food coma coming on, we treat ourselves to the works: massages, facials, aromatherapy, you name it. Then we enjoy the facilities, completely refreshed, and bask in our blissful glow. A spa half-day, if you want to get technical."

Nolan looks like he got lost at the word 'indulgent,' but he smiles, nonetheless. "Sounds like hygge on steroids."

I nod enthusiastically, leaping out of bed with excitement. "Spa-going is a serious sport. I'm not suggesting some amateur rub-down. This is maximum 5.14d-grade relaxation." I cock an eyebrow. "Think you can handle it?"

He laughs, a competitive heat flashing in his eyes. "I trust that I'm in the hands of a trained professional." By the way he pulls me in, gripping my ass cheeks, I can tell he's not referring to a massage therapist. "You sure you don't want to warm up though? I could give you an amateur rub-down right now."

A tempting offer, but despite Nolan Wells's supreme stamina, I have yet to meet a man who can come so hard he sees stars and still have enough energy to sweat out the rest of his bodily fluids in the sauna.

I bite back my typical retorts when I'm trying to defer something at work—*let's put a pin in that, we can circle back later*—because I'm not about to spoil a spa day with corporate clichés.

"No time for warm-ups," I insist, stepping out of his grasp before we get carried away. There's no guarantee that Granite Grove will be able to squeeze us into the spa without a reservation, so dilly-dallying any further is a risk I'm not willing to take.

"But if you prove that you can relax like a pro," I say with a wink, "then I promise you can give me an elite workout, one-on-one, in my hotel room tonight."

I'D PUT the Granite Grove spa on my Yosemite bucket list the second I went on sabbatical, but I didn't anticipate it taking this long before I could check it off. When I was with Nolan, I put myself under too much pressure, trying to keep up with him on the rock. And when we were apart, due to me breaking the cardinal rule of belaying, I refused to book an appointment no matter how loudly my muscles ached for relief. Wellness experts say you don't need to earn rest, but going to the spa has been my reward for a job well done since I was sixteen. It felt wrong to treat myself when, by anyone's definition, I didn't deserve it.

This experience with Nolan, however, has been therapeutic in more ways than one. I can't say I've ever learned anything while face-down in a massage donut, since it's the perfect opportunity to turn my brain off. This session represented something different. I finally spoke up and advocated for myself with a romantic partner, and said partner took a page out of my book for once and let himself relax. Getting rubbed down with pucks of polished granite has made that lesson a particularly valuable one for both of us.

"You know," Nolan says, as we head into the caldarium and sink into reclining lounge chairs that have no business being this comfy, "if someone would have told me that hot stone massages were a thing, I would have gotten one a long time ago. It felt like El Cap was giving me a warm hug."

I feel the same way about this facility. I've enjoyed many a day spa, but Granite Grove knows what's up. The room where we had our facials and couple's massage was appropriately restorative, with its low lighting, new age music, and distinctive scents of citrus blossoms. But I can tell this open, co-ed area is what keeps guests coming back for more. Along the perimeter are various amenities, like a sauna, steam room, and cold plunge. Hot tubs line a large indoor pool, complete with a lavish fountain in the middle. If you were to look up hedonism in the dictionary, the definition would include a snapshot of this spa's Greco-Roman decor. I feel right at home and can't imagine today getting any better.

And then it does when our server comes by to drop off the

mojitos we ordered. I lift mine in a toast. "To the finer things in life."

Nolan grimaces from behind his glass, and Hammy's fretting immediately pushes me into fix-it mode. "Oh, did your drink have a bad batch of mint? We can order something else—"

He reaches out to stop me from calling over the server. "The mojito's fine." He sips for several seconds to prove his point.

"Then what's wrong? Why did you pull that face?" I ask with concern. I should drop it and enjoy the heated chair's warmth against my lower back, but hiding our true feelings is what got us in trouble in the first place.

Nolan must also recognize the risks of returning to unhealthy patterns because instead of changing the subject, he takes another gulp and sighs. "It's just something my parents would say all the time. They were very fond of the *finer things*."

My face falls when he spits out the words with sarcasm, and he's quick to reach across and hold my hand. "You didn't do anything wrong, Tania. I have nothing against boozy brunches and spa days. Even without my sprained ankle, my body needed to recharge more than I care to admit, so I'm glad you took charge and planned this."

I squeeze his fingers. "I'm sensing a but."

He chuckles under his breath. "You couldn't have known because you've never met them, but my mom and dad didn't want me to take over their financial advisory business so I could help future generations build wealth. It was so I could continue their tradition of hoarding their own. They never understood why Ryan and I sacrificed creature comforts to chase our dreams, never cared to learn. They held our inheritance over our heads as a way to get us to do their bidding. So when the accident happened and they threatened to cut me off for good if I didn't ditch soloing for running Monte Carlo simulations, I told myself I'd never allow affluence to control my life. They could let their legacy of first-class flights and designer clothes die with them. The finer things in life mean jack shit if you value them over your own family."

Hearing Nolan's pent-up resentments towards his parents makes everything click into place. Of course, he would resist my desires for the hygge life: to him, wanting to be surrounded by pleasure and luxury was more than an incompatibility. It felt like yet another loved one rejecting him and his whole worldview.

I suck down my mojito, enjoying the sweet and sour notes on my tongue. I'd have to pace myself. It's been so long since I've enjoyed a craft cocktail that I'm tempted to down four of them. And that's when my therapist's advice comes rushing back to me.

"It doesn't have to be all or nothing," I insist. "There's a lot of middle ground between a stoic, spartan existence or total debauchery. We can stay true to who we are without pushing each other away. The finer things in life include both bougie spa days and the magnificent views when we summit. And what's most important is we can enjoy them *together*."

"For the most part, that's true." Nolan fidgets with his drink, tapping his fingertips on the glass and stirring the straw in circles. "After we summit using ropes. But like the word implies, soloing is something I do alone. And assuming I survive the Dawn Wall, you know I'm just going to move the goalpost and attempt even more dangerous climbs. Are you going to be okay with me risking my life on a regular basis?"

He flashes a sheepish smile, as if he understands at his core that what he's asking of me is inherently selfish. It's something I've been called on countless occasions when I share that I'm childfree by choice. But at the end of the day, all we have is ourselves. And as selfish as it sounds, we're not obligated to maximize our lifespans and usher in the next generation.

With that perspective, I can't be that surprised that Nolan is broaching the subject of free soloing so soon after reconciling. It's the same reason why I'd bring up family planning on first dates. There's no sense in making a major commitment to someone who isn't going to accept us exactly as we are.

I set my drink down and join Nolan on his lounge chair, making sure to give his sprained ankle enough space. It's a good thing these chair-shaped clouds can fit two people easily.

"Honestly, I questioned how this relationship would work way before I found out about you free soloing. There's a reason why couch potatoes don't usually end up with elite athletes. It's already hard enough to date your polar opposite. So if you had asked me when we first met, I would have said I'm absolutely not okay with you playing the rock-climbing equivalent of Russian roulette. Because what else could I expect, knowing the risk, if the worst were to happen?"

Nolan's mouth opens in protest, and I rub my hand across his chest to settle him. No one in the spa has bothered him for a selfie or autograph, thankfully, but I don't need to give strangers a front-row seat to a scene.

"Hold on, don't get your harness in a twist. I was going to add that my biggest challenge will be learning to live with that risk. I don't know how exactly, but I want to try because I know you're worth it. I'm not going to lie and say I fully understand why you want to free solo, because I don't. But I do know that when you're out there, free and unencumbered, that's when you feel most alive. That's when you feel the most —period. Who am I to take that away from you?"

Hot tears pinprick my eyes, and I pull Nolan closer, grateful to have him by my side. "You were the first person who asked me what I *wanted* to do with my life, not what I think I *should* do. I may not have figured that part out yet, but all I can hope is that I find the thing that makes me feel the way you do when you're climbing." I kiss his weathered knuckles. "I'm done dreaming small, because when I'm with you, my world is bigger than I could ever have imagined."

His eyes, also swimming with tears, lock with mine. There's a sense of peace between us that has nothing to do with the tranquility of the spa. We never know how much time we'll have with the people we love, but the Seneca quote on Ryan's gravestone is right. If the life we build is well-lived, it will be long enough.

"You know what?" Nolan coughs back his emotions before gulping the rest of his cocktail. "I take back what I said about the finer things. Because I would have traveled to every spa in the world had I known the finest thing in my life would be you."

Phew. I was planning on taking a dip in the hot tub, but with a declaration like that, it turns out I'm already soaked. Entwining my legs with his on the oversized lounge chair, I can't help ogling Nolan's thirst-inducing thighs that have peeked out of his terrycloth robe. He tips my chin up and I'm about to offer a mea culpa for such blatant objectification, until I meet his gaze and see all the sentimentality has been replaced with a wry sinfulness. The sauna's all the way across the room, and yet with one look Nolan has raised the temperature by thirty degrees.

"Alright, we're taking the spa day back to your room," he says, abruptly standing and adjusting himself through his robe. Good thing this is an adults-only facility, because one wrong move and Nolan would be showing off way more than his massive calves. "Time to pick up where we left off this morning, wouldn't you agree?"

Without waiting for an answer, he leads me to the locker room to quickly gather our belongings. I'm surprised when he shuffles us out of the spa before we can change back into our clothes. What if a guest snaps a pic and tomorrow my face is plastered on the climbing equivalent of TMZ?

Then again, there would be no better way to show off that we're back together than being seen in nothing but bathrobes.

That thrill of exhibitionism calls to us as we make our way to my guest room. I must take a few milliseconds too long to fish the key out of my bag, because before I can process what's happening, Nolan pins me against the door to ravage my mouth in a kiss.

Immediately, I snake my hands under his robe, appreciating the way his abs tense under my fingertips. God, how I missed his hard body on mine. Nolan leans down to place his lips on my neck, right on the pulse point behind my ear. He must sense that I'm this close to collapsing into a puddle at his feet the way he wraps my legs around his waist. His cock strains against me, and I moan into his mouth, tempted to fuck him right here and now. After being apart for nearly two weeks, we need to make up for lost time.

"Ahem!" We turn around, still interlocked, to see a meat-head-looking dudebro covering the eyes of his preschool-aged daughter. A vein pops out of his forehead like he's going to give us a piece of his mind, but his lecture on poisoning young minds dies on the tip of his tongue when he recognizes Nolan, who gives him an arrogant smirk—the kind that says he can get away with anything, anywhere he pleases in this valley.

"Um, carry on, Mr. Nolo." Dudebro gives him a thumbs-up and whisks his daughter off to their room a few doors down. As soon as they're out of sight, we fall apart in a fit of giggles.

Afraid that the mood may have been killed, I run through the options of how we can turn the night around as I fish for my key. "Should we open my last Napa cab? Put on a *Married at First Sight* marathon?"

He shakes his head, lust returning in his eyes. "Not until

I'm done taking my sweet time with you. We're going to wash off that little interruption in the tub—and once you've been thoroughly cleaned, I'm going to fuck you dirty all over again."

～

"The Unofficial Ranking of Olympic Sports by Their Level of Sexiness," by The Send-It Sisters on Friday, March 25

It doesn't matter what year it is—we've always got the Olympics on our brains. To pass the time until that iconic torch is lit, we're announcing our unofficial list of sports, ranked not by their level of difficulty but by how sexy they are as a whole.

That's not to say that there aren't fine-as-hell athletes in every sport, but we believe some games curl our toes more than others. Let's just agree that the next Olympics can't come fast enough, and neither can we.

Forever Disqualified

We'll start with the sports that are banned for their utter lack of sexiness.

- *Country Club Games*: These are ultra-bougie sports that come with a degree from a "school in Massachusetts." Sorry, equestrians, sailors, rowers, and golfers—you may have a magnum-sized trust fund, but we'll never call you Daddy.
- *Covered Up*: It goes without saying that you can't be attractive when we can't see most of you. Call up Netflix because while love may be blind,

unfortunately for fencing, bobsleigh, and luge, it
still has taste.

- *BDSM Disappointments*: Enough jokes have been
thrown at curling, badminton, and table tennis,
but maybe it's because their equipment is so
wimpy? Hit us up when you're slapping around
pucks and ping-pong balls with canes and floggers
instead.

BRONZE MEDALS

Third place goes to the sports that have the potential to be
sexy but are still missing that certain something that will melt
our panties.

- *Tired Teams*: Yes, we know that athletes in
football, basketball, and hockey technically have
game, but who's impressed by your one-night
stand with someone who shoots hoops? As
Miranda Priestly would say, it's about as
groundbreaking as florals in spring.
- *License to Yawn*: Elves and bounty hunters are hot
—Olympic archers and shooters are not. Have you
seen those highly robotic weapons? They make C-
3PO look like Casanova. If you've got that much
metal going on, you won't be getting us off.

SILVER MEDALS

With second place, we're finally getting somewhere. They
may not be slam-dunks for the sexiest sports, but we wouldn't
complain about getting cozy with these athletes.

- *Marital Artists*: No, that's not a typo, because
nothing says husband material like a man with
major "who hurt you?" energy. If you do judo,

taekwondo, or karate, we can trust you to be a
fighter in the streets and an epic lover in the sheets.

- *Throwing Our Weight Around*: You only have to
  sneak a peek at boxers, wrestlers, and weightlifters
  to understand their inherent eroticism. They lift
  things and roughhouse! We volunteer as tribute.

- *Send Us into a Tailspin*: If 360 means anything to
  you as an athlete, we'll be there for 365. Nobody
  does loop-de-loops on our hearts like skiers,
  skaters, snowboarders, gymnasts, and BMX babes.
  We're dizzy just thinking about what you could
  bring to the bedroom.

Gold Medals

The Olympics may be the ultimate competition, but it's
no contest with these sports that take first place in our hearts
—and ovaries.

- *Keep Your Shirt Off*: It's not fair that the hottest
  sports take place in the hottest weather. No shade
  to the Winter Games, but nobody has a more
  unfair advantage than surfers, swimmers, divers,
  water polo players, and beach volleyballers. If
  Chris Hemsworth could play you in your biopic,
  we are on board.

- *Climb on Me*: Okay, we admit we're biased on this
  one, but while climbing may be late to the
  Olympics, we've been early adopters of these sexy
  athletes. Few sports can be as effortlessly applied to
  the outdoors, so we're dying to get these guys out
  of the gym and their hands on our softer holds.

chapter
twenty-five

"Are you sure about this?"

You'd think I'd have taken yes for an answer by now, but I find myself feeling less confident each step we take —from Nolan slamming the door behind us, to tugging me by the loops of my robe straight into the bathroom, to running the water in the Japanese soaking tub. Even if it's deep enough to have a bench along the perimeter and has soothing jets like a jacuzzi, my anxiety still manages to spike given his injury. There's a reason why I didn't propose taking a dip in the hot tub at the spa. Doesn't he know that you're eleven times more likely to die from slipping in the bathroom than in a terrorist attack?

Using his good foot, Nolan kicks aside his climbing bag. "I've never been so sure of anything in my life, Tania. And if you don't join me, I'll pull you in, waffle weave and all."

He smirks as he slips out of his robe, clearly enjoying me enjoying the view. It should be criminal for his body to look that chiseled and perfect.

"I should wash that *obnoxious* look off your face." I don't bother with a striptease, instead throwing off my robe as quickly as possible so I can help Nolan before he attempts to clamber into the tub by himself.

He takes my hand and gingerly swings his legs around, sinking into the hot water with a contented sigh. "Don't lie— you love when my ego is on full display."

I follow his lead, taking a seat on the opposite end of the tub to give his sprained ankle some berth. "It's not your ego," I counter, trying to put my finger on what exactly is so appealing. "It's the dichotomy that's attractive. You're so humble and down-to-earth all the time. Compared to the bros I'm used to in the Bay, you're this adorably dorky loner—and I mean that in the nicest way possible. But when you're in your element, your confidence is sky high, and you transform into this ultimate version of yourself. You're still matter-of-fact, but you're not afraid to be brutally honest about being the best."

Nolan slides closer, cornering me, and I raise my knees to my chest so I can avoid accidentally kicking his right leg. "I'll admit when you scale thousands of feet without ropes, people let you get away with pretty much anything. What power can they hold over me when I can do what they don't dare to? But this is the first time I've felt drunk on that power outside of free soloing. Your body's even more addicting than El Cap, and I have to conquer it again and again."

He attempts to pull me into his lap, but I resist. "You talk a big game, *Free Nolo*, but as much as I'd love to be your most thrilling conquest, I'm afraid you'll make one wrong move, and I'll be driving you back to urgent care."

It's the first time I've called him by his nickname, after hearing it from so many of his overfamiliar fans. But instead of annoying him, I'm rubbing him the right way. It's like I'm tapping into his most competitive nature, and it's revving him up faster. "I don't know if you've heard, Tania, but I've got a reputation for being methodical . . . deliberate . . . and precise in my movement." With each word he stretches out, his hands travel up my legs and waist, gliding through the water until his thumbs graze under the curve of my breasts. I arch my back, lifting my aching nipples toward his mouth, but he doesn't take the bait. "If anyone's going to lose control of their body, it will be you."

I exhale my frustration in a huff. "So what are you suggesting we do about that?"

Nolan looks around the room. "Do you remember your impression of me when you first stepped into my van?"

I chuckle, reminiscing fondly on our not-so-cute meet cute. "I saw your ropes hanging on the driver's seat, and the life of a climber was so beyond my imagination, I assumed you were a serial killer instead." That's when I follow his gaze to the gear bag lying on the bathroom tile next to the tub. "Don't tell me you were playing the long game."

He laughs at the accusation. "Not at all, I promise. But if you trust me, I can murder your ability to squirm. So how about it?"

He gestures to the towel rack above me, and I nod. Let's face it, I'm way too intrigued by giving up all control to Nolan to turn down the temptation. "Climb on."

I'm not sure what the consequences will be now that our climbing commands are doubling as safe words, but worse things can happen than getting a jolt of arousal every time we give each other the go-ahead at the gym. It cuts to the chase, and that's all that matters. The sparks in Nolan's eyes have grown into full flames, and I know it's on now.

He leans over to pull down one of the white towels to the broad rim of the tub, before picking me up by my ass and setting me on it like it's a cushion. "Sit on your knees," he commands, watching as I adjust. I may not be the most sexually adventurous person, but I can guess what awaits me next.

Nolan pulls a rope out of the bag and makes quick work

of the knots, first to tie my arms behind my back, then to attach them to the towel rack above my head. It leaves me incredibly exposed but I'm secure in knowing there's no way I can unintentionally kick his shin or step on his toes.

After double-checking that my circulation isn't threatened and I'm as comfortable as I can be while unable to move, Nolan grins at his handiwork. "I must say I'd much rather use ropes on you than on the rock."

I take in the orange cords snaking up my arms. "Is this how you feel when you're soloing—naked and completely vulnerable and like you could die at any moment?"

"The exact same climb can be terrifying one day and exhilarating the next. The height of the mountain doesn't change—only the way you feel about it does." He smiles like the Cheshire Cat. "We just have to stretch your comfort zone until the mountain isn't scary anymore."

On that note, he firmly grips my thighs and pushes my knees apart, prying me open. I'm not proud to say my first thought is to be grateful we aren't bathed in harsh fluorescent lighting because I no longer have the luxury of being coy and demure, with my sex at Nolan's eye level. But it's hard to be self-conscious when he's staring like a starving grizzly bear who's come out of hibernation to feast.

With me incapacitated, Nolan honors his promise to take his sweet time, kissing so slowly up the inside of my thigh that I'm leaning back just to get him closer to his destination. I may no longer be in the water with him, but by the time he runs his tongue up my slit, I'm drenched.

He dives in more fearlessly than anyone who's ever gone down on me, relishing how my moans get louder and more urgent with every flick of my clit. He teases me so effortlessly I refuse to believe he was ever inexperienced with women, because after just a few weeks, he's eating pussy like a pro.

"Mmm, get as loud as you like," he says as my pleas for

more echo off the bathroom tile. "I want to know how close you are."

As if that was up for debate. "Please, I need it," I whimper, trying to thrust against his tongue in a race to release. "I'm going to—"

"Oh, I know, honey. I know. I can feel you're almost there." He stretches me out even further. "Just keep that pussy nice and open for me. Atta girl, that's it. Show me how wet you are."

I strain against the ropes to meet his mouth, but with my arms wrapped behind my back and my legs spread-eagled, I can't get any leverage. And from the way Nolan chuckles in response, he finds my futile attempts amusing.

"My poor baby," he hums against my clit. "So desperate to fuck my face. Just remember—you wanted the day off. You can't have your cake and control it too. You're at my mercy now, so you better get used to it. You're gonna take what I give you, Tania, or I'll leave you to fend for yourself."

"Please, no, I'll be good, I promise." Well aware there's zero chance of coming without his help, I babble a string of reassurances that I'll be on my best behavior.

"That's right." Satisfied by my obedience, he continues stroking me with his tongue, which is both torture and the most indulgent treat. I do what I can to keep my body still, but the closer I get to cresting over the edge, the more I buck and writhe to increase the pressure. Addicted to taking charge, Nolan refuses to let me budge, doling out pleasure on his terms. It's not until his breaths are coming out as ragged as mine that he takes pity on me.

"There you go," he coos when my moans hit a fever pitch. "Let it out, that's my girl."

When gratification is no longer delayed, euphoria can feel overwhelming. My climax comes crashing hard over me and I attempt to clamp my knees shut, but my body doesn't stand a chance against Nolan's Olympian-level grip.

"That's it, you did so well," he murmurs. "But I need you to hold on, because I'm not even close to being done with you." He slides my ass forward, and as my ability to form coherent thoughts disappears, all I keep coming back to is how lucky I am that I wasn't saved by a sprinter or a drag racer, because whatever Nolan's faults may be, lack of endurance is not one of them. And the silver lining to being tied up is all I have to do is sit back and enjoy it.

But as he slips one oversized finger and then another into me, I'm dying to pull him so close that you can't tell where I end and he begins. "Nolan, *please*. Fill me up—I can't take it anymore."

He obliges, reaching over to grab a condom from the climbing bag. I expect him to untie me and carry me to the bed, but in a few deft moves, he uses the towel rack like a pulley to lift my ass into the air. "Who knew that hauling gear up big walls would come in handy like this?" He maneuvers to sit behind me, with my pussy hovering right above the tip of his cock. "Now let's see if we can get you to scream—"

And with that, he lets go of the rope that's keeping me suspended and impales me. "Fuck!" I groan from the impact.

His lips curl into a smile as he pulls my hair to the side and leaves a trail of kisses down the back of my neck. "Your wish is my command."

Now I'm not saying Nolan's trained his whole life for this, but I'm also not saying he hasn't. Because it is certainly a feat of physical prowess the way he's able to bounce my full weight up and down on his dick while keeping one hand on my clit at all times. It's honestly smart to hold me together with these ropes because I'm afraid without them, I would instantly melt into a puddle of jelly.

"Aw, running out of stamina, are we? And you didn't even

have to put in any of the work." His teeth graze the sensitive spot behind my earlobe, sending a shiver down my spine. "As it should be, because I can go forever for the both of us. All I ask of you is to come harder than you have in your entire life."

He wraps my hair around his arm like it's another rope and pulls, jerking my head back as he thrusts deeper. I cry out as yet another orgasm ripples through my body, and I clench down hard around him, until he releases his grip along with the rest of his self-control, spilling himself into me with a groan.

I fall back against Nolan's chest, more exhausted without moving than I've ever been after a day of climbing. "I bet that pearl-clutching dude from earlier heard us despite being several rooms away."

He laughs while quickly undoing the knots so he can massage my aching arms. "I hope he did, so he can go tell everyone around here, because I'm prouder of that performance than I was free soloing Half Dome."

No longer constrained, I slowly swivel around, with Nolan still inside me, so I can pull him in for a deep kiss, enjoying the taboo of my taste on his tongue. "Keep fucking me like that, and I'll let you solo Everest."

With all the anxiety that typically courses through my veins, I should be a complete mess on the last night of my sabbatical, consumed by the stress of packing my stuff, parting ways with Nolan, and preparing for a long-distance relationship.

But whether Hammy has finally settled down or simply been fucked to sleep, my eyelids struggle to stay open. I don't know what the morning will bring, or the next week, or the years to come. For once, I am at peace with the not knowing.

Because once we're cleaned up and snug in bed, skin to skin, for the first time I fall asleep, not to the incessant worry of it all going wrong, but to the possibility of it going right.

~

Text conversation between Tania Beecher and Dahlia Cruz, LCSW, on Friday, March 25, at 10 p.m.

Tania Beecher: I know it's super late, Dahlia, so I'm not expecting you to respond, but I wanted to say thank you. Not only was Nolan able to forgive me, but I was also able to forgive myself, and now we're better than ever. It might be the mind-blowing sex talking, but he could be the one. I'm still terrified it will all fall apart, but I guess you can't achieve happily ever after if you don't try.

Dahlia Cruz, LCSW: I'm glad to hear from you, Tania. When we're scared to do something but do it anyway, that's courage. Be proud of your bravery, and know that regardless of what happens in the future, your happy ending has been inside you all along.

chapter
twenty-six

When I stayed the night in Nolan's van, I heard the rain and snow pelt the frame, felt the gusts threaten to topple us over. But even though I can see the formidable winter weather looming through the hotel window, we're insulated from the storm in this cozy suite. Instead of forcing down cold muesli and hiking at dawn, I finally get to spend my last morning in Yosemite the way I imagined: waking each other up with some lazy lovemaking and ordering breakfast from room service.

As Nolan enjoys his avocado toast and I devour my eggs benedict, my nerves begin to set in. It's not an acute panic, but rather that restless energy of feeling untethered, like the blustering wind outside is picking me up and carrying me away. Pretty soon, I'll be in the elements, no longer protected by the lodge's walls and the cocoon we've built around us to keep out the real world.

"What happens now?" I ask after I've finished packing my bags. The only to-do item left is to check out, so the question isn't logistical but existential.

Nolan pulls me into his arms and holds me tight. "I've got an ankle boot on, remember? I'm not going anywhere."

I sigh. "I know. That's part of the problem. Getting an annual park pass isn't the issue, but what am I supposed to do? Drive four hours every Friday night to visit you after a monstrously long week at work, only to return on Sunday and rinse and repeat until it breaks us?"

He pauses to think for a moment. "It's still the off-season and I'll be recovering for several more weeks, but once I'm back on both feet, I can travel to see you too. We can balance the burden."

"How romantic. Burden is exactly the word I want to use to describe our relationship."

"Hey, I'm not saying I'm an expert at dating, but even with climbing, eighty percent is pure bliss for me, and twenty percent is a grueling, miserable workout. Everything has its burdens, but that doesn't mean they aren't worth it."

I pull back, skeptical. "But shouldn't love be easy and effortless?"

"Loving you *is* easy and effortless, but even if this is the most stable, communicative relationship I've ever had, it will take effort to keep it that way. Don't take this the wrong way, Tania, because I know when you're off the clock, you prefer every moment to be simple and snug, but nobody achieves anything great living the hygge life." He gives me a playful grin. "If we want to maximize both our personal happiness and professional performance, we'll have to take risks—together."

Damn, and here I am, thinking I'm the wordsmith. I nod, conceding his point. He's always saying that everything will work out, and for both our sakes, I have to believe him.

"In that case, I'll keep climbing at Pacific Pipeworks. I don't want to lose all the progress I've made."

Nolan shakes his head. "Normally, I'd be encouraging of anyone interested in hitting up the climbing gym, but I can't bear the thought of you being belayed by some dude who works there. The routine can wait until we're attached at the literal hip again." He touches his forehead to mine. "Until then, I'll call from Granite Grove's business center after every send just to hear your voice."

With tears clouding my eyes, I wrap my arms around his neck and try not to squeeze the life out of him. "I hate the thought of something bad happening to you while you're climbing all alone."

He rubs my back slowly until I let out a ragged sigh. "Between you and Ryan being with me in spirit, I know even when I'm soloing, I'm never alone." He kisses the top of my head. "Thank you, Tania. For everything. I know we had a bit of a down-climb there in the middle, but we got through the crux, and we're going to summit stronger than ever. I promise."

My bottom lip trembles, and I have to practically shove him out the door before I break down and permanently move into the hotel just to avoid saying goodbye. "Go climb on now. I'll be back before you know it."

I'm not sure if it's true, because as soon as the door clicks shut, the ground feels shakier beneath my feet.

So now I'm left on my own, save for Hammy, who has awoken from his deep slumber to remind me of everything in my old life I should be worried about: the aftermath of Habit-uall's security incident, the First Party conference just days away, managing team morale leading up to performance reviews at the end of the quarter, avoiding my parents' insistent phone calls about coming home for Easter, a holiday I no longer want to celebrate—and oh god, should I drive straight to my therapist's office to save myself a trip?

There's no point to standing around when I have a long drive ahead of me. With an exhale of resignation, I gather up my belongings, throw my backpack over my shoulder, and drag my suitcase down to the lobby, secretly hoping that Nolan's waiting to beg me to stay.

"He's already left."

I turn around from the entrance to see Summer staffing the front desk. We may have put our conflict behind us, but I'm still taken aback to see sympathy on her face.

She chuckles at my surprise. "You and me both, sister. Who would have thought that in a single day I'd go from wanting to kick you out to wishing you could extend this sabbatical of yours. You sure you can't work from here remotely? I thought all you techies ditched the office anyway."

I sigh again, annoyed that it's already returned as a regular part of my communication. "We did, until the market took a major nosedive. When investors get scared, companies clamp down on perks, including working from home."

Summer tilts her head. "So what's the plan—give your boss the middle finger and become a renowned rock climber like Nolan?"

I grimace at the ridiculous notion. "I'll leave the climbing to the experts, thank you very much. All I can hope is that Nolan has a long, illustrious life ahead of him."

"I'm not sure about illustrious given the danger he throws himself in on the daily, but his life will be better with you in it." We exchange a warm smile, before she pulls up my reservation. "And you're good at what you do too, Tania. If you ever go off to do your own thing, just know you'd already have one client waiting in the wings."

I admit I'm intrigued by all the immediate tasks I could tackle. How I could help refresh the lodge's website, update all the collateral, revamp its social media strategy—basically brush the dust off their stale playbook and appeal to the burnout generation that needs to log off and get outdoors.

We finish checking out, and Summer comes around the front desk to give me a genuine hug, insisting we do a girls' climbing trip next time I'm in the park. And as I'm driving home, I wait for Hammy's worries to dominate my brainspace, expecting the dread to fill my lungs until it's difficult to breathe.

But even though my mind is whirring, Hammy is nowhere to be found. I'm no longer fretting about my old life—I'm dreaming of a new one. I've always been the kind of person who'd move mountains for my friends, but now I realize I'd climb mountains with them too.

Nolan's words from last night make another appearance. *The exact same climb can be terrifying one day and exhilarating the next. The height of the mountain doesn't change— only the way you feel about it does.*

He's right—taking a leap of faith is scary, but it's also thrilling. Hammy isn't ever going to vanish completely, but I have more control over him than I realized. He actually shuts up when I jump headfirst through my fear.

I know now why Nolan is obsessed with free soloing and why I'm obsessed with him. The pounding in my ears, the racing in my chest, the urge to roll down the car windows and scream at the top of my lungs—it's not anxiety.

It's adrenaline.

I pull up my phone contacts on my car's menu screen and tap the number I'm looking for.

John picks up on the second ring and greets me through my speakers. "Hey, Pinky, what's up? Is your sabbatical over already?"

"Yep," I reply cheerily. Before, that fact would put me in a deep depression, but now I'm too excited for what's next. "And it's time to take over the world." I pause. "Okay, maybe not the world. But I think I know what we can name our marketing agency."

❧

Tania Beecher's search history on Sunday, March 27

What you need to start marketing agency
    How to get health insurance in America that doesn't suck
    Does Nolan Wells insure his giant hands
    Is a CPA and a "tax guy" the same thing
    Is wine a deductible expense
    How to start business with bro without murdering him
    Is it rude to quit after a sabbatical
    How to quit job but like in a nice way
    Setting team up for success after you leave
    Thank you gifts for coworkers
    Where do Yosemite folks live
    Oakhurst real estate
    How big is an acre
    Would I make a good "horse girl"
    Pets with less maintenance
    Too soon to buy a house with boyfriend of two months
    What to do in the middle of nowhere
    Can Doughbies cookies deliver outside the Bay Area
    Doughbies cookies recipe to make at home
    How to get into baking
    Starting sourdough starter
    What to cook for housewarming party
    Can your boyfriend carry you over a threshold
    Too soon to get engaged after two months

chapter
twenty-seven

By the time I arrived at my apartment in Oakland, I knew I would be handing in my resignation, but I didn't want to tell Nolan until we could meet again in person. I could hear the disappointment in his voice when I told him he'd have to wait two weeks, but he took it in stride. Thank goodness he's been so fiercely independent, he's unlikely to push back and ruin the surprise.

And a surprise it will be—at least to Habituall. Out of hierarchal etiquette and common courtesy, I decide to tell Evan first, because as CEO he is my boss. And because he's also the boyfriend of one of my best friends, I have to keep quiet about my decision with Casey and the glam fam as well. I feel like the worst friend ever being purposely obtuse in the group chat, but I can't risk the news getting out before I have the chance to inform everyone properly.

It feels awkward that the first thing I plan on doing when I return to the office is quit, but it's better to rip off the bandage sooner rather than later. So Monday morning, before the leadership meeting, I pull Evan into a conference room and give him my two-week notice.

"Which tech CEO am I going to have to murder for poaching you?" Evan blurts out, only half joking.

I chuckle nervously. "Trust me, the only man capable of stealing me away is the greatest athlete of our generation."

Evan softens, and I can tell by his expression he understands what it's like to upend your life for love. "I'm happy for you. I really am. But you're one of our OGs, Tania. Are you sure this is what you want?"

I nod. Although my decision to resign may have been influenced by Nolan, it's one I'm making on my own. "When I joined Habituall six years ago, I was just the content marketer who wrote pun-heavy blog posts and took care of replying on social because nobody else wanted the job. But I had the goal of being a VP of marketing, and because of you, I've accomplished that and so much more. And for a while now, I've been restless to figure out what's next. Sure, I could keep climbing the corporate ladder until I'm some high-powered CMO at a Fortune 100. But then I met Nolan, and he made me see that I could climb completely different peaks."

A smirk tugs at Evan's lips. "So I am going to see you on the cover of *Nat Geo* hanging off a cliff."

I balk. "Oh god, no. I mean, who knows what climber I'll be under Nolan's wing, but not anytime soon. No, it's time for me to take everything I've learned here and forge my own path as a freelancer."

He blinks, and his expression is both impressed and skeptical. "Entrepreneurship isn't for the faint of heart. I would know. People think working a 9-to-5 is hard, but that pales in comparison to being your own boss."

"I thought so too, at first," I concede, "because we grew up in the Wild West of tech startups. But Nolan's shown me that there are so many ways to make a living. If your only vision of running a business involves coding all-nighters and begging for venture capital, you probably don't think work-life balance is possible. But I don't want to build an empire. For once, I'm going to keep my ambition in check and enlist some help. I'm partnering with my brother, and we're only going to take on select clients that deserve special attention—and don't worry, we're happy to have Habituall on that roster if you're interested. I just don't want to live to work anymore. I want to work to live." I break into a giddy smile. "I'll always enjoy the finer things, like a bougie Napa cab, but the finest things are free: fresh air, rest, and a whole lot of love."

Evan gives me a hug, not the one from a superior but from someone I'm lucky to call a dear friend. "From one founder to another, you are going to crush it. And no matter what happens, you'll never be alone, because we're going to be here, rooting you on every step of the way." He squeezes tighter. "I wish you all the best. My life is better in every way now that Casey is in it, and I'm glad you and Nolan found each other. I expect an invitation to the wedding."

I wave him off. "That's putting the cart way before the horse."

He shrugs. "I don't know about that. Nolan Wells seems like the kind of man who, once he makes a decision, commits three hundred percent."

We laugh, and after we inform the rest of the C-suite and nail down the offboarding plan, I tackle the rest of my to-do list, starting with telling my marketing team. And for what it's worth, my fear that they would be fine without me around on sabbatical is now what reassures me that they'll be fine without me, period.

THE TWO WEEKS FLY BY, and our First Party conference goes off without a hitch. Despite the team's exhaustion after putting another annual event behind us, they all insist on throwing me a farewell party, which is how I find myself here on the rooftop of our office building. It's Friday afternoon, and I keep being reminded of all the lasts—the last happy hour with this panoramic view of San Francisco, the last time we empty the fridge of our booze stash, the last time I raid the swag closet for extra T-shirts and hoodies, and the last time I'm stunned by how much crap Jennifer can keep on her desk.

Harris laughs when I list off everything I'll miss. "If that's what makes you nostalgic, I'll have her petition the government to turn her workstation into a national historic site, so her twenty takeout containers and empty boba cups will be preserved forever."

Casey clinks her wine glass against mine as we take in the cityscape, the stark-white Bay Bridge jutting out of the horizon in the background. "You're moving to the mountains, not the moon. It's not like you'll never come back to visit Habituall. Heck, I'm not even an employee, but I'm here so often I might as well be."

"Betches, get over here—it's photoshoot time!" I turn to see Som waving us over to the rooftop's edge, where the glam fam is corralling the rest of the company. No matter how many times Alex and her friends make an appearance, it's still wild to have the world's most famous celebrity at your office—entourage, security guards, and all.

While Som makes quick work of sorting coworkers by height and instructing them how to pose against the skyline, I walk over to Glen, Tori, and Alex for a group hug. "The princess has graced us with her presence! How did you get the paparazzi to leave us alone?"

Alex blushes while Glen rolls his eyes. "Don't worry—she bribed the staff in the lobby with selfies and autographs if they barred anyone from entering the building for a couple of hours—"

"Because this day is all about you, not me," Alex insists,

looping her arm in mine and pulling me to the center of the throng of people. "Let's go, Tori—move that caboose!"

"Hey, are you seeing what I'm seeing?" Tori looks over the lip of the building, brows furrowed.

Som snaps her scarf at her. "Yeah, betch, it's called golden hour, and it's rapidly closing, so let's take this group shot already."

Tori turns back, eyes wide as saucers. "It's not the light—someone's climbing the fucking building."

My heart seizes in my chest. I don't have to take in the sight with my own eyes, because I know immediately who would be foolish enough to scale a tower of stone and glass. *"Nolan!"*

I sprint to the edge where Tori's standing, and lo and behold, when I follow her gaze, I see Nolan Wells smiling up at me. "What the hell are you doing?"

He doesn't pause his ascent, alternating his arms and legs in a move I learned is called chimneying because of its resemblance to how Santa might climb back up to his sleigh after dropping off presents. "I wanted to surprise you with a visit," he shouts, "but for some strange reason, nobody would let me in the building."

I groan, kicking myself for just moments ago thinking of Alex as smart for locking down the place. But how was I supposed to know that my impatient boyfriend would take matters into his own giant hands?

I pace back and forth along the railing like an agitated tiger trapped in a cage, and Hammy's making everything worse, rattling the bars. *This is it,* he screams. *He's going to fall, and his insides will splatter across the concrete. You'll end up exactly like Summer, losing the one person you love the most.*

Bristling with indignation, I tell my anxiety hamster to back off. Summer wouldn't have traded her time with Ryan for the world, and I feel the same. As much as I want to run away and fall apart in hysterics, I'm going to stay put and support Nolan no matter what. So I won't tell you again, Hammy—shut the *fuck* up.

Thankfully, by the time Nolan came into Tori's view, he was almost near the top. I've pressed the elevator button up to the office enough times to recall that this skyscraper is twenty-four floors, and based on how many windows remain above him, he must only be four floors away.

After a few more minutes, Nolan pulls himself over the edge, biceps bulging in his North Face T-shirt, and we rush into each other's arms. From the way I'm ready to collapse in an exhausted heap, I expect him to be drenching sweat after a feat like that. And yet, he's barely breathing any heavier than he would be after a few sends in the gym.

"Gotta say, that was pretty rad," Nolan says, beaming. "Been forever since I did an urban solo—did you know this building's facade is granite? Nothing like El Cap, of course, because it's only a tenth of the size, but it was cool none-theless."

Squeezing him tight, I'm grateful he's back on solid ground, but right when I'm about to ask him again why he's even here, he swivels around to absorb the crowd surrounding us. "Hey, are you having a party?"

I step back. This wasn't how I'd planned on breaking the news, but now's as good a time as any. "It's my farewell party. Today's my last day. When we first met, you asked me what I would do with my life if I stopped pretending, and I've decided I want to join you on the road less traveled. It's time I try soloing for myself, at least when it comes to starting my own business."

Anticipating a barrage of questions, I start rambling about how I've given it a lot of thought and I can sleep at my parents' house whenever we get tired of being cramped together in the van. And I definitely keep to myself that I've already been researching real estate around the park, because I'm sure talking about buying a house would be moving way too fast—

But Nolan isn't listening to a word I'm saying, because all of a sudden he drops to one knee and I'm standing there, wondering whether my coworkers are gasping or I'm just hyperventilating.

"It only took one night alone to realize I never want to be without you again. I know it's outrageous for me to climb up here and propose like this, and I'm not saying we have to rush an engagement, but it's not as outrageous as the idea of spending any more time apart than we have to."

He pulls out a black velvet box and pries it open, chalk rubbing off everywhere, to reveal a stunning ring. Gold band, emerald-cut diamond with emerald accents, like the sheer wall of El Capitan bathed in the sunrise and surrounded by trees. "Tania Beecher, do you want to keep doing what we're doing, for the rest of our lives?"

I nod, tears of relief pouring out of me, and not just because he's safe from falling down this skyscraper. After months of struggling to see eye to eye, we're finally on the same page. It won't make Nolan's calling less scary or my future career less uncertain, but if we're together 'til death do us part, it makes our lives worth every moment in between.

I grab Nolan's face with both hands and kiss him deeply, to the cheers of my closest friends and colleagues. "Climb on."

~

"*NOLAN WELLS, the World's Boldest Climber, Is on Top—in More Ways Than One*" by *Climbing.com on Monday, October 17, at 1:00 p.m.*

. . .

IT's an epic day for both the climbing community and the entirety of humanity as famed rock climber Nolan Wells has made history today for his free solo ascent of the Dawn Wall of El Capitan in Yosemite, Calif. Wells conquered the hardest route in the world in record time—and that's *without* ropes and safety equipment, a feat widely considered by experts to be physically impossible.

Although Wells has called Yosemite home for over a decade, living in a refurbished van at the base of El Capitan, he's never before discussed his intention of free soloing the Dawn Wall. But those closest to him felt it was only a matter of time once he completed the first ascent within a single day —making it much more likely that he could solo the route without succumbing to exhaustion. And after years of laser-focused preparation, Wells achieved the unthinkable, topping out after eight grueling hours on the wall.

As if this triumph wasn't enough cause for celebration, it comes on the heels of Wells's unexpected marriage proposal in April to Tania Beecher, founder and CEO of marketing consultancy Beecher Media. Any man can drop to one knee, but only Wells has managed to do so after free soloing her former employer's headquarters to prove his devotion. At 338 feet tall, the San Francisco skyscraper isn't even on the Wikipedia page for the city's tallest buildings—first place going to the 1,070-foot Salesforce Tower—but we're told the grand gesture took Beecher by surprise all the same.

Could love be behind Wells's motivation to take on even greater death-defying stunts? Neither Nolan nor Tania could be reached for comment, so only time will tell. For now, sources say the lovebirds are blissfully keeping busy remodeling their new home in Oakhurst, Calif., and planning their upcoming nuptials. Cheers to the happy couple!

epilogue

I t's not uncommon for Nolan to leave for El Capitan early in the morning, whether we were sleeping in the van or at our four-thousand square foot farmhouse in Oakhurst—a home that sounded atrociously lavish until I realized that a four-bed, five-bath property on eight acres in the foothills cost way less than your average West Oakland condo.

But when October arrived and he started requesting a brief moratorium on my visits to the park, that's when I knew that D-Day was upon us. The day that Nolan Wells would attempt to free solo the Dawn Wall. I'm not even religious, but I pleaded to any available deity that I wouldn't be made a widow before we had the chance to tie the knot.

So when Summer texted me at six this morning to tell me Nolan had indeed scaled the first nine pitches before sunrise, I grabbed my already-prepped go bag and drove as fast as the winding mountain roads would let me. By the time I join the onlookers at the base of El Cap, Nolan's already halfway up, navigating the downclimb around the dyno that's unreachable without ropes.

The irony of being a childfree-by-choice couple is that I've never felt more like an expecting parent than I do now. Except Nolan's the one doing all the work, and I'm the clueless dad scuffling a permanent circle in the grass beneath my feet. The closer he gets to the top, the more I understand how our lives will forever change when—not if, because I can't entertain the thought—he catapults into the history books.

Four hours of labor later—after rejecting everyone's attempts to feed me because if my fiancé is going to be delirious and hungry, so will I—we witness Nolan birth his own miracle, summiting without so much as a fist in the air. He's never been one for theatrics, but the assembled crowd makes up for it. Every single person in the park is screaming and crying at merely watching him achieve the impossible.

The second miracle that day is that Nolan is able to get cell service and FaceTime me once he's safe at the top. I yell at everyone to stand back before accepting the call.

We've been together for eight months, and I've never been threatened by the place El Cap has in Nolan's heart. When he appears on my screen, he's smiling harder than I've ever seen him smile. Every muscle is crinkled in pure elation, and my heart soars at seeing him be the happiest he's ever been.

"Good to see you again, babe," he says with a chuckle, and I roll my eyes at Nolan greeting me as nonchalantly as if he just got back from the supermarket.

"How do you *feel*?" I squeal, dying to hear his first thoughts after achieving the moon landing of rock climbing.

He blisses out like he's on a high stronger than any drug. "So delighted . . . That was pretty satisfying." Pretty satisfying. You heard it here first, Guinness Book of World Records.

"So what's next?" The bottle of Veuve in my go-bag begs to be popped.

He shrugs. "I don't know . . . I was probably gonna hang-board later."

This man, I can't. "Babe, I say this with all the love in my heart, because I'm so glad you didn't plummet to your death, but if all you want is to stick your fingers in something and try to last as long as you can, I have way better ways we can celebrate tonight."

THE END

thank you

Thank you for reading *Love on the Rocks*! It would mean the world if you'd consider writing a review on Amazon and Goodreads, as well as recommending the book on social media. Word of mouth has a huge impact on an author's success, and it helps other readers discover new books to enjoy.

Can't get enough of Tania and Nolan? To gain access to a special bonus epilogue from Nolan's point of view, visit alyssa jarrett.com/love-on-the-rocks

acknowledgments

Now that my second novel is published, I realize that I'm thanking most of the same people as I did for my debut. How incredibly grateful I am that my village of support has been constant for so many years.

First, of course, to editor and author whisperer Kristen Tate at the Blue Garret. Like Nolan, you have saved me from falling over the edge of many metaphorical cliffs. When it comes to both writing books and living life, thank you for teaching me to have a plan, but hold it lightly.

To my therapist Daisy Cervantes. I have struggled with capital-A anxiety for as long as I can remember, but you brought me out of one of my most serious bouts of it. I'm so proud of the progress I've made because of you and amazed at how much better life can feel when I trust myself.

To everyone who read the earliest drafts of *Love on the Rocks* and steered me in the right direction, especially to Sophia Le, Joanna Furlong, Lindsey Lanza, Taleen Voskuni, and Rebecca Wise. You all were unanimous in your support of Tania's story, so I'm glad I decided to make her part of the glam fam.

To Susan Velazquez Colmant at JABberwocky Literary Agency. Not many unagented authors are lucky to receive such extensive editorial feedback, so I'd say my time spent in the query trenches was worth it just to get connected to you. You were right—Nolan's parents were cartoonishly villainish and didn't need to make an appearance. Good riddance.

To all my closest friends for being constant reminders that

art is only worthwhile when the people you care most about can appreciate it. Please keep inviting me to parties to give me excuses to leave my house.

To my brother and forever business partner Nick Jarrett, who took on the task of designing the cover of *Love on the Rocks* even when life itself was rocky enough. Maybe one day, when we have all the time in the world, we can create those comic books we always dreamed about as kids.

As always, to my husband and fellow indoor cat, Tom. This book wouldn't even exist if you hadn't taken me climbing. I don't see us ever graduating from the gym to the big walls of Yosemite, but it was so fun imagining it all the same.

And, finally, to you, my readers. Publishing a book is an arduous journey, but connecting with you all makes the climb worth it every time. I would move mountains for each and every one of you. Thank you.

about the author

Alyssa Jarrett is a romance author and tech marketer based in the San Francisco Bay Area. When she's not telling steamy, satirical love stories, she can be found drinking an iced tea or cuddling with her husband and three cats.

You can subscribe to her newsletter, Grumpy + Sunshine, on Substack, and follow her @authoralyssajarrett on Instagram, Threads, and TikTok.

alyssajarrett.com
alyssajarrett.substack.com

Follow Alyssa online: